"Welcome to Love, David."

David was probably the best-looking guy Tara had ever seen in her life.

"Hi there," Tara said, walking over to him.

"You are Tara Moore?" he asked, sounding surprised. He had a slight, sexy accent.

"I am," Tara replied. "Why, don't I look like a Tara Moore?" she asked flirtatiously.

She expected him to toss her a compliment in reply. He didn't.

"I have no idea," he said seriously.

Tara smiled so her dimples showed. "Welcome to Love, David." She leaned over and gave him a light kiss on his cheek, all the better for him to smell her perfume.

She expected him to comment on it, or at least to inhale with appreciation.

He didn't seem to notice. In fact, he really didn't seem to notice Tara at all.

Other Scholastic titles
you will enjoy:

The Bridesmaids
Cherie Bennett

Malibu Summer
Jane Claypool Miner

Unforgettable
Caroline B. Cooney

GIRLS IN LOVE

CHERIE BENNETT

SCHOLASTIC INC.
New York Toronto London Auckland Sydney

Copyright © 1996 by Cherie Bennett.
All rights reserved. Published by Scholastic Inc.

ISBN 0-590-88030-6

12 11 10 9 8 7 6 5 4 3 2 1   6 7 8 9/9 0 1/0

Printed in the U.S.A.

First Scholastic printing, November 1996

For Jacqueline Oosterkamp and Shelly Barton, our gracious hosts at the Chateau de Lesvault writers' retreat in Onlay, France, where I wrote this novel.

And for my very significant other, Jeff Gottesfeld, for his research and knowledge of winter sports.

Chapter 1

"I'm in love!" Tara Moore sang out, as she burst into her best friend Erin Kellerman's living room.

Erin was sitting on the couch; her feet, clad in oversized pink bunny slippers, were perched on the coffee table in front of her, a copy of *Cyrano de Bergerac* open on her lap. She barely glanced over at Tara, then turned back to her book.

"Erin Kellerman, I just told you that I am in love," Tara repeated, her southern-accented voice commanding Erin's attention.

"Of course you're in love," Erin replied, her eyes still on her book. "We live in Love. It's the name of our town. Love, Michigan. Tiny, quaint, and very boring."

"That joke is old and tired," Tara drawled, snatching the book from Erin's hands and sitting down next to her. "You study too much, you know," she told her, her dimples showing as she grinned. "Besides, as one of my two best friends in the entire world, you are obligated to squeal with excitement when I tell you that I'm in love."

"Squeal-squeal," Erin said, reaching behind Tara for her book. "Come on, I still have Act Three to read and a paper to write on Rostand's use of allegory. Today is Saturday. It's due on Monday. And I don't write fast."

"*Cyrano de Bergerac,* written by Edmond Rostand," Tara recited. "It's the most successful play he ever wrote. Most people believe he wrote it back in the sixteen hundreds, but in fact he actually wrote it at the turn of this century."

Erin just stared at her friend's huge green eyes, perfect long, wavy blond hair, and curvy figure. "It isn't fair, you know," Erin said. "You're gorgeous *and* smart."

"I know," Tara agreed solemnly. "But I have thick ankles, which, may I remind you, have prevented me from winning more than one beauty pageant in my thirteen years of competition — "

" — And you're seventeen now," Erin

marveled. "No offense, Tara, but that's kind of scary."

"Tell that to my bank account," Tara replied, "which just happens to hold four thousand dollars of money for college that I have won at various pageants." She set Erin's book down on the coffee table. "So, let's talk about guys. I just met the cutest, finest guy on my way over here — "

"The one you are now in love with," Erin clarified.

"Of course," Tara said. "And I'm thrilled to know that you've been hanging on my every word. He was ice skating over at Shatner's Rink. I stopped by to see if Noelle was practicing, but Anne Gladstone told me she was in the gym doing her routine minus the ice. So this guy — his name is Lyle — asks me what time it is — "

"Oh, well, then I see what you mean," Erin teased her friend. "When a guy asks me what time it is, I fall in love, too."

Tara swatted her friend's arm playfully. "Then he asked me if I skated, and then we got to talking, and he had the most gorgeous eyes with these really long, thick eyelashes. He's a freshman at Love College, and I have a date with him tonight."

"But tonight we have the last big Winterfest Student Committee meeting," Erin reminded Tara. "You *have* to be there! We're only seniors in high school, and we actually got picked for the committee and you can't just — "

"Erin, sweetheart, take a deep breath and say your mantra or something," Tara suggested sweetly. "You Yankees get so intense about things!"

Erin made a face at Tara. "This is not a northern versus southern thing, Tara."

"I'm going on my date *after* the meeting," Tara explained. "So you can quit pitchin' a fit." She snuggled back on the slightly shabby couch and stared dreamily into the air. "I love college guys, don't you? They're so . . . collegiate."

"Tara," Erin began patiently, "you have an IQ of 150. And the best you can come up with is that college guys are 'collegiate'?" She reached around Tara for the copy of *Cyrano*. "Besides, this Lyle guy goes to Love College. Right here in Love, Michigan. Which is, as I said, tiny, quaint, and boring."

"Well, aren't we in a lovely mood," Tara drawled. "What's got you all bothered?"

"My life," Erin muttered.

"Tell me every detail," Tara suggested,

easing the book away from Erin again. "I only have five minutes, though, so please kind of summarize the boring parts."

"Very funny," Erin commented. She sighed and knocked her bunny slippers together. Then she sighed again. "It's my crazy family. They're driving me nuts."

"Nuts how?" Tara inquired.

"Tara, hi!" a cheerful voice called from the doorway.

Both girls turned around. It was Erin's aunt Daisy. Daisy was about forty, with lively, close-set blue eyes that appeared to be slightly crossed, but weren't, and very long hair that she put into a messy bun at the nape of her neck every morning, like a woman from the turn of the century. By ten o'clock most of the hair had escaped its confines and straggled around her face and, along with her large, slightly off-kilter blue eyes, tended to give her a rather strange look. At the moment her hands were encased in latex gloves, and even though Daisy wore no cosmetics, there was a line of petal pink lipstick on her chin.

More than one of Erin's acquaintances over the years had referred to her aunt as Crazy Daisy.

This was because, in addition to Daisy

Kellerman's rather odd looks, she spent all of her time with dead people.

On purpose.

But then, so did all of Erin's family.

Kellerman Funeral Home had been, and continued to be, the only funeral home in the town of Love for almost a century. Erin's dad, like his father and grandfather before him, was the mortician. Erin's mom was a nurse at Love Hospital, leading to smirking jokes about a pipeline to the family business. Erin's aunt Daisy was the cosmetician who made the faces and hair of the newly deceased beautiful for their final resting place.

In other words, she was a makeup artist and hair stylist. For dead people.

"Oopsie!" Daisy exclaimed. "I left Mrs. Deederman in hot rollers. I'll be right back!" Daisy dashed out of the room.

Erin closed her eyes. It was just too horrible. Mrs. Deederman was, of course, dead. She had keeled over into her Jell-O at the Early Bird special (half price before five-thirty P.M.) at the local diner the day before. Erin's mother had tried to resuscitate her at the hospital, of course, but hadn't had any luck.

My life is like some horrible joke, Erin thought, and I'm the punchline.

The entire Kellerman family lived on the grounds of the Love town cemetery. The large house with a white-pillared front porch would have been beautiful set just about anywhere except on the grounds of Love Land.

Love Land. Where Your Loved Ones Rest Happily Ever After.

Erin cringed just thinking about it.

And now Erin's family was trying to get her to help out with the family business part-time, to help earn money for college next year. They couldn't understand why it was that Erin wanted to have absolutely nothing to do with dead people at all, ever.

And Erin certainly didn't want to help her crazy aunt put petal pink lipstick on dead ladies' lips. It was all just too . . . horrible.

Erin's family was so weird, and Erin herself was so, well . . . normal, actually, that it didn't even seem as if she belonged in her family. Even her two younger brothers and two sisters were unfazed by the death business. In fact, they often dressed up as characters from *The Addams Family* and charged kids in the neighborhood fifty cents to tour the Kellerman property.

All Erin wanted was to be normal. "Normal" meant a lot to Erin, who had been known since grade school as Erin "Death" Kellerman, the girl who lived at the cemetery. It wasn't exactly an easy thing to live down in a town as small as Love, where everyone knew everyone. Because of her family, people expected Erin to be bizarre. Being called normal was the greatest compliment she could get.

With her pretty auburn hair, regular features, and smattering of freckles, she was girl-next-door cute, but not a raving beauty. She got good but not spectacular grades, and she had a cute, nice, but not spectacular boyfriend, Pete Cole, who had been her boyfriend since the eighth grade.

In fact, if it weren't for Erin's bizarre family and her two spectacular best friends, Erin would have been just as ordinary as she claimed she wanted to be.

Her two spectacular best friends, Tara Moore and Noelle Le Blanc, would stand out anywhere, but in the tiny town of Love they were notorious. And while Erin herself had no desire to stand out from the crowd, she was actually gratified that her friends were so unique and special.

First, there was the one and only Tara Elizabeth Moore, who had moved with her mother to Love at age ten from another college town, Starkville, Mississippi, when Tara's parents divorced. Tara's mom, a no-nonsense feminist who taught women's studies at Love College, often looked at her daughter as if she had given birth to a Martian.

Tara had been perfect-looking at ten, and her looks had only improved in the following seven years. She had a melodious southern accent that was just as thick now as it had been the day she arrived in Love. Since the age of twelve she had never been seen in public without mascara and a manicure.

Tara had entered — and won — a dazzling array of beauty pageants over the years, from Little Miss Sunshine to Apple Princess at the Michigan State Fair. As she had often told Erin, if it weren't for her thick ankles, she would go for Miss America. According to Tara, thick ankles kept you out of the really big time.

Whereas this beauty pageant thing could have made Tara unutterably icky, it just added to her quirky appeal. Because Tara Elizabeth Moore was brilliant. Super smart. Smarter than any of the dozens of guys who had fallen crazily in love with her. She fell in love with them, too, for about a day and a half, after which they usually bored her silly, and then she stopped returning their phone calls.

This only made them want her more, of course.

Guys were forever pledging their undying love to her. One boy wrote poetry and signed it with his own blood, which even Tara, with her penchant for the dramatic, found a little excessive.

And then there was Erin's other best friend, who had the incredible name Noelle Le Blanc. Noelle was as incredible-looking as her name — small, seemingly slender but actually extremely muscular and strong, with glossy, straight black hair and dark, intense eyes.

Noelle was a world-class figure skater who spent nearly all her time practicing.

Noelle's family lived in Detroit, but Noelle lived in Love with her skating coach, Olympic gold medalist Jack Preston and his wife, Sandi. She was tutored at the Prestons' home so that she could devote most of her time to skating. Recently, Noelle had just missed qualifying for the American Nationals by one tenth of a point. For weeks she had been inconsolable. And then one day she began training again, harder than ever. Her plan was to make the next Olympic team, American Nationals or no American Nationals. And to prove it, she would place first in the women's skating championships at the Love Winterfest, which was now only three weeks away.

The town of Love was famous for Winterfest, a winter carnival and sports championship for select high school and college athletes from around the country.

When Winterfest was started ten years earlier, it had actually saved Love from bankruptcy. And in the decade since its inception it had become a world-class, nationally known sports event.

Each year, several hundred high school and college athletes were invited by a selection board to compete at Winterfest. And each year, six high school seniors and fourteen college students were named to the prestigious Winterfest Student Committee. Although almost everyone in Love would be assigned an athlete to guide, the Student Committee members were matched with the high-profile athletes — the ones the media wanted to know about. Their job was to shepherd their athletes through Winterfest and to be there for any and all interviews with the media.

This year, both Tara and Erin had been selected for the committee. Erin had been shocked to find out she'd been chosen. After all, the group was mostly all college students. And everyone in the group was so outstanding and, well, wonderful. Like Tara.

And being known as "Death" Kellerman would hardly qualify me, Erin thought.

But after Tara had badgered her for two weeks, she'd finally submitted her name, and had been chosen.

It was kind of funny, Erin mused, that she, Tara, and Noelle had ever become friends. They had met seven years ago, the year both Tara and Noelle had moved to Love. All three of them were singing in the Christmas chorale, going door-to-door singing carols in really bad three-part harmony. By chance, Tara had been on Erin's left, and Noelle had been on her right. Erin still remembered how Tara had looked that day, wearing a red velvet coat with a white fake fur collar and cuffs and a matching red velvet hat that set off her blond curls. And Noelle had worn a tiny white skating skirt over green-and-white tights, and a green sweater with white skiers on it. After the caroling she planned to go right back to skating practice, so she had simply worn the outfit she planned to skate in.

Erin remembered how serious Noelle had looked, how she kept looking at her watch to see if she would be late for practice. And she remembered how — even then — Jimmy Berchin, the cutest boy in their class, kept throwing snowballs at the beautiful Tara to get her attention.

And I so badly wanted them both to like me, Erin recalled. *I kept trying to think of something I could do that would impress them.*

She couldn't think of anything, so she just kept singing.

Jimmy Berchin got frustrated because Tara was ignoring him, Erin remembered. That's when he yelled at her, "Hey, did you know the girl next to you loves dead people?"

Tara had glanced over at Erin, whose face burned bright red with embarrassment. She just kept on singing, "Joy to the world . . ."

"I mean it," Jimmy went on. "Her name's Death Kellerman. If you touch her, you die." He reached around Tara and touched Erin, then dramatically and loudly strangled himself, falling in the snow in a heap.

The chorale director had thrown him out, but it was too late. Other kids thought that what Jimmy had done was just hilarious, and they had reached out to touch Erin and then pretend they too were dying. Most of the girls began to giggle and move away from Erin, squealing and reaching for each other in fake terror.

And I wanted to die, too, Erin recalled. *No. I wanted to kill all of them, and then I wanted to die.*

She would remember for the rest of her life what Tara did at that moment. Tara shook her perfect blond hair off her face, then she casually put her arm around Erin and kept right on singing. On the other side of her, Noelle did the same thing. And so the three of them were joined, singing Christmas carols in bad three-part harmony, and suddenly it didn't matter anymore that she was "Death" Kellerman, the laughingstock of Love Elementary School through no fault of her own at all.

And then, arms still entwined, Tara began to change the lyrics to the carols, making them funny, until she had both Erin and Noelle practically falling over from laughter. Other kids began laughing, too, and suddenly Erin was a part of the group instead of outside it.

I'll remember that forever, she realized, a smile on her lips.

After that, Tara had managed to convince Noelle to go to practice a little late, and the three of them had shared hot chocolate with tiny marshmallows at Tara's house. A lifetime friendship had been born.

Actually, it was both the first and the last time Erin could remember Noelle going late to practice.

Come to think of it, it's amazing that I still feel so close to Noelle, considering how single-minded she is about her skating, and —

"Okay, Mrs. Deederman's curls have been saved!" Daisy called cheerfully as she came back into the living room, pulling off her gloves.

"So, Daisy," Tara said with a grin. "How's business?"

"Well, I could say that business is dying," Daisy said with a chuckle, "but it's actually booming! Frankly, I could use a little help!" She eyed Erin when she said this, and

Erin shook her head vehemently.

"No, no, never, never," Erin said flatly.

"Okay, sweetie," Erin's aunt said easily. "But if you change your mind, you know where to find me!"

"Only too well," Erin agreed.

"Would you girls like a snack or something?" Daisy asked, ignoring Erin's comment.

"No, thanks, Aunt Daisy," Erin said. "We're supposed to meet Noelle over at the rink."

"Okay, then, well, I'll see you later," Daisy said, smiling a sweet smile and crossing her strange eyes as she padded out of the room.

"Do you ever think about her making you a nice little snack and then having those same loving fingers smoothing blue eyeshadow on Mrs. Deederman?" Tara asked.

"All the time," Erin admitted. She looked at her watch. "We need to go over to the rink. I guess Cyrano will have to wait."

"I'll tell you what happens," Tara said, as Erin reached for her coat, which was lying over the end of the couch. "He doesn't get the girl, and he dies."

"What a depressing play!" Erin exclaimed, pushing out of her bunny slippers and slipping on her shoes. She then reached for the backpack she always used instead of a purse.

"Oh, well," Tara said blithely, "one thing worked out for him. At least Crazy Daisy didn't do his makeup before he was laid to rest!"

Noelle Le Blanc was in her own perfect world. Breathing heavily, gliding along on the ice, all she could hear was the pounding of her own heart, and the swoosh-swoosh-swoosh of her blades as they slid along the ice.

"Give me a double axel!" Jack Preston, her coach, called to her from where he stood at the side of the rink, watching Noelle with fierce intensity.

"Remember to center your weight this time, Noelle!"

A double axel, Noelle thought unconsciously, as she circled the rink preparing for her move. *Named for its inventor, Axel Paulsen. The only jump that takes off from a forward position. If I want to win Winterfest, I need to do a triple lutz. Two triples, maybe. Perfect triples. I have to be able to do double axels in my sleep.*

Noelle took two more powerful glides across the ice, prepared, then leapt into the air, spinning neatly, her body in perfect alignment. Then she landed on one blade, the other leg held out at the perfect angle, her arms gracefully extended away from her sides.

"You wobbled on the landing!" Jack yelled with disgust. "You wobbled on a damn double, Noelle! Just what do you think you're doing?"

Erin and Tara traded looks from their spot on the other side of the rink. They had heard Jack yell at Noelle many, many times, but they had never gotten used to it.

Noelle, still skating around, her hands on her hips, looked over at her coach.

"Just do it again," Jack commanded. "Do it until you're perfect, do you hear me? Or quit wasting my time!"

Noelle ducked her head into her shoulders for just a moment. *He's right,* she thought. *It wasn't perfect. And it was only a double.*

"Head up, shoulders back, you look like a turtle!" Jack barked.

Noelle raised her head and threw her shoulders back. She skated faster, whirling around the ice, then she prepared to jump again.

This time she nailed it. She knew it. She could feel it. She turned to Jack, eager for his praise.

"One jump doesn't make you a champion," Jack yelled to her. "And it was only a double. That jump didn't even get you to the Nationals!"

Only a double. Jack was right. A double was nothing. Less than nothing. She thrust herself forward again, doing double after double, finally stopping after a series of six perfect leaps. Then she skated even faster, her body a whirl of black hair and royal blue skating skirt on the ice, forcing air into her lungs, forcing herself further and further. Then she ripped off a perfect triple salchow/double axel combination.

There! Noelle thought. *That should satisfy him.*

She glanced over to her coach.

He was talking on the pay phone on the wall. He hadn't even seen the last combination.

"Hey, Noelle!" Tara called from where she and Erin were sitting in the spectators' bleachers. "Y'all are supposed to be on a break now!"

Noelle turned back to the rink, took a few more strides, did another couple of double axels, and a dazzling layback spin, then she skated over to her friends. "Hi," she said, breathing hard as she stopped in front of them. "Is it six o'clock already?"

"After," Erin said. "We were going to Pizza Bob's for dinner, remember?"

Noelle shot a look over at Jack, who was now off the phone and scowling at her from across the rink. "I don't think I can go," she said. "I'm not having a very good day."

"But you have to eat," Erin pointed out. "Have you eaten anything today at all?"

"A bagel, I think . . ." Noelle said vaguely.

"But you need some food," Erin protested.

"Oh, I'll just grab an apple or something," Noelle said, pulling her leg warmers up higher on her calves.

"Honey, you weigh just about nothing now," Tara said. "You need more than an apple."

"Jack says I need to take off a few pounds," Noelle explained. She was still panting heavily, as if she couldn't catch her breath.

Erin looked over Noelle's tiny body. "From where?"

"Skaters are skinny," Noelle explained. "You should see Nancy Kerrigan or Oksana Baiul in person. They are so *little*." Her words came out breathlessly.

"Are you okay?" Erin asked. "You're breathing so hard."

"Noelle, are we skating or baking cookies today?" Jack yelled.

"I have to go," Noelle said.

"But — " Erin began.

"I'll meet you at eleven when I'm done," Noelle promised quickly.

"Tara can't," Erin said. "She has a date with the new love of her life."

"Oh, I'm pretty sure I'll be completely over him by eleven," Tara said seriously. "You know how love fades."

"Noelle, I mean it!" Jack thundered.

"So I'll see you guys at eleven at . . ." But here Noelle stopped speaking. It seemed as if she couldn't get her breath.

Erin reached out to touch Noelle's hand. "Noelle? Are you sure you're okay? You don't look right."

But Noelle didn't answer. Instead, even as her coach screamed at her from across the rink to get back to work, Noelle, with perfect grace, slid to the ice in a dead faint.

Chapter 2

"Sure beats grits," Tara drawled, as the waitress placed the large, all-vegetable Pizza Bob's special pizza she and her friends had ordered on the red-and-white tablecloth. Noelle and Erin could hardly hear Tara's voice — Pizza Bob's was *that* crowded.

"It's a total madhouse in here," the harried waitress, who was obviously a college student, said to them over the noise and the music blaring out of the jukebox.

"I guess it's because some people have already started arriving for Winterfest," Erin said loudly, as the music changed on the jukebox to something by S.W.V.

"This'll be my third Winterfest," the waitress said wearily, shoving some of her blond hair behind her ear. "Every year it's the same insanity."

"You must make good tips, though," Erin pointed out.

"Not worth it," the waitress commented. "My feet are killing me. And I have a headache. What did you guys want to drink, again?"

"A pitcher of Coke," Tara said.

"*Diet* Coke, please," Noelle corrected quickly.

"Coming right up," the waitress said, sticking her pencil behind her ear, "or you might never get it at all."

It was a little after eleven o'clock that night, and, as they'd arranged earlier, Erin, Tara, and Noelle had met at the best of the three pizza places in town, Pizza Bob's, to hang out and to compare notes. Not that Pizza Bob's had great pizza, but it was by far the best that Love had to offer.

Erin had been the first to arrive, and then Tara had come in, exactly at eleven. Tara was always exactly on time, a habit her friends had gotten used to. Erin had to smile, watching Tara work her way through the crowd. Tara had on one of her perfect, color-coordinated outfits, while Erin wore corduroy jeans and a Love College sweatshirt.

Tara wouldn't be caught dead in what I'm

wearing, Erin realized. *And if I wore one of her "outfits," I'd feel as if I were in some kind of play.*

Then, right behind Tara, Noelle had come in, wearing jeans she had thrown on over her rehearsal tights, and an oversized ski sweater that made her look even tinier than she really was.

She looked so terrible this afternoon when she fainted, Erin recalled anxiously, thinking of the horrible moment when Noelle slid silently to the ice. Everyone had rushed over to her, and Jack gave her smelling salts. The smelling salts had worked; Noelle opened her eyes immediately.

She swore she was okay, Erin reminded herself, as she watched Noelle make her way through the crowded restaurant. *She did get right up afterward. And she looks fine now.*

It must just have been the pressure of the competition coming up.

"I have to eat fast," Tara told her friends, wiping some tomato sauce off her pinky. "I still have to drive to the airport to pick up David Benjamin tonight."

"He's getting in so late?" Erin asked in surprise.

Tara nodded. "It's some kind of special cheapo flight or something," she explained. "He doesn't get here until twelve-thirty."

Erin looked over at Noelle, who suddenly looked pale and tired to her. "Are you okay?" she asked Noelle.

Noelle was staring into the distance, clearly lost in thought.

"Noelle?" Erin said, touching her friend's hand.

"Hmmmm?"

"I asked if you were okay," Erin repeated.

"Oh, sure," Noelle said. "I was thinking about the way I hold my hands on the triple lutz, maybe I need to spread my fingers more — "

"Earth to Noelle," Tara called, reaching for a second slice of pizza. "This is pizza-eating time. This is flirting-with-guys time. Forget skating for a brief moment of your life."

Noelle shrugged. "That's easier said than done."

The waitress returned with their pitcher of diet Coke and left. Noelle poured herself a glass and drained it quickly.

"Have some pizza," Erin urged Noelle, pushing what was left of the pie toward her.

"Can't," Noelle said. "I shouldn't even be here. Jack would kill me if he knew."

"What is he, the prison warden?" Tara asked, making a face.

"You live with him and Sandi," Erin pointed out. "Where did you tell them you were going?"

"I didn't," Noelle admitted. "Jack's speaking at some sports banquet in Grand Rapids, and Sandi went with him." She looked around the pizza joint as if there might be someone there who'd report her to her coach.

"What are you looking for, Noelle?" Tara asked. "You think they have spies out looking for you?"

"I wouldn't put it past them," Noelle said seriously.

Tara shook her head. "Well, all I have to say is that you do not make big-time figure skating look as romantic and heavenly as it does on TV." Her glance fell on two cute guys in a booth across the room. "Oh, seriously cute," she said, smiling flirtatiously.

"How can you do that?" Erin asked.

"What?" Tara asked, her eyes still on the guys.

"Flirt like that," Erin explained. "I mean, as many times as I've seen you do it, I still don't get it. I would feel like the world's biggest fool grinning at those guys."

"Practice makes perfect," Tara sang out, turning back to Erin and Noelle. "I could give you flirting lessons, you know."

"That would be as unnatural on me as . . . as wearing your cute little outfits," Erin admitted.

"Only because you refuse to try," Tara maintained. "Now watch; I will demonstrate perfect flirting technique on the next male that walks through that door."

All three girls turned to the door and waited. It opened. A guy walked in.

"Oh, no! It's Bile Lyle!" Tara screeched, sliding down in the booth.

"Who?" Noelle asked, staring at the guy who stood in the doorway, looking around at the crowd.

"My date," Tara hissed, trying to remain completely hidden in the booth. "The guy I met this afternoon at the rink!"

"Didn't you show up for your date?" Noelle asked.

"Of course I showed up," Tara replied. "I have manners, you know. But the date was so hideous. The last book he read was some unauthorized biography of Stephen King, and I think he used the Cliff Notes."

"So he's not exactly an intellectual, you mean," Erin translated, looking over her shoulder at the guy. "But why 'Bile Lyle'?"

"Gas," Tara reported, still hunkered down in the booth. "Terminal gas. Everything Lyle ate gave him gas. He carries Pepto-Bismol around and swills from it."

"Ick," Noelle said, making a face.

"Please tell me he isn't coming this way," Tara begged.

"He isn't," Erin reported. "He's walking to a table of guys in Sigma Pi sweatshirts. You can come up for air."

Tara tentatively peeked over the top of the booth. "Ah, the coast is clear." She sat up and fluffed her hair daintily.

"It was really that bad a date, huh?" Noelle asked, eyeing the slice of pizza.

"I've had more fun watching paint dry," Tara replied. "Not that he got the hint. He asked me out again, and asked for my phone number."

"You didn't give it to him," Erin asked warily.

"No," Tara said. "I gave him yours."

"You didn't!" Erin cried in dismay, and then she realized that Tara was teasing her. All three girls laughed.

"No, you lucked out, but I should have,"

Tara said. "You could use a change from Mr. Pete."

"I love Pete," Erin said loyally, taking a sip of her Coke.

"And I love pajamas with feet," Tara said, "but I wouldn't wear them for five consecutive years. You and Mr. Pete have been an item since eighth grade. And it's a big world out there, chock-full of guys."

"And you plan to date the majority of them," Erin said.

"Once," Noelle added with a grin.

"Can I help it if I have very high standards?" Tara asked loftily.

"And can you help it if every guy between the ages of fifteen and fifty asks you out?" Erin added with a laugh.

"Not boring Mr. Pete," Tara pointed out. "He is utterly faithful to you."

"That's true," Erin agreed. "And he's not boring. I'm really lucky."

Pete Cole had been Erin's boyfriend forever — well, since eighth grade, which certainly *felt* like forever. He was medium height, with curly brown hair and sweet brown eyes behind round glasses. He was smart and nice, and he was totally and completely in love with Erin.

And I love him, too, Erin thought. *I can't*

even imagine my life without Pete. We do everything together. And we never fight. I suppose we'll go to the same college and one day we'll get married and . . . live happily ever after. Which is good. Really.

I guess.

"Don't you ever wonder what it would be like to kiss a guy other than Pete?" Tara asked, as if she had been reading Erin's mind.

"No," Erin said a little too forcefully. "Why would I?"

"Because, as I said, there are a zillion cute guys on this planet," Tara explained.

"But there's only one Pete," Erin said.

Tara sighed. "What am I going to do with the two of you? One of you is practically married, and the other lives like a nun on ice."

"You can't make it to the Olympics and think about guys at the same time," Noelle explained, still staring hungrily at the pizza.

"Why don't you eat it, Noelle," Erin urged her. "Really. One slice of vegetarian pizza can't be so bad for you."

"No, I can't," Noelle said forcefully, pushing the pizza away from her. "I can't even think about it." She poured herself another glass of diet Coke.

"I just worry about you," Erin began.

"She doesn't want you to become a family client anytime soon," Tara teased.

Erin shot her a look of disgust. "Very funny."

"I know," Tara agreed. "I *am* amusing." She reached into her purse and pulled out a small, thick, spiral-bound book with a photo of a skier on the back cover, putting it on the table next to the pitcher of Coke.

"What's that?" Noelle asked.

Tara flipped the book over.

"Winterfest 10: Athletes in Love," the cover read.

"It's the Winterfest guide to the athletes," Erin explained. "We heard all about it at the committee meeting. This is the first year they've put this out. I got one, too. You're in it, Noelle." She reached for the guide on the table, and quickly turned to the section on figure skating.

"Here!" she said, thrusting the guide at Noelle. "There you are."

Noelle took the guide and looked down at a thumbnail-sized head-and-shoulders photo of herself — immediately worrying that her smile wasn't perfect enough — and then read the short biography under it:

NOELLE LE BLANC, age 17, lives right here in Love, Michigan, though she was raised in Detroit. One of America's finest young figure skaters, she just missed qualifying for the national championships. A major threat to win the junior women's figure skating at this year's Winterfest.

"Nice bio," Erin said to her friend encouragingly.

"It's okay," Noelle said. The part about how she had "just missed" qualifying for the national championships echoed in Noelle's head.

Just missed.

"I like that 'major threat' part," Tara said supportively.

Noelle shrugged. "Being a major threat to win and winning are two different things." She handed the book back to Tara.

"Y'all check this out," Tara said. She flipped through the pages until she came to the section on men's alpine skiing. Then she looked carefully until she found the photo she wanted.

It was a very handsome young guy, with short dark hair, and startlingly light-colored eyes in a very tanned face. He wore a black turtleneck and he looked serious.

"David Benjamin," Tara read aloud. "Age nineteen, a native of Tel Aviv, Israel, now an exchange student majoring in American Studies at Colby College, Waterville, Maine. Since bursting on the college skiing scene with his shocking win in the downhill event at the New England Small College Athletic Conference championships, David is being touted as Israel's first hope for winter Olympic gold. A win at Winterfest would show the way."

Noelle raised her eyebrows. "He's your athlete?"

"All mine," Tara purred. She glanced at her watch. "I'm picking him up in an hour. And I get to guide him through Winterfest for the next two weeks. What a tough assignment."

"Who did you get assigned?" Noelle asked Erin.

"His name is Luke Blakely," Erin said. "He's a ski jumper. I have to meet his bus tomorrow afternoon."

"Maybe you and Luke Blakely will fall madly, passionately in love," Tara suggested wickedly.

"Tara, I am in love with Pete," Erin said patiently.

"For a girl who finds Love, Michigan, so boring, your love life is not exactly adding to the excitement of the town," Tara pointed out. She stared at David's photo again.

"I'm sure you'll make up for that," Noelle told her.

"David Benjamin will fall madly in love with you, like every other guy," Erin said with a sigh.

"Oh, well," Tara said blithely, "so many guys, so little time."

"He sounds like a great skier," Noelle remarked.

"I am more interested in other qualities, quite frankly," Tara admitted.

"Such as his talent at first dates?" Erin asked.

"Something like that," Tara agreed, gazing at David Benjamin's photo. "I just have a feeling about this," she said.

"What?" Noelle asked, trying to ignore the growlings of her empty stomach.

"Destiny," Tara said dramatically. "David Benjamin and I are destiny."

* * *

I think that's him, Erin thought with shock, as she saw the broad-shouldered guy climb out of the University of Colorado's chartered bus, which was parked in front of one of the dorms at the college, go to the luggage bin underneath the bus, and pull out two pairs of long jumping skis. *That's got to be Luke Blakely,* she decided. *He doesn't look like his picture. Not much, anyway.*

Erin stood up and wrapped her arms around herself, trying to rub the cold out of her body. She had on three layers under her ski jacket, but the temperature was heading toward zero, and she was freezing.

Frankly, he's a lot cuter than his photo, she admitted to herself.

As she watched Luke gather up his things, his bio from the Winterfest guide flashed before her eyes.

LUKE BLAKELY, age 19, was raised in Alamosa, Colorado, and attends the University of Colorado. A ski jumper since the age of nine, Luke is majoring in psychology and hopes to be a college ski coach after graduation. He also competes on the University of Colorado tennis team.

While his bio had sounded interesting, Erin had not been impressed with his photo. His hair had been buzz cut, the picture was blurry, and Luke had been kind of scowling at the camera.

But here was an entirely different Luke. His hair was now longer, his dark eyes sexy and intense rather than scowling, his muscles clearly visible through his unzipped parka.

As Tara would say, hush mah puppies.

Well, I'd better go meet him, Erin thought, starting to hurry down to the bus. *He looks like he could use help with those skis, and I'm supposed to be his host!*

"Hi," Erin said shyly, as she approached Luke, who was still hunched over his skis and training pack. "Are you Luke Blakely?"

Luke stood up and grinned.

"Yeah," Luke said. "Are you the welcome wagon?"

"I'm — "

"You're Erin Kellerman," Luke said.

"How did you know?" Erin asked.

"The printout," Luke explained. "Mine

said my guide to Love would be Erin Kellerman."

"And it is," Erin said. "I mean, I am." She smiled again, feeling ridiculous and flustered.

He's just a guy, she told herself. *You are acting like an idiot.*

"So, can I help you with your stuff?" Erin offered.

"Yeah, thanks," Luke said. Together, Erin and Luke carried his skis and boots — ski jumpers don't use ski poles, that much Erin knew — and all his other gear up to the check-in desk at the dorm.

Quickly and efficiently, the registration desk got Luke installed in one of the few single rooms in the dorm. And then, Erin politely asked Luke, as she'd been instructed in her welcoming materials, if she might show him around Love.

"Oh yeah, sure," Luke said easily.

"Really?" Erin asked with surprise.

"You just offered, didn't you?" he asked with a bemused grin.

"Well, yeah," Erin acknowledged. "But only because they told us we have to. I didn't really think you'd take me up on it."

"Why not?"

"Well . . . because there's nothing to see!" Erin blurted out.

"Wrong," Luke said. "There's the jumping hill. That's about all I care about, frankly. Could we go check it out?"

"Sure," Erin agreed, and they walked to her parents' car.

Thank God we've got a Ford Taurus in addition to the family hearse, Erin thought, as they got in the car.

"The jumping hill is fifteen minutes out of town," Erin explained as they drove along. She pointed out the sights — such as they were — the local Wal-Mart, Shatner's Rink, where Noelle practiced, the college's impressive athletic facilities, and even Pizza Bob's.

"Like I said, there isn't anything to see," Erin said apologetically.

"That's cool," Luke said. "I didn't come for the sights."

Right. Of course he didn't, Erin reminded herself. *He came to jump. And to win. Or try to.*

She sneaked a look at him out of the corner of her eye. He was so great-looking. He even smelled great all the way across the front seat. Erin felt nervous sitting just a couple of feet away from him.

She turned on the radio, just for something to do, and tried to act normally. But suddenly she couldn't remember what "normal" was.

You are in love with Pete, she told herself. *This is just some bizarre hormonal thing, and it doesn't mean anything at all.*

"So," Luke asked her, as she finally turned her car up the winding access road that led to the ski jumping facility, "what's it like to be in Love?"

"It's fantastic," Erin said earnestly, as she maneuvered the car carefully on the icy access road. "Pete is so terrific. I mean, I really am in love, and it's so perfect, and — "

"Who's Pete?" Luke asked.

Erin glanced at him and turned her eyes back to the road. He was staring at her, an amused look on his face.

"I mean what's it like to be in Love, Michigan? You know. To live here."

Erin felt the hot rush of blood to her face.

Right. Of course. How could I have been so stupid? Luke doesn't even know about Pete, and he probably doesn't care either, Erin thought, totally mortified.

"I feel like a total idiot," Erin admitted,

wishing she could just sink into the ground and disappear.

"Hey, forget it," Luke said easily. "Actually, I think it's kind of cute."

"You do?"

"Sure," Luke said. "You must really love that Pete dude, that's all I have to say."

"Right, I do," Erin said. "He's great. Really."

"I believe you," Luke said.

"Good," Erin replied. "You should. Because he's terrific."

"You already said that," Luke reminded her. He was smiling into her eyes, and she could see flecks of gold in the dark brown.

Pete's eyes, Erin instructed herself. *Think about Pete's eyes.*

"So, we should get out of the car," Luke suggested.

"Right," Erin said. "Here's your hill."

Luke got out and stared up at the hill. The sun had just begun to set, creating exquisite patterns of gold and crimson against the stark white snow.

"I can feel it," Luke muttered.

"What?" Erin asked, sticking her mittened hands under her arms for warmth.

"The ride," Luke said, still staring at the

top of the hill. "The rush." He turned to her. "You ski?"

"Yeah," Erin said. "But not very well."

"What do you do well?" he asked. "Really well. Better than anyone else."

Erin thought a minute. Nothing came to mind. "I guess I'm not really an . . . outstanding kind of person," she admitted.

"Wrong," Luke said softly. "Everyone is. It's just that some people haven't found what they're outstanding at yet." He looked at her, a half smile on his face. "Maybe you're outstanding at loving that guy, what's-his-name?"

"Pete," Erin said.

"Right," Luke agreed, turning back to the hill, a blissful look on his face.

Outstanding at loving Pete, Erin thought.

For the very first time since eighth grade, that didn't seem like such a wonderful thing to be after all.

Chapter 3

"How was dinner?" Sandi asked Noelle pleasantly.

"Great," Noelle told her. "Just great."

"Glad you liked it," Sandi said, reaching to clear off the empty dinner plates.

Noelle felt as if she could grab the plate and chew it into tiny china bits, that's how hungry she still was.

Dinner that night had consisted of three nearly tasteless tomato slices with no salt or salad dressing, a broiled chicken breast minus the skin, some steamed spinach, and some canned asparagus.

Lunch had been an apple.

Breakfast had been a plain fat-free yogurt and orange juice.

And tomorrow promised more of the same.

Noelle thought about Erin, who was at

that very moment meeting her athlete at his bus. She thought about Tara, who had called while Noelle was studying English with her tutor to inform her that David Benjamin's flight from Maine the evening before had been canceled because of a snowstorm, and he was arriving Tuesday afternoon instead.

Tara had been chewing something as she told Noelle this information over the phone. Noelle, always interested in what other people could eat, since she was never allowed to, had asked Tara what she was eating.

A chocolate candy bar.

Chocolate. Noelle couldn't remember the last time she had had chocolate.

"How did the jumps go today, Noelle?" Sandi asked, as she loaded the dishwasher with the dirty dishes.

"Not good," Jack said, answering for Noelle. "She doesn't work hard enough."

Noelle bit her lower lip. She had heard Jack say the same thing to her every day, it seemed, since she had moved in with him and Sandi seven years ago.

Jack still looked like the Olympic gold medalist he had been so many years ago, and Sandi retained her preppie Love College homecoming queen look. The Prestons had never had any children. Instead, for the past ten or fifteen years, one or another elite young figure skater had lived with the two of them, ever since Jack had given up competing and had turned full-time to coaching.

But so far Jack had never coached an Olympian. It was something he wanted, more than anything in the world. And he believed that Noelle was his shot.

Noelle Le Blanc had been Noelle White for the first seven years of her life in Detroit. It was there, at the Detroit Skating Club, that Jack Preston had spied little Noelle twirling and jumping across the ice.

He told Noelle's parents, Jimmy and Shirley White, that their daughter could be a champion, but only if she devoted her life to it. He painted pictures of dollars, of the fame, fortune, and glory of being an Olympian.

Jimmy and Shirley White fell for it, hook, line, and sinker.

And so Noelle's last name had been changed to the ethereal-sounding Le Blanc, and a few years later Noelle's parents agreed to allow their ten-year-old daughter to move to Love and train full-time with Jack Preston.

Not that Noelle hadn't wanted this, because she had. Nothing mattered more than pleasing Jack. Nothing. Pleasing Jack meant reaching her goal, the Olympics. And sure, sometimes she missed her parents, her brother, Buddy, and her sister, Claire, but she just kept telling herself that she was different, special, destined for greatness.

Everyone that Noelle knew — except for maybe Erin and Tara — thought she was the luckiest girl alive.

Noelle agreed, too, most of the time.

She heard her stomach growling, and put her hand over it, as if she could will the empty feeling away. Maybe tonight Sandi would bring an apple or a pear over for her for dessert? It happened every once in a while. So maybe . . .

But Sandi was wiping off the counter. And her hands were empty.

Noelle tried to take her mind off food. She looked around the kitchen walls, which were covered with blown-up photographs of coach Jack, mostly taken at the 1976 games. Then, Jack Preston, just turned eighteen, had surprised everyone by winning the gold medal in the men's singles figure skating competition, beating such notables as the 1972 Olympic champion, Ondrej Nepela of Czechoslovakia.

There was Jack, in midair, in the middle of a triple lutz.

There was Jack, in midair, in the middle of a triple salchow.

There was Jack, being interviewed by skating legend Dick Button on ABC television, waiting for his scores to be announced.

There was Jack on the medal stand, holding a tiny American flag in his left hand, his wavy blond hair neatly combed, waving to the huge crowd, a bright gold medal glinting as it hung around his neck.

That could be me, Noelle thought. *It has to be me. It just has to.*

But you missed the Nationals, a voice said in her head. *Maybe you just aren't good enough. Maybe you'll always choke. Maybe you're going to be a total failure and let everyone down.*

Noelle's eyes fell on another photo, of Jack and Sandi together, two years after his Olympic win. In this photo they were both in skating outfits, their arms around each other. Noelle knew that that photo had been taken of them on their honeymoon. Sandi had been one of Jack's choreographers, and they had fallen in love. Now Sandi choreographed Jack's protégée's routines.

Noelle turned at the sound of Sandi crunching into a juicy apple, and her mouth watered.

"How's your weight?" Jack asked.

"Okay," Noelle said evasively. She knew the question was a waste of time. Jack always knew exactly what she weighed. This was just his way of telling her she wasn't going to get an apple.

"Five more pounds need to go before Winterfest," he reminded her.

"I remember," she said, trying not to look at Sandi and her apple.

"So, what's on your agenda for tonight?" Jack asked, leaning back and folding his arms.

"Mirror practice," Noelle reported. "Then homework. Then sleep."

"I'll do mirror practice with you," Sandi offered.

"Don't forget to call your parents," Jack reminded her. "It's Sunday night. They're expecting your call."

"I won't," Noelle promised.

"And there's no need to mention that little incident at the rink yesterday," Jack instructed her. "Don't worry them. You worry them, you worry yourself."

"Got it," Noelle acknowledged.

Jack leaned over and ruffled her hair. "Good girl," he said, and Noelle basked as if the sun were shining on her and her alone.

"You ready for mirror practice now?" Sandi asked.

Noelle nodded.

"Great," Sandi said, throwing her apple core into the trash. "Let's go into the bathroom. It has the best acoustics."

Jack looked on as Sandi and Noelle together walked the short distance from the kitchen to Jack and Sandi's bathroom off their bedroom. Sandi was right — the bathroom did have the best acoustics in the house — it duplicated the cavernous sound of most competition rinks — and acoustics were important in mirror practices. In fact, Sandi kept a small boom box in the bathroom for just this purpose.

"You ready?" Sandi asked, as Noelle positioned herself in front of the full-length mirror.

Noelle nodded assent, as Sandi snapped on the tape recorder. The lilting saxophone of the Paul Desmond jazz standard "Take Six" filled the bathroom, and for the next two minutes and forty seconds — the regulation length of the compulsory technical program, one of the two programs that Noelle would skate in the competition — Noelle practiced in front of the mirror each and every facial expression she would do as part of her skating routine.

When she finished, Sandi had her do it again. And again. And again and again. Which wouldn't have been so bad, except for the fact that Noelle and Sandi had been doing mirror practices four times a week for the last year and a half. To the same music.

When Sandi was satisfied with Noelle's work on "Take Six," she snapped a different cassette into the recorder — a four-minute version of Ravel's famous classical piece *Bolero*, which was the music that Jack and Sandi had chosen for Noelle's free skate program.

For the next hour — until Noelle's jaws ached from smiling so much at herself — Sandi and Noelle worked on the *Bolero*.

Finally, Sandi said she actually had to use the bathroom.

"Why don't you go call your parents now," she suggested, "and then come back. We can work some more."

"Sure," Noelle said.

"Because you need the work," Sandi intoned meaningfully.

"I know," Noelle acknowledged.

"All over the world, girls who want to be champions are doing their mirror work," Sandi said, repeating an axiom that she and Jack had repeated to Noelle ever since she had moved in with them. "You don't work, you don't win."

"I know," Noelle repeated, which was the only permissible response to any of Jack and Sandi's familiar axioms.

Sandi smiled at her. "You've got it, Noelle. You've got what it takes. Jack and I both know that. Do you know how much that means?"

"Yes," Noelle said quietly. "I do."

"Good." Sandi ruffled Noelle's hair, just as Jack had done. For a moment something fiery and rebellious lit up inside Noelle.

Quit doing that! she wanted to scream. *I am not your obedient little dog, so quit petting me!*

But she didn't say a word.

Instead she swallowed the bad feeling, as she had so many times before, and dutifully headed for her own room to call her parents.

"You'll show them all!" Sandi called out, as she shut the bathroom door.

Will I? Noelle wondered anxiously, as she made her way to her room. Her mind flashed back six months to the Midwest Regionals, the competition that determined which two skaters from her region would qualify to go to the Nationals.

"You'll show them all!" Sandi had told her that day, too.

Only Noelle had finished third.

Two skaters went to the Nationals, but not Noelle Le Blanc.

And there was no reason for me to finish third, Noelle recalled. *My program was going great! And then, in the last fifteen seconds, I two-footed a landing on a double axel, and then Jack says that threw me so I lost my smile for just an instant . . .*

And I finished third, by one-tenth of a point.

Jack says it's because I don't work hard enough in practice. And he's right. Jack says —

"Did you call your parents yet?" Jack

asked, cutting into Noelle's thoughts.

"I was just going to," she explained, heading toward her room.

"Good," Jack said. "Use the phone in the family room," he suggested, "and after that I'll meet you in there and check out your mirror work."

Noelle nodded, and dutifully walked down the long hallway of their expansive ranch house, until the hallway led into the family room, with its two trophy cases.

One held Jack's dozens of skating trophies; the second, smaller one held Noelle's trophies.

Noelle sat down gratefully on the couch, picked up the portable phone, and dialed her parents' number in Detroit.

"Hello?" answered her mother's familiar voice, after the phone had rung only once.

"Hi, Mom," Noelle said, trying to keep the tiredness and the hunger she was feeling out of her voice. "It's me."

"Noelle!" her mom cried, happiness oozing out of every millimeter of her vocal cords. "Hold on a sec. Hey! Jimmy! Noelle's on the phone!"

Noelle waited patiently for her father to pick up the extension.

"Hey, doll, how you doin'?" Noelle heard her father ask gruffly. Actually, Noelle was surprised that her dad was at home. It was still the football play-offs, and that usually meant that he'd be moonlighting as a bartender at a local tavern frequented mostly by auto workers.

"Fine," Noelle said, remembering what Jack and Sandi had told her to say.

"That's great, honey," her mother said. "Are you doing everything that Jack and Sandi tell you?"

"Everything," Noelle promised.

"Hey, honey," Jimmy told her. "Guess what? A sportswriter from the *Detroit Free Press* wants to interview us tomorrow. About you! How about that?"

"That's great, Dad," Noelle told him. "Just don't tell him my weight. Jack would kill me."

Shirley laughed, but her tone was anxious. "Now, sweetheart," she said to her daughter, "you haven't gained any weight, have you?"

"No, Mom," Noelle said honestly. "Still five foot three and a hundred five. But Jack wants me at ninety-five for Winterfest. He says he'll settle for a hundred."

"You just do what he says, sweetheart,"

her mother instructed. "Imagine that, my daughter being trained by an Olympic champion!"

Noelle closed her eyes. She had heard this same litany hundreds of times.

"I think you take after me, Noelle, honey, I really do," Shirley continued. "I used to be a very good dancer, you know."

"Until you packed on fifty pounds," Jimmy pointed out cruelly.

"Oh, Jimmy," Shirley chided him. "So, how are you feeling, sweetheart?"

"Great," Noelle lied. She wasn't about to tell her mother about fainting on the ice Saturday afternoon, or that sometimes, late at night, she felt like her heart was racing.

After all, she reminded herself, as her parents argued about who needed to take the garbage out, *a week ago I had the same routine physical that all the athletes competing in Winterfest had to have, and the doctor told me I was fine.*

Of course, I didn't mention anything about my heart racing. But if something was really wrong with me, he would have been able to tell, I'm sure.

"Noelle, honey?" her mother called into the phone.

"What?" she asked, shaking off her thoughts.

"I said Claire and Buddy send you their love, honey," Shirley repeated. "They're at Aunt Gussie's house watching their new big-screen TV."

"I miss them," Noelle said, and suddenly she felt really sad.

"They miss you, too, honey," Shirley said.

"They're so proud of you, dollface," her father said. "Just as proud of you as we are. They tell all their friends about their famous big sister."

"Oh, I didn't tell you!" Shirley exclaimed. "We're all coming to Winterfest! Aunt Gussie and Uncle Jerry and all their kids, too. We're renting a camper!"

"We're all coming to see you win, doll," Jimmy added.

"That's right," Shirley agreed. "I just can't decide what to wear! You know how they love to show the parents on camera, honey."

"You'll think of something nice, Mom," Noelle said.

"I'm gonna be so proud when you're up there on that podium," Jimmy predicted. "My kid. Jimmy White's kid, up there, a winner."

"I'll try to make you proud," Noelle said, swallowing hard.

"You about ready to start again?" Sandi asked, coming into the family room.

Jimmy overheard her and laughed. "Guess we're getting our money's worth, Shirl," he said to his wife. "Go to it, doll."

"We'll see you at the competition," Shirley promised her daughter.

"Okay, Mom," Noelle said.

"Great!" Jimmy replied. "So, bye!"

"Bye, honey," Shirley added.

"Say hi to Buddy and — " Noelle started to say, wanting her parents to say hello to her younger brother and sister for her. But her parents had already hung up.

"I'll get your tape," Sandi told her, and hurried out of the room.

Noelle sighed and leaned back on the couch. Directly in front of her was her trophy case. In it, arranged on racks and shelves, were dozens of trophies, ribbons, and medals that she had won at scores of competitions, ever since she'd laced on her first pair of skates when she was six years old. Jack had insisted that her parents ship all the trophies from Detroit to Love when Noelle had moved in with Sandi and him. Her parents had protested at first, but, like with everything else, they finally did what Jack told them to do.

There was, however, one unusual thing about the trophy case. Noelle noticed it every time she looked at it.

There was one trophy missing. Actually, not a trophy. There was a spot for a medal.

In its place, Jack had placed an enormous handlettered sign that Noelle had read many times each day.

OLYMPIC GOLD MEDAL, the sign read. IF IT'S NOT HERE, ALL THE OTHERS AREN'T WORTH DOODLY-SQUAT.

"You ready?" Jack asked, coming into the family room.

"Absolutely," Noelle said firmly, eyeing Jack's handlettered sign and picturing a gold medal in its place. She stood up and held her head high. "Let's get back to work."

Tara found a seat in the no-smoking waiting area, crossed her legs, and checked her watch. Perfect. David Benjamin's plane from Maine was due to land in five minutes.

Well, it's about time I get to meet him, Tara thought crossly. She had spent an hour getting to the airport Saturday night before finding out that his flight had been canceled due to a snowstorm in Maine.

When she got home, she'd checked her computer for e-mail. David had left her a message telling her he'd be on the flight arriving at 4:15 P.M. Tuesday. He had asked in the e-mail how he would know her. Tara had e-mailed him back, saying that since she had his picture in the Winterfest guide, she would know him.

Per usual, Tara liked having the upper hand.

She looked around, immediately catching the eye of two collegiate-looking guys who were walking by with backpacks slung over their shoulders. They smiled at her in that way she had known all her life, that told her how pretty she was, and how much they'd like to meet her. And of course, Tara smiled back.

She looked down at the outfit she'd chosen to wear to the airport: winter white wool trousers with a short, fluffy, pink-and-white angora sweater that delicately exposed the tiniest portion of her perfectly toned stomach. Her nails were painted a delicate pale pink that matched the slender ribbon in her wavy blond hair and the blush on her cheeks and her lips, compliments of Estee Lauder. The entire effect, Tara knew, was both very demure and very sexy. And per usual, she had planned it that way.

Also per usual, her mother had just about flipped out when she saw how Tara was dressed.

"You're wearing *that* to the airport?" her mother had said, looking up from the papers for Advanced Women's Studies she was grading, as Tara walked into the living room.

"No, Momma, I'm going naked, it's just that I have yet to shuck my clothes," Tara drawled.

Her mother frowned and shook her head. She was used to her brilliant daughter's sarcasm. She didn't like it, but she was used to it. "Why is it that Playboy bunnies come to mind when I look at you, Tara?" she asked wearily.

"I wouldn't know," Tara said, reaching for her purse, which of course matched the rest of her outfit. "I mean, I don't mind looking as if I could have been one, but as you know I would sooner own the franchise."

This got a small smile from her mother's pale lips. "What happened to oversized flannel shirts and jeans with holes in them?"

Tara smiled at her mother, who, at the moment, was clad in just such an outfit. "You own them all, Momma," she replied. Tara sprayed herself with perfume — something wonderful and French — and put the vial back into her purse. The perfume was compliments of a boyfriend who had lasted a whole week, which in Tara's experience was a long relationship.

Her mother studied her, a look somewhere between amusement and disdain caught on her face. "I guess you just completely take after your daddy," she said softly, and to Tara the implication was that "taking after your daddy" was the worst thing in the world.

She remembered her daddy, even though she hadn't seen him for seven years. He had been big and blond and handsome, an All-American football player at Mississippi State University. He was also brilliant — even Tara's mother admitted that.

It was the only good thing she ever said about him.

The question is, why did they ever get married in the first place? Tara wondered for maybe the zillionth time. *He was studying business, and she was studying feminist poetry. It's not like they had anything at all in common.*

Whenever Tara asked her mother why she and her father had married, her mother always said the same thing: "I was young and stupid and I mistook hormones for love, Tara."

Great, Tara thought. *And out of those hormones sprung little ole me.*

Tara strongly suspected that her parents had really married because her mother had gotten pregnant with her. She had been born seven months after their wedding date, but her mother claimed that Tara's birth was premature.

Tara didn't buy *that* for an instant.

Her parents had stayed married for ten years, both becoming professors at Mississippi State University. And while they were always civil to each other, they just never seemed . . . well, like a family, really.

Of course, now Tara's father lived in Saudi Arabia, where he was a big executive for Shell Oil. And he had a new wife, Brenda, who was as pink and white and girly as Tara's mother never was. And a new daughter, who wore a huge pale blue ribbon in her hair in the one photo Tara had ever seen of her. He sent Tara one birthday card and one Christmas card per year, along with a big, fat check.

So, Tara sometimes mused, was she really just like her father? Would she trade one family in for another if it suited her purposes, just the same way that now she was always trading one date in for another?

"I guess you're right," Tara agreed stiffly. Her mother often told her she was "just like her daddy." And to Tara it felt as if her intense mother was rejecting everything about her.

"You know, I don't know why you didn't just give him custody of me in the divorce," Tara added.

Her mother stared directly into Tara's eyes. "Because he didn't ask."

Oh, that's cold, Tara thought, and she felt as if she had been slapped.

She stood up and pulled the strap of her bag over her shoulder. "I'll be back when I get back," she said, turning on her heel.

"Wait, Tara, I didn't mean it like that — " her mother called from behind her.

But Tara never turned around.

She recrossed her legs and checked the time again. *Why do I always fight with Momma?* she asked herself. *It's like she hates everything about me except my brains, and even that she considers wasted on a girl who color-coordinates her lipstick and hair ribbons..*

Well, everyone in the world is not Miss Super-Feminist, Momma, she told her mother in her head. *Everyone in the world does not march in perfect, politically correct step with you.*

At that moment people began to pour out of gate 7G, which had to mean that David Benjamin's plane had landed. Tara stood up and looked over the arrivals. And then she spotted him. He looked like his photo, only better: more than six feet tall and very tanned, with short brown hair and huge, electric blue eyes that a black-and-white photo hadn't done justice. He wore jeans and a blue T-shirt that matched his eyes, underneath a well-worn brown leather jacket. He carried a sports sack in one hand, and a garment bag that seemed almost empty was slung over his shoulder.

He was probably the best-looking guy Tara had ever seen in her life.

"Hi there," Tara said, walking over to him.

"You are Tara Moore?" he asked, sounding surprised. He had a slight, sexy accent.

"I am," Tara replied. "Why, don't I look like a Tara Moore?" she asked flirtatiously.

She expected him to toss her a compliment in reply. He didn't.

"I have no idea," he said seriously.

Tara smiled so her dimples showed. "Welcome to Love, David." She leaned over and gave him a light kiss on his cheek, all the better for him to smell her perfume.

She expected him to comment on it, or at least to inhale with appreciation.

He didn't seem to notice. In fact, he really didn't seem to notice Tara at all, except as a human body that would transport him to his dorm.

"Thank you," he said formally. "It was nice of you to come and meet me."

"Well, that's just the kind of girl I am," Tara said, grinning again. "Can I help you carry anything?"

"Oh, no, it's not necessary," David replied.

"The baggage claim is this way," Tara said, cocking her head toward a corridor to the right.

"This is my baggage," David said, indicating the two pieces in his hands.

"Really?" Tara asked. "Lord, I carry that much with me for an overnight!"

She expected David to laugh. He didn't.

"Then you must overpack," he said seriously.

"No skis? Boots?"

"Shipped," he said.

She led him out to the Subaru she shared with her mom, and pulled out of the parking lot.

"So, tell me all about yourself, David," Tara said.

"To tell you all would take a long time," he said seriously in his Israeli-accented voice.

"It's just an expression," Tara explained.

He turned to study her. "I know."

"Oh, you were pulling my leg!" Tara said with a laugh.

"Yes," David agreed. "I was pulling on your leg." He studied her again. "You have an accent, you know."

"Oh, and you don't!" Tara said, laughing again.

"Southern," he said, still studying her.

"I'm from Mississippi," Tara said, turning the Subaru onto the expressway.

David didn't seem very interested. He looked out the window. "Very little snow."

"But there's some in the forecast," Tara told him. "So, David, I'd be more than happy to show you around Love," Tara offered. "We could take a tour, then go get some dinner, if you'd like."

"No thanks," David said. "Maybe later."

Tara smiled at him again. "Why, David, how can you turn down the chance to spend the afternoon with me?"

David studied her again. "Because I have other plans," he replied.

Ouch, Tara thought. *This is not going well.* A spasm of irritation radiated up her spine.

Maybe it's an Israeli thing, she thought. *Maybe he's already wild for me, but he just doesn't want to show his feelings.*

She checked him out again. He seemed totally oblivious to her, staring out the window. Well, Tara was definitely not oblivious to *him*.

"So, David," Tara began anew, "I'm just so curious. How did a guy from Israel become a downhill racer?"

David shrugged, still staring out the window. "I like a challenge."

Tara glanced at him quickly. "But how did you even get interested in it?"

"Patrick Ortlieb," David replied.

"Patrick who?"

"Ortlieb. He won the downhill at the '92 Olympics," David explained. "No one believed he could do it. Everyone thought that the French would take the medal. But Ortlieb showed them all. He was like a cement truck with power steering going down the hill. I looked at him and I thought, 'I want to do that, too.'"

"Just like that?" Tara asked.

"Just like that," David agreed. "As I said, I like a challenge." He turned his attention back to the passing road signs out the window, ignoring Tara once again.

Well, David Benjamin, Tara thought to herself, *I like a challenge, too. And I have a feeling you're going to be mine.*

May the best man win.

Chapter 4

"Noelle Le Blanc?" the middle-aged nurse called out, in a clear, strong voice.

"Right here," Jack replied, from where he and Noelle sat together on one of the waiting room couches. "She's right here with me."

The nurse regarded the two of them, bemused by Jack's answering for Noelle.

"The doctor will see you now, Noelle," the nurse told Noelle.

"That's your call," Jack said to Noelle, with kindness and encouragement in his voice. "I'll be right here when you get out."

"Thanks," Noelle said, a knot forming in the pit of her stomach. She stood up to follow the nurse into the area of the examining rooms.

"Hey," Jack said, "no way do I want you distracted by anything. It's smart you talked to me. Okay, now it's in and out."

"Thanks," Noelle said again, as she followed the nurse's gesture toward the examining room.

The night before, just before going to bed, she had screwed up all her courage, and confided to Jack and Sandi her ongoing worry about her health, especially her heart.

"Sometimes I just feel so exhausted," she had nervously told them. "And then it feels as if my heart is just, like, racing or something."

She had waited for their stern voices of disapproval, of their angry voices saying that she was babying herself, that she wasn't acting like the winner she should be.

But it hadn't come.

Which shocked her. Many times they had insisted that she continue to train in the face of minor, sometimes even major, injuries. In fact, about a year ago Noelle had crashed attempting a new jump, and had landed directly on her right wrist. It had really hurt, and it kept hurting for weeks afterward. Jack and Sandi had assured her it was simply a bad sprain, and, hey, she didn't have to skate on her hands, did she?

It was only when the pain wouldn't go away and she'd been X-rayed, that she discovered that she'd actually sustained a hairline fracture of her wrist.

Even then she had continued training.

And many times, when she'd had a cold or even the flu, Jack had insisted that she continue to practice, even if she had a fever.

"They're not going to cancel the Olympics if you have the flu," he'd often told her, and she could see his point. She would have to find a way to overcome any health obstacle if she wanted to be a champion.

No one cares if the champ didn't win because the champ has the flu, she constantly reminded herself. *They only care that the champ didn't win, period.*

So when she'd told Jack and Sandi that she was worried about her heart, she pretty much expected that they would tell her it was nothing, that she should ignore it, and that she shouldn't look for excuses to lose.

But it wasn't that way at all. That very morning, at eight o'clock, Jack made an appointment for Noelle with the best cardiologist — heart doctor — in Grand Rapids, and now, at two o'clock in the afternoon, she was sitting in an examining room with her coach out in the waiting area.

How Jack had gotten the appointment on such short notice, I didn't ask.

Sometimes it helps to have an Olympic gold medal, she thought, as she nervously undressed and put on the paper gown, as the nurse had instructed her. Then she climbed up onto the examining table to wait for the doctor.

She didn't have to wait long.

The door opened, and the nurse walked in with a doctor. He was middle-aged, balding, and he wore wire-rim glasses that were slipping down his nose.

"Noelle Le Blanc?" he asked, pushing his glasses up.

"Yes," Noelle replied nervously. She was surprised at how small her voice sounded.

"Jack Preston told me you're worried about your heart," the doctor said.

"Well, it's probably my imagination," Noelle said. "I mean — "

"I'm Doctor Paul Westfall, chief of cardiology here at Grand Rapids Medical Center," he said, cutting her off. "I understand you're a skater."

"Yes, sir."

"So, let's check you out." He smiled at her, as did the nurse. Their smiles made Noelle feel better, more confident.

For the next thirty minutes, Dr. Westfall gave Noelle a thorough examination, including something that he called an echocardiogram. Noelle thought that she saw him raise his eyebrows briefly when the results of the test came through, but all Dr. Westfall said when he was finished was for Noelle to get dressed and for her and Jack to meet him in his office in five minutes.

Noelle did as she was told. She dressed and went out to the waiting room, where Jack gave her a thumbs-up sign and she dutifully gave one right back to him. Then they found their way to Dr. Westfall's office, where the doctor was already waiting for them.

"So, how's my champ?" Jack asked, even before Noelle and he could settle in their seats.

"She'll be just fine," the doctor reported, looking at Jack and not at Noelle. "Nothing that should get in the way of her competing."

"Great!" Jack replied, touching his hand

lightly on Noelle's arm. "Feel better, champ?" he asked her heartily.

Nothing that should get in the way of my competing? Noelle thought, sweat beginning to form under her armpits. *What does that mean? Is something wrong with me?*

"She does have a heart murmur," Dr. Westfall added.

"I do?" Noelle asked, her hands clenched into fists of fear. "A heart murmur?"

"It's nothing, really," Dr. Westfall assured her, pushing his glasses up his nose again.

"But . . . what is it?" Noelle asked, feeling frightened. "What does it mean?"

"It's nothing," Dr. Westfall repeated. "Lots of teenagers have it. Here, read this."

He reached in his desk and pulled out two sheets of paper, handing one to Noelle and one to Jack. They were information sheets on heart murmurs and something called mitral valve prolapse.

Noelle quickly read the sheets of paper. Heart murmurs are sounds caused by the flow of blood through the heart, she read. Most times, they are only heard through a stethoscope, and are very, very common in adolescents — in fact, between twenty and forty percent of teenagers have murmurs discovered during routine physicals. And most times, murmurs are totally harmless.

"Yours is caused by mitral valve prolapse," Dr. Westfall explained. "It's even more common in girls than in boys."

"What is it exactly, Paul?" Jack asked.

"The mitral valve controls blood flow in your heart," Dr. Westfall said. "If it's thicker than normal, it billows upward when the valve closes, or it can open as it billows. That causes a murmur."

"You're sure it's okay that she competes?" Jack questioned.

"Totally," Dr. Westfall said. "You'll want her to take antibiotics before she goes to the dentist, because we don't want any infections of that valve, but otherwise, she checks out."

"Great," Jack said, grinning broadly. "Oh, one other thing. She had a fainting spell the other day. Related?"

"What's she eating?" Dr. Westfall asked.

Nothing! Noelle wanted to scream, but she kept her mouth shut.

"Oh, the usual precompetition diet," Jack reported.

"High-protein, low-calorie?" Dr. Westfall asked her coach, winking at him.

"You know the drill," Jack nodded.

"Give her an extra power bar now and then," Dr. Westfall instructed. "Or an extra meal. She won't faint then."

Then the doctor turned to Noelle. "You understand all this?"

"Yes, sir," Noelle answered politely.

"Good," the doctor said. "Now, go out there and win Winterfest. Next time I see you, I want you to be up on that podium!"

"Yes, sir," Noelle said again.

"If I know your coach," Dr. Westfall said, leaning back in his chair and giving Jack a sideways look, "you're not going to have much choice about it!" His glasses slipped down his nose again, and he smiled at Noelle.

"That's right," Jack said, turning to Noelle. "You ready, champ?"

"Sure," Noelle replied, getting up from her chair.

She was fine. The doctor had said so. The fainting and her racing heart were nothing. Nothing at all.

"Wow," Traci Campbell said, as Noelle edged through the swinging door into the ladies' locker room at the rink. "You were fantastic today! That was, like, the best I ever saw you skate!"

"You think?" Noelle asked, wiping the perspiration from her brow.

"Absolutely," Traci assured her. "Your triples were unbelievable!"

"I didn't even know you were watching," Noelle said, unlacing a skate.

"You never do," Traci replied with a smile. "You're always concentrating so hard."

Other than Tara and Erin, Traci Campbell was Noelle's closest friend. She didn't hang out with Traci the way she did with Tara and Erin, but Traci was a skater, so they had a lot in common.

For the last thirty minutes, Traci had sat in the stands, watching her friend and learning. She had come over after school in order to do her own practicing. But Noelle knew that Traci's goals in skating were very different from her own. Traci went to Love High School, and practiced only three hours a day at the most, because she was simply hoping to get a skating scholarship to a good college. She lived at home and had an actual life and a boyfriend.

Noelle could barely even imagine it.

"It was a good practice, you're right."

"Better than good, Noelle," Traci said, unwrapping a Snickers bar. "Seriously. I get inspired every time I watch you!"

"That candy bar inspires me," Noelle said, staring covetously at the candy bar in Traci's hand.

"Want a bite?"

"Jack could probably smell it on my breath," Noelle said with a sigh.

"He's tough," Traci said, taking another bite. "I couldn't give up candy. No way."

Noelle took in Traci's pretty face and dark eyes, her smooth brown skin, her long, tightly curled black hair now held back in a bun, and her strong, curvaceous body. Noelle knew that Traci had been inspired to skate by another black skater, the beautiful and powerful Surya Bonaly, from France. And like Surya, Traci looked almost womanly, whereas Noelle still looked dainty and childlike on the ice.

Dainty and childlike won championships these days. Womanly did not.

Noelle turned away from Traci and her Snickers bar, and unlaced her other skate.

"Jack says no candy until after Winterfest," Noelle explained.

"Not if you're going for the Olympics," Traci agreed, as she continued to lace up her own skates.

"If I win, I think I get one Hershey's kiss,

then it's back to skinless chicken breasts."

"Ugh," Traci said, making a face. "Better you than me. If I had to give up my mother's fried chicken, it just wouldn't be worth it."

Fried chicken. Just the thought of it made Noelle's mouth water.

When is the last time I ate fried chicken?

"So, how did it go at the doctor's?" Traci asked, sitting down on the bench next to Noelle.

That morning, Traci had called to see how Noelle was doing, and Noelle had told her about the doctor's appointment. Funny, because she hadn't told Tara or Erin.

"It went fine," Noelle reported. "I was all worried for nothing."

"You sure?" Traci asked. "What about that heart-racing thing you told me about?"

Noelle shrugged. "Nothing. Evidently lots of people's hearts race."

"I never heard that," Traci said doubtfully.

"I'm fine," Noelle insisted. "You just told me how great I did today, didn't you?"

"Yeah," Traci acknowledged reluctantly.

Jack had driven Noelle directly from Dr. Westfall's office to the rink, where he had put her through a hard, complete practice that included both conditioning drills, during which Noelle skated at top speed for fifteen minutes at a time, and artistic elements. In fact, Jack had made Noelle skate both her long program and her short program four separate times, and then gave her a beat-by-beat critique of each routine.

And she had done great.

"Frankly, I'm surprised Jack even agreed to take you to see that doctor," Traci said, getting up to do some warm-up stretches.

"He's not an ogre, you know," Noelle said.

Traci gave Noelle a look and kept stretching.

"Well, he's not!" Noelle insisted. "He just wants me to win, and so do I!"

"Uh-huh," Traci agreed, but her tone of voice sounded doubtful.

Noelle fiddled with the laces to her skates. "The doctor did say I have a heart murmur," Noelle admitted, her voice low.

"A *what?*" Traci asked, stopping mid-stretch.

"Forget it! It's nothing, I shouldn't have even told you!" Noelle exclaimed. She grabbed a handful of tissues and wiped off the blades of her skates.

"Noelle, a heart murmur isn't 'nothing'!" Traci insisted.

"This is," Noelle said. "There's no problem with me competing. He says I have mitral valve something-or-other."

"I'm going to ask my mom about it," Traci said, her face serious. Traci's mom was a doctor at Love Medical Center.

"Traci, your mom is a podiatrist and this has nothing to do with my feet," Noelle said dryly. "Besides, I just saw a heart specialist. Don't you think he would have told me if there was anything wrong with me?"

"I don't know," Traci replied, her hands on her hips. "How good a friend of Jack's is he?"

"That is *totally* unfair," Noelle said.

"Maybe," Traci said grudgingly. "I'm just looking out for you."

"I appreciate that," Noelle answered as she packed her skates into her skate bag. She could have left them in her locker, but Jack insisted that she bring her skates with her and not leave them at the rink. Too much temptation for somebody, he said.

"Listen, you have a great practice and don't worry about me, okay?"

"Someone needs to worry about you," Traci said huffily.

"Traci, I'm fine," Noelle insisted. "And after I win the gold at Winterfest, we'll split a Snickers bar to celebrate. Deal?"

"Deal," Traci agreed, hugging her friend.

But she was still staring pensively after Noelle long after Noelle left the locker room.

Erin scanned the sky, searching for signs of snow. *It isn't Winterfest without snow,* she thought, *inches and inches of wonderful, freshly fallen snow.*

She was in a giddy and strange mood, brought about by none other than Luke Blakely. Because as much as Erin liked him, it seemed to her that . . . well, he liked her, too.

Erin stood in a small knot of people at the bottom of the impressive steel seventy-meter ski jump hill that had been built outside of Love — the same jumping hill to which she had taken Luke just after he came to town.

She was bundled up in many layers of padding against the twenty-degrees-and-dropping cold. The sun was in the process of setting behind the low-slung hills in the distance.

Fortunately for the jumpers, the jumping

hill was entirely floodlit; the gleaming steel structure glinted in the harsh white fluorescent light. The steep run-out area, which emptied into a wide, flat, stopping area — where the ski jumpers landed and came to a skidding halt — was bathed in even more white fluorescent light.

Luke would be jumping soon.

Luke.

Even saying his name silently in her own head made Erin feel breathless.

She tried out Pete's name in her mind, to see if it had the same effect. *Pete*, she thought. *My boyfriend, Pete.*

Pete.

Nothing.

I refuse to feel guilty, she told herself, stomping her feet for warmth. *I just won't let myself. Besides, I haven't done anything to feel guilty about!*

But I'd like to.

When she'd last seen Luke, he told her that he was going to be practicing that afternoon and offhandedly he'd asked her whether she might want to come watch him.

"Maybe I can even get you into these skis," he joked easily. "Jumping is easier than tying your shoelaces, you know."

"It looks dangerous," Erin pointed out.

"It's not dangerous at all," Luke told her. "Of course, the first time I did it, I was so scared I felt like my butt was going to jump into my stomach."

Erin had laughed, and Luke had laughed, and everything had been perfect.

Still, that morning, when Erin woke up, she had no intention of going to the ski jump to watch Luke practice. Not in a million years.

I have a boyfriend, she told herself. *I love my boyfriend. My boyfriend is there for me whenever I need him to be. My boyfriend even puts up with my crazy family, and that's no little thing. Besides, I'm supposed to study with Pete after school, for the history exam on Friday. So no way can I go watch Luke practice.*

But at school she found herself mumbling some excuse to Pete, and when four o'clock came around, she borrowed the Taurus again, saying that she had to do some shopping downtown. It was as if there were some unseen cosmic force pulling her toward the jumping hill.

She couldn't stop herself.

And, she had to admit to herself, she wasn't trying very hard.

And now here she was, watching Luke. Earlier, Luke had spotted her in the spectators' area, and he'd even stopped by and chatted with her after his last practice jump, clearly pleased that she was there. Erin noticed another girl from the welcoming committee, a serious snob named Sierra Bagley, look at Erin with new respect when she saw Death Kellerman with Luke Blakely.

Looking up to the top of the hill, Erin spotted Luke, ready for his final jump of the day.

Erin watched, holding her breath, as he stepped off the flat holding area at the top of the structure and launched himself into the twin ski tracks that had been carved out by countless jumpers before him.

Luke went into a tight tuck as he flashed down the jumping structure, heading right for where the track ended and pure air awaited.

He hit the take-off area and exploded off of it into the early evening sky.

Whoosh! Luke flew into the air, stretching his body well out, so that he was almost parallel to the ground that loomed up ten or fifteen feet below him. Then he quickly spread his skis into a wide V-shape, trying to trap the maximum amount of air under himself, as if he were a kite.

He'd explained the aerodynamics of ski jumping to Erin during their drive around town. But it was one thing for him to explain it, and quite another for Erin to see it firsthand.

Luke flew and flew and flew.

And finally, he pulled his skis back together and landed in the stopping area before skidding to a parallel stop not twenty feet from where Erin and the others stood watching.

The fifteen or twenty people standing near Erin burst into spontaneous applause. It was an awesome jump — the best they had seen all afternoon. Even some of the other competitors who were waiting to ride the Snocat lift that would take them back up to the top of the jumping hill applauded. Sierra looked over at Erin again, and Erin couldn't help it — she gave her a smug grin.

"Who is that guy?" Sierra asked her.

"Luke Blakely," Erin said. "He's from the University of Colorado."

"He's your athlete, huh?" Sierra asked, pushing some of her curly red hair up under her ski cap.

"Yep," Erin said proudly.

Sierra shook her head. "I got a speed skater from the University of Pennsylvania who does macramé in her spare time," she said. "Lucky you."

Erin just smiled. *Yes. Lucky me*, she thought. *Lucky, lucky me.*

Luke unhooked himself from his bindings, picked up his skis, and walked directly over to Erin.

"So, what'd you think, champ, you ready to try?" he asked, smiling good-naturedly.

"Thanks but no thanks," Erin replied.

Luke bumped his shoulder into hers playfully. "Chicken?"

"Frankly, yes," Erin admitted.

"Maybe we could go together, you know, some tandem kind of thing," Luke mused, flashing that winning smile of his again — the smile that made Erin's knees go weak.

"I never heard of tandem ski jumping," Erin said, trying not to melt at his hand on her shoulder.

"Well, we could invent it," Luke suggested. He smiled into her eyes.

He should not be doing this to you, she told herself. *He totally should not be doing this.*

But he is.

"So, where can you take me for some food?" he asked.

He wants to go out with me, Erin thought. *It doesn't mean anything. Yes, it does. No. Yes. I think I'm losing my mind.*

"Uh, how about the diner?" Erin suggested.

"Sounds great," Luke agreed. He gently touched Erin's waist and they began walking toward her car. Even through all her layers of warm clothing it felt as if her skin were on fire.

"Listen, you were really great up there," Erin began, determined to keep the conversation from turning personal.

"I'm glad you thought so," Luke said. "It's a great hill. I really dug it. So, where's this diner we're going to?"

"No, uh-uh!" a young voice yelled frantically. "Don't go there! Not the diner!"

Erin and Luke both turned around. There stood a little kid — he looked like he was about ten years old — who had a really worried look on his face. Standing next to him was another boy, also young, but quite a bit taller. The two of them were obviously together.

"There's something wrong with the diner, kid?" Luke asked good-naturedly.

"Yeah," the boy said. "It's like this poison diner, I'm not kidding!"

"The food isn't *that* bad!" Erin said.

"I'm telling ya, it's poison!" the boy insisted, walking over to Erin. His taller friend followed him. "My grandma died in there like a few days ago and all she did was eat the stupid Jell-O . . ."

At that moment he stopped midsentence, staring at Erin. He nodded and pointed at her. "Hey, I know you. You're a Kellerman, right?"

"Right," Erin answered, a sinking feeling in her heart. His grandmother had swan-dived into the Jell-O at the diner. That could only mean one thing. This was dead Mrs. Deederman's grandson.

"Your picture's up in the funeral home!" the boy exclaimed. "There's, like, this family portrait thing on the wall, right?"

"Right," Erin admitted, her face turning red. She could feel Luke's eyes on her.

"You buried my grandma! You know, Mrs. Deederman?"

"*I* didn't bury her," Erin hissed. "*I* had nothing to do with burying her."

"I was there, too," the taller boy piped up. "It was so cool, except they wouldn't let me touch the body. I'm Caleb Narroway, and this is Dinky Deederman."

"Dinky?" Luke echoed.

Caleb nodded. "His name is really Derrick, but everyone calls him Dinky 'cause he's so short. Ya know. Dinky. Get it?"

"Shut up, Caleb," Dinky said to his friend.

"Wow, you're like, famous," Caleb told Erin. " 'Death' Kellerman, that's what everyone calls you, right? That's what my big sister Angie says."

"Only when I was a little kid — " Erin began, her face so hot with embarrassment that she could practically feel the steam rising off her flesh.

"Hey, I think it's monsterly cool!" Caleb insisted. "Last year I went on your little brother Sam's death-house tour — you know, where he dresses up like he's in *The Addams Family*? It cost fifty cents. We got to see caskets but they were empty. Kind of a rip-off, if you ask me."

Erin smiled weakly.

"So, what are dead people really like?" Caleb asked eagerly.

"I wouldn't know," Erin said, her voice low. "We have to go — "

"What, you're telling me they call you 'Death' Kellerman for nothing?" Caleb asked dubiously. "I mean, I saw your picture up there on the wall at the funeral, you know."

"It's a family picture," Erin said. "I'm related to them. That's all."

"I take it your family is in the funeral biz," Luke commented.

Oh, this is just great, she thought miserably. *Did Luke really have to know that my family has the monopoly on death in Love, Michigan?*

"That was my father who buried Mrs. Deederman," Erin replied, trying to maintain her dignity. She turned to Dinky and Caleb. "My *father*, not *me. Mr.* Kellerman. *He's* the funeral home owner. It's *his* business."

"Aw, come on," Caleb jeered loudly. "Like I said, everyone here in Love knows that you spell 'death' K-E-L-L-E-R-M-A-N."

"Shut up, Caleb," Dinky instructed his taller friend, who poked Dinky in the ribs again.

More blood flushed into Erin's face. She gave a quick glance at Luke, who looked amused.

"Hey," Caleb said, ignoring Dinky, "undertaking is way cool. Dinky's grandma looked great dead. Who did her hair? Your aunt? My mom says everyone calls her 'Crazy Daisy'!"

Erin pictured herself wrapping her fingers around little Caleb's throat and squeezing until he required her father's services, but she restrained herself. "Well, lovely talking to you, kids," she said. "But we have to — "

"Your aunt is Crazy Daisy, right?" Caleb went on enthusiastically. "Too cool, man! I bet she did the makeup and you did the hair, right? So what does dead people's hair feel like? Is it, like, different and stuff? Hey, can you do mine? If I die, I mean."

"Shut up, Caleb!" Dinky remonstrated with his friend, but Caleb just poked him in the ribs again.

Erin turned to Dinky. "I'm sorry about your grandmother, Dinky — I mean, Derrick."

"Yeah," Dinky said, shuffling his feet on the frozen ground.

Caleb turned to Luke. "Hey, aren't you that ski jumper dude?"

"Yeah," Luke replied.

"Cool," Caleb said. He turned to Erin, a wicked smile on his face. "So, can you ask him for his autograph for me? Or can you only get autographs of dead people?"

Luke threw his head back and laughed out loud, which only made Caleb think he was the cleverest human on the planet.

"Sure, kid," Luke said, "she can get my autograph for you. And I don't even have to die first."

Caleb eagerly held out a pen and a piece of grubby-looking paper, and Luke signed with a flourish. And finally Dinky and Caleb ran off to see who else they could annoy.

"Sounds like you have an interesting family," Luke told Erin.

"Uh-huh," she mumbled as they headed for her car.

"Remind me not to have any serious accidents while I'm here," Luke added.

Then he threw his head back and laughed again, until even Erin had to join in.

It was the very first time she had ever laughed at the idea that in the town of Love, death was spelled K-E-L-L-E-R-M-A-N.

Chapter 5

I cannot imagine any guy in the world being able to resist this, Tara thought to herself as she bounded easily up the outside stairs of the dormitory, a square box filled with fragrant pizza balanced in both her hands, and her purse perched on top of the box.

He's a skier. He works hard. He's a guy. Guys love surprises. So I think I've brought him the perfect surprise. In addition to me, of course.

It was Wednesday afternoon, and all day Tara had been replaying over and over again her meeting with David the day before.

Replaying how he had totally ignored her.

It was, Tara had to admit, a first. It really irritated her, to tell the truth. But the more irritated she felt, the more she knew she just had to do something about it.

And so, as she had sat in her last class, advanced calculus, where she was the only student who got straight *A*s, she had devised her plan.

Right after school, Tara had made a quick phone call to the athletes' dorm at Love College to make sure that David was there and not out on the ski slopes practicing. The registration desk checked its records and said yes, David Benjamin was in the dormitory. In fact, he was hanging out in one of the television lounges and would Tara like to speak to him?

"No," Tara said, "I would not like to speak to him, but please tell him that someone's sending over a surprise he's sure to like."

Then, Tara went home to change clothes. She went all out, donning white stretch ski pants (the ones her mother said looked as if they had been spray-painted on by a lecherous graffiti artist) and a white cashmere sweater, that, like her angora sweater, bared a bit of her stomach. Then she added tiny diamond studs to her ears, redid her understated but perfect makeup, and sprayed herself with yet another of her French perfumes.

She stood in front of her mirror, taking in her image. "Well, if I were a guy, I couldn't resist me," she told herself. "Time to put Operation Get David into full gear."

Tara drove over to Main Street near the college, and parked right in front of Pizza Bob's. Then she went in and picked up the Pizza Bob Big Bob special, which basically meant the pizza had every ingredient in the kitchen on it as a topping. Then she drove over to David's dorm — fortunately, her car had her mother's preferred faculty parking sticker on the windshield, so she could park in the nearby faculty lot.

No sense wasting time walking, Tara thought as she pulled into an empty space.

And now, here she was, the perfect gift carrying the perfect gift.

It's heavy artillery time, Tara thought to herself. *Let's just see how cool you are now, David Benjamin.*

"Al-lo!" she cooed in a heavy French accent, as she sailed through the dorm doors and presented herself to the uniformed attendant at the athletes' registration area. "I haf ze delee-ver-ee for Dah-vid Ben-ha-meen."

"For who?" the guard asked, confused.

"Ah, it iz my ack-sant," Tara said, nodding. "For ze athlete David Benjamin," she said carefully. "Ze speed skee-yeer, no?"

"And you are?" the guard asked.

"Ze deliveree pair-son, of course," Tara replied lightly. "For to make ze deliveree. *Le livraison,*" she added, in perfectly accented French.

She smiled at him prettily, hoping that her ruse would work.

No way do I want this guard to announce to David that Tara Moore is here to see him, she thought. *That would give David a chance to say no, maybe. And today, I am not taking no for an answer.*

"Some ID, please," the guard demanded.

"Comment? Je ne comprends pas rien," Tara answered. "I do not to speak ze Engleesh too well, I ahm so veh-ree sah-ree."

"ID," the guard asked again. "Identification?"

"So sah-ree, but I do not under-stahnd. Where ees *Monsieur* Benjamin?"

The guard looked baffled, thought for a moment, and then told Tara that she could find David Benjamin in the first-floor lounge.

"Sank-you, *merci, je vous en prie, monsieur, à bientot, vive la France,*" Tara replied, sailing through the lobby. She caught a quick look back at the guard, who had already turned his attention back to his crime novel.

"I sure hope they aren't counting on the security here," Tara muttered. "They'll let anyone in!"

Just as she went through the door, she heard the guard pick up the phone, dial a number, and announce a pizza delivery.

Well, at least there's nothing wrong with his olfactory nerves, Tara thought, sniffing in the great scent of hot pizza.

Tara walked slowly down the hallway, peering into open rooms. Finally, at the end of the hall, she came to a lounge with a large-screen TV. And, sure enough, David was in there, his back to her, playing some sort of video game on the television.

Even the back of his head is to die for, Tara thought.

"Surprise!" Tara said gaily.

David turned around, startled by Tara's voice.

On the video screen in front of him, a cartoon skier crashed into a tree. "Ouch!" said the canned, metallic voice from the television.

"Oooooou!" went the sound of a disappointed crowd. Then, two little cartoon guys ran across the snow carrying a stretcher, picked up the little cartoon skier, and carried him off the slope.

"You just crashed," Tara said helpfully.

"What are you doing here?" David asked her.

"I brought you a present," Tara said brightly.

"The guard said a pizza," David said, eyeing the box in Tara's arms.

"Well, dang, I guess nothing gets past him, huh?" Tara exclaimed, walking around the couch. She plopped the pizza down on the coffee table in front of David. Then she sat down next to him. "Glad to see me?" she asked.

"Very nice," David said politely. He didn't particularly sound as if he meant it.

"You do like pizza, don't you?" Tara asked. She opened the box and carefully took out a slice, holding it up to David's mouth. "Bite."

Instead of opening his mouth, David took the slice from Tara's hands and then bit into it. "It's very good," he said dutifully, like a well-bred young man talking to his annoying ancient aunt.

"So, David, how was practice today?" Tara asked brightly, crossing her legs. She cursed the thick ankles that made her live in pants instead of cute, short skirts, sure now that her legs were the thing that would get David to notice her.

"Good," David said, chewing the pizza. "My times were fast."

"Fast enough to win Winterfest?" Tara asked.

"No," David said honestly. "I am not the best. Not yet. But I still have more than a week." He bit into his pizza again.

"Well, that's a wonderful attitude," Tara said. "I just admire it to death."

"To death?" David repeated.

"Oh, it's a southern thing," Tara said gaily, wincing as the silly words popped out of her mouth. "What I mean is, I admire that kind of intensity," Tara amended, leaning over to pick an imaginary speck of lint off of David's ski sweater.

"And what are *you* intense about?" David asked curiously, reaching for another slice of pizza.

You, she wanted to say. But she didn't.

"Oh, you know, this and that," Tara said vaguely.

"You can't be intense about 'this and that,' " David said. "You can only be truly intense about one thing at a time."

"Oh, really?" Tara asked coolly.

David nodded.

"Well then, Mr. Benjamin," Tara said, "right now I am intense about the Winterfest athletes' dinner dance Friday night. How's that?"

"Dinner dance?" David asked blankly.

"But you must know about the dinner dance!" Tara exclaimed. "It's in your itinerary."

"I haven't read my entire itinerary," David admitted.

"Well, you should have," Tara said. "Friday night is the big dinner dance for all the athletes. It's in the Kennedy Room at the student union. All the heads of Winterfest will be there, and the heads of the college, and the welcoming committee — that would be me — and all the athletes."

"Very nice," David said politely.

"And you're supposed to go with your host," Tara added pointedly.

"Which would be you," David said.

Tara smiled. "Right the first time. And what's really exciting is that they will be announcing the Winterfest Court!"

David looked at her blankly.

"The six girls who will make up the Winterfest Court," Tara explained patiently.

"You know, like a beauty pageant. Actually, I've won quite a few of those," she added demurely.

"Where you parade around in a bathing suit and give plastic answers to plastic judges?" David asked.

"I happen to have saved thousands of dollars toward college from pageants, thank you very much," Tara said, her temper flaring.

David just reached for a third slice of pizza.

"Anyway," Tara continued, "Friday night they'll choose six princesses, and one of those girls will be crowned Queen on the last night of Winterfest."

"And will that be you?" David asked.

"I haven't even been picked for the court yet!" Tara replied.

"But you will be, I think," David said.

Tara cocked her head at him flirtatiously. "Don't you think I might qualify?"

"I have no idea," David said.

Oh, I could just strangle him, Tara thought. *He is totally impossible!*

Even though she had vowed not to eat any of the pizza, she found herself reaching for a slice and angrily chewing half of it down.

"Don't choke," David warned her, as she swallowed a huge mouthful of lukewarm pizza.

She put the slice down and willed herself to remain in control. "So, David," she said, deciding to change the subject completely. "What was life like for you in Israel?"

"Very different from here," David said.

"I imagine so," Tara agreed.

"And I imagine you don't know anything about it," David replied.

Tara smiled at him coolly. "I imagine that the first kibbutz in Israel was Deganyah Aleph, founded near Lake Kinneret, well before the Second World War. I imagine that you're happy now that the Israeli shekel has stabilized against the American dollar, and that the inflation rate is under control, though you might have taken a severe hit when the Tel Aviv stock exchange crashed in 1994. Oh, and one other thing. Most everywhere, the movie theaters are closed on Friday night and Saturday, although I understand you can still rent videos in Haifa. So if you want to see some movies while you're here, I'd be happy to take you."

David's jaw hung open, and Tara, who knew a good exit line when she was about to create one, jumped to her feet.

"Gosh, David, gotta run. It was just so lovely chatting with you. I'll see you soon. Shalom, y'all!"

Then she picked up her purse, swiftly kissed his cheek, and bounded out the door.

Take that, David Benjamin, she thought. *Now the score is tied.*

Israel 1. Mississippi 1.

"I think I'm losing my mind, Noelle," Erin said, her head in her hands. "I think about him all the time! It's like some sickness or something!"

It was late Wednesday afternoon, and Noelle and Erin were together in the Mighty Cup, a new coffeehouse that had recently opened just across the street from Shatner's Rink. Erin had ended up bringing Luke to the Mighty Cup after his practice — she'd decided not to risk the diner. In fact, she and Noelle were sitting at the same table, toward the rear, where she and Luke had sat.

Noelle was on an hour break from skating practice — she was not the only student who was training with Jack Preston, although of course she was by far the most accomplished. At the moment, though, Jack was working with a class of eight-year-olds who had only been on skates a year or two.

"Watch out, Noelle," Jack had warned her just before releasing her for this one-hour break. "In eight years, one of these girls will be the new you, and you're going to be toast."

Noelle had paled at Jack's words, looking over the eight-year-olds as if she could pick out the girl who was going to replace her.

"Just keep it in mind," Jack said. "You'd better do it now, while you've still got it, or it'll be all over. See you in an hour. Or less."

Noelle took a sip of her sugar-free cocoa and tried to clear Jack and his warning from her mind. "Luke Blakely-itis," Noelle said. "What if there's no cure?"

"I'm serious!" Erin exclaimed, raising her head. "I've never really had this happen to me before."

"What about Pete?" Noelle asked, sipping her cocoa.

Erin sighed. "I lied to him the other day so I could be with Luke. I hate myself."

"Oh, come on — "

"No, I really hate that I did that," Erin said. "I *love* Pete!"

"I know you do," Noelle said. "But now you have a crush on Luke."

"It's just so . . . so weenie!" Erin exclaimed, and Noelle burst out laughing.

"I have the solution for you," Noelle said.

"What's that?" Erin asked eagerly.

"You have to be so totally consumed with something else that you don't have time to think about guys at all," Noelle explained. "Then all your problems will be solved."

"I have a feeling I'd be thinking about Luke if I were climbing Mount Everest," Erin moaned.

"That must be kind of fun," Noelle said wistfully.

"It isn't," Erin said.

Noelle put her cup down. "Do you realize I've never been out on a date?"

"I know," Erin said, "but — "

"I've never been kissed," Noelle continued. "I'm seventeen years old, and I've never been kissed. God, I'm pathetic!"

"No you're not," Erin insisted. "You're a champion!"

Noelle ran her pinky around the rim of her cup. "Sometimes I think my friend Traci has the right idea," she murmured. "She's got a boyfriend. She's going to get a great skating scholarship to college. I mean, maybe I'm crazy to — "

At that moment, Noelle's gaze fell on something beyond Erin, and her face paled.

"What is it?" Erin asked with concern.

"One of the skating judges from Winterfest just walked in," Noelle said in a low, intense voice. "I recognize her."

"So?" Erin asked, taking another swallow of her hot tea. "She's allowed to buy coffee."

"What if she wants to talk to me?" Noelle asked, her voice starting to get a little panicky. "Jack isn't around."

"Why would she want to talk to you?" Erin asked, puzzled. "She's judging you."

"Judges talk to skaters and their coaches all the time," Noelle explained, her voice still low. "But one's never talked to me before alone, and so — uh-oh . . ."

"What's the matter?" Erin asked.

"She's coming this way," Noelle said frantically. Instantly a very fake smile crossed her lips, through which she mumbled, "Be cool. Follow my lead."

"But — "

"Ssssh!"

A well-dressed woman in her forties, about five foot five, with prematurely gray hair held back by a black velvet headband, strode over to Noelle and Erin's table.

Yep, that's her all right, Noelle confirmed, the fake smile still plastered to her face. *I remember she always wears that stupid black velvet headband. She was one of the judges at the Midwest Juniors two years ago. Thank God she didn't judge me this year when I lost.*

I think she liked me, Noelle thought, crossing her fingers under the table in the few seconds before the woman reached her. *I think —*

"Excuse me," the woman said, looking directly at Noelle, "but aren't you Noelle Le Blanc, the skater?"

Noelle flashed that fake smile even wider. "Why yes," she said, in a simpering tone of voice that Erin had never heard before. "I am. I'm so honored that you recognized me."

The woman smiled. "It's a pleasure to see you again. I'm Constance Connolly. I'm one of the judges for Winterfest. I'm so glad you're competing this year."

"It's an honor to be here," Noelle said humbly. "Please meet my friend Erin Kellerman."

Constance Connolly gave Erin a smile that was just as fake as Noelle's had been, and then turned her attention back to Noelle.

"I hear Jack is working you hard," Ms. Connolly said to Noelle.

"We're working very hard," Noelle agreed.

"I spoke with him just a few days ago — he has high hopes for you for this competition."

"I'm very anxious for it to begin," Noelle intoned. "I will do my very best."

"I'm sure you will, dear," the older woman said. She glanced quickly at Erin, then back at Noelle. "Uh, Noelle?" Ms. Connolly said. "Could I, uh, speak to you privately for a moment?"

Noelle looked over at Erin. Erin quickly got to her feet. "I'll go . . . make a phone call," she invented quickly. Then she hurried off to the ladies' room, completely baffled by what was taking place at the table.

Noelle turned back to Constance Connolly. "Won't you sit down?" Noelle said politely.

Constance sat, taking in Noelle's cup of cocoa, her eyebrows raised.

"Sugar-free," Noelle said quickly.

"Of course," Constance said. She folded her fingers together and leaned toward

Noelle. "I wanted to speak with you before we got too close to the competition," Ms. Connolly said carefully.

"I'm always eager to hear the opinion of the judges before my performance," Noelle said, trying to recall all the instructions Jack and Sandi had given her about what to do if a situation like this were ever to arise — where a judge would want to talk to Noelle without her coaches' being present.

Listen carefully, Jack had said, over and over and over. *Agree with everything the judge tells you,* Sandi had added. *Smile your best smile and be polite. And for God's sake, don't go out dressed in torn jeans or a ratty T-shirt or with your makeup or hair out of place. Because that's when you are going to run into a judge. It always happens.*

Noelle breathed an inward sigh of relief at this last thought. Even though she was leaving the rink for only forty-five or fifty minutes, she had put on black leggings and a lovely scarlet-and-black sweater from her aunt Gussie. Her hair was up in a neat bun and she had on lipstick and mascara.

No points deducted for appearance, Noelle thought quickly. *Not this time.*

"It's not your performance I'm concerned

about," the older woman said. "You've got everything it takes."

"Thank you," Noelle replied, breathing another inward sigh of relief. "You think I'm attaining sufficient altitude on my double axel?"

"Absolutely," Ms. Connolly said, smoothing some invisible stray hairs back into her headband. "There's just one thing I want you to think about before this performance."

Noelle smiled brightly. "What's that, Ms. Connolly?" she asked.

"Your teeth," Ms. Connolly said bluntly.

"My . . . my teeth?"

"Yes," Ms. Connolly said. "The little gaps in your teeth. You ought to get your teeth fixed."

Noelle froze.

Sure, I've got gaps in my teeth, she thought. *But they're so tiny. Aren't they? Wouldn't Jack and Sandi have said something to me if it was a problem?*

But it must be a problem. This judge would not be telling me this if it wasn't a problem.

Noelle smiled, but this time her smile was unbelievably self-conscious. "Thank you for bringing that to my attention," she said to Ms. Connolly. "I appreciate it very much."

"My pleasure," Ms. Connolly said, rising from her chair. "I truly believe it will make a difference in your artistic impression."

"You've been very helpful," Noelle said dutifully.

"You're a lovely girl, Noelle," Constance said warmly. "And in any case, I very much look forward to your performance."

"I look forward to skating for you," Noelle said in a stilted voice. She stood up and offered her hand to Ms. Connolly, who shook it before she walked away.

Noelle sat back down, stunned. Ms. Connolly bought her coffee and left, waving at Noelle. Erin finally returned from her hideout in the ladies' room.

"What was that all about?" Erin asked, sliding into her seat.

"I am so screwed," Noelle replied. She dropped her head into her hands.

"What?" Erin asked, uncomprehending. "What happened? Does she hate how you skate or something?"

"No," Noelle answered, picking up a spoon and swirling it around in her now lukewarm cocoa. "She likes how I skate."

"So then — "

"She hates my teeth."

"She *what??*" Erin asked.

"She says my teeth suck and I need to get them capped," Noelle explained.

"But I don't understand . . ." Erin began.

"It's not so complicated," Noelle said, an edge to her voice. "Ms. Connolly basically just said that I'm not going to win Winterfest unless I get my teeth capped."

"But that's crazy!" Erin protested. "What do capped teeth have to do with skating?"

"A lot," Noelle answered, "evidently."

"Wait, wait, I am, like, totally confused here," Erin said.

Noelle sighed. "Female skaters are judged on their appearance as well as their skating," she explained.

"No way," Erin uttered.

"Totally true," Noelle insisted.

"But . . . but that's not fair!" Erin exclaimed. "Does a ski jumper have to have capped teeth to win his event? If a skier has zits, do they deduct points?"

"It's not the same thing," Noelle said doggedly.

"Well, I just think we should all protest this," Erin fumed. "This is not right!"

"You just don't get it," Noelle said. "Figure skating isn't skiing. It's not the luge, or speed skating, or any of the other winter sports."

"They're all sports," Erin insisted. "And the best person should win. Period."

"Right," Noelle said. "So, tell me the names of three Americans who recently won Olympic gold medals in skiing."

Erin looked stumped. "I can't," she admitted.

"Okay," Noelle asked, "tell me the name of the last American to win a silver medal in figure skating."

"That's easy," Erin replied. "Nancy Kerrigan. Remember? We watched the whole competition together with Tara."

"Who'd Nancy beat?" Noelle asked.

"Tonya Harding," Erin answered. "And that girl from France — "

"Surya Bonaly," Noelle said.

"And Midori Ito from Japan," Erin added. "I remember."

"And who beat Kerrigan," Noelle continued, "to win the gold medal?"

"That skater from the Ukraine . . . what's her name . . . Oksana Baiul. She was so terrific."

"And tiny. And feminine. And perfect-looking," Noelle added. "And who's the American skater who won the gold medal at the Olympics before?" Noelle quizzed her friend.

"Everyone knows that," Erin answered. "Kristi Yamaguchi."

"I rest my case," Noelle said. "Skiing and skating may both be Olympic events, but there's no comparison between the two. You know how much money Nancy Kerrigan made in endorsements after she won the silver medal? Ten million dollars."

"Really?" Erin asked. "Ten million?"

Noelle nodded. "And she got her teeth capped, after the '91 World Championships. Linda Fratianne got her nose done before she competed in Lake Placid, at the 1980 games," Noelle continued. "Too bad Annett Pötzsch lost ten pounds right before the competition and beat her."

"But —"

"There's another skater who had her breasts reduced," Noelle went on, "because a judge told her coach she thought it would improve her artistic impression."

"Noelle, no offense, but this is kind of scary — " Erin said slowly. "All this has nothing to do with being a real athlete!"

"Nothing to do with being an athlete," Noelle agreed. "But everything to do with winning. That judge just told me I should get my teeth capped. Now, if you were me, what would you do?"

"Get the judge fired," Erin steamed.

"Right," Noelle said. "I should go right to the Winterfest organizers and tell them to can Ms. Connolly. That's my ticket to victory. Sure thing."

Erin was silent for a long moment.

And her silence said everything.

"So now you get the picture," Noelle said with a sigh.

"So, can you?" Erin asked in a low voice. "Get your teeth capped, I mean?"

Noelle gave a short, bitter little laugh. "Oh, sure," she said. "I'll just call up my father, the factory worker who moonlights as a bartender to pay for my coaching and my skating costumes, and my mother who hasn't had a new dress in two years, and ask them to send me thousands of dollars they don't have so I can get caps on my teeth before Winterfest."

"Noelle, I wish there was something I could do," Erin said, reaching out to touch her friend's hand.

"I've got to think of something," Noelle said, tears coming to her eyes. "Because if I don't, I can kiss Winterfest — and the Olympics — good-bye."

Chapter 6

"Oh, hi, honey, you're home," Erin's mother said, sticking her head in the doorway of Erin's bedroom.

Erin smiled at her mother. Mrs. Kellerman was in her mid-forties, with hair a deeper auburn than her daughter's, and crinkly laugh lines around her round, hazel eyes. She was dressed in her nurse's whites, just about to leave for her shift at the hospital.

"Doing my nails," Erin said, holding out one hand where the nails were now colored bright red. "What do you think?"

Her mother walked over to her bed and peered at her daughter's fingers. "I don't think I've ever seen you in red nail polish before."

"I never wore it before," Erin admitted, waggling her fingers. "Does it look stupid?"

"No, not at all," her mother said, sitting down next to Erin on the bed. "It's kind of terrific."

Erin smiled at her mother. *My parents are so sweet,* she thought. *Just because they're in the death biz doesn't really make them weird, contrary to what everyone in Love might think!*

"So, what's the occasion for the red nails?" Mrs. Kellerman asked. "Big date with Pete?"

Oh, God, Pete, Erin thought, her heart sinking. She checked her watch quickly. Pete was due over in ten minutes, and what she had to tell him was not going to make him happy.

"Something wrong?" Erin's mom asked. "You look like somebody died."

"Please, no death humor," Erin said. She screwed the cap back on the nail polish, even though only one hand was done. "I have a major problem."

"Can I help?" Mrs. Kellerman asked.

"It's a guy thing," Erin admitted.

"I remember guy things," her mom said. "I'm not that ancient."

Erin fiddled with the top to the polish. "Tomorrow night is the athletes' dinner dance — you know — for Winterfest," she

began. "And I'm supposed to take my athlete."

"So far, so good," her mom said, nodding.

"Well, my athlete is a guy," Erin continued. "A cute guy. A really, *really* cute guy,
Luke Blakely. But Pete thinks I'm going
with him, Pete."

"Okay, now you just lost me," her mom
said. "Why can't you go with Pete and escort the athlete?"

"Because I just checked my tickets, and
they admit only two — me and my athlete,"
Erin explained. "I didn't know. I mean, I
just assumed I could bring a date . . ."

"And you haven't told Pete yet," her mom
surmised.

Erin nodded.

"Well, he'll understand, honey," Mrs.
Kellerman said. "It's not like you don't want
to go with him. I mean, this Luke isn't your
date."

Erin bit her lower lip.

"Oops," her mom said. "I spoke too soon,
huh?"

"I don't know," Erin confessed. "I mean,
it's not a date but it *is* a date . . . or something."

"Well, discretion being the better part of
valor, I suggest you downplay the 'date' el-

ement when you explain all this to Pete," Mrs. Kellerman said.

"Yeah," Erin mumbled.

"I mean, keep in mind that Luke what's-his-name will soon be gone back to . . . wherever he's from, and you certainly don't want to break Pete's heart."

"No, I don't," Erin agreed. "You're right."

Mrs. Kellerman glanced at her watch and jumped up from the bed. "Gotta run, honey. I'm doing a double because so many nurses are out with this flu thing that's going around." She kissed her daughter's cheek and hurried out.

She's right, Erin thought, staring into space. *In one and a half weeks all of this will be over, and Luke will be back in Colorado. And I love Pete. I really do. And—*

"Hi!"

Erin looked up. Pete was standing in the doorway of her bedroom. She took in his curly brown hair, open, honest face, and the sweet smile she knew so well. And she felt . . . guilty.

Not so much because she had goofed up in asking Pete to escort her to the dinner dance, but because she was deep down so glad to find out that he couldn't do just that.

"Hi," Erin said. "Come on in."

Pete walked over to her and lifted her right hand. "Red on one hand only?" he asked. "You starting a trend?"

"I just didn't finish yet," Erin explained.

"Tomorrow night should be a blast," Pete said, sitting on the bed where Erin's mother had been sitting. "I'll pick you up at seven-fifteen, okay?"

"Uh . . . there's a problem," Erin said.

"What?" Pete asked.

"Oh, *please* don't be mad at me," Erin said in a rush. "I did a totally stupid thing — "

"I could never be mad at you," Pete said.

"Never say never," Erin suggested meekly. "The thing is . . . well . . . I checked the tickets, and I only have two."

Pete made a face. "I don't suppose your athlete has his own ticket . . ."

"Right, he doesn't," Erin said. "I guess I'm not allowed to bring anyone, and I never checked. I mean, I just assumed —"

"Bummer," Pete said. "Wow, I was really, really looking forward to taking you."

"Me, too," Erin said. "I'm so sorry — "

"Hey, forget it," Pete said, leaning over to kiss her cheek. "I would have made the same mistake."

"You're not mad?" Erin asked.

"I told you, I could never be mad at you," Pete said, playing with a lock of her hair.

"You're too nice to me, you know," Erin said, an edge to her voice.

"Hey, that's just the kind of guy I am," Pete said cheerfully. He stood up and stretched. "Man, I am so glad school is finally out for Winterfest break." He turned around to face her. "So, tell me about your athlete. All I know is that his name is Luke and he's a jumper."

"Oh, well, there isn't much to tell," Erin said evasively.

"Nice guy?" Pete asked.

"He's okay," Erin said carefully.

"Cute?" Pete asked.

Erin shrugged.

He walked over to her and lifted her to her feet, looking deep into her eyes. "Erin, this isn't, like, a *date*-thing with him, is it?"

She pulled away from him. "Of course not," she said. "I'm just doing what everyone on the committee is doing!"

"Okay — "

"I don't know how you could accuse me of that!" Erin ranted. "That is totally unfair!"

"Hey, Erin, chill out," Pete suggested, taken aback.

"Well, I just don't like to be accused of

things," Erin said, sitting back down on her bed.

Pete stared at her and scratched his chin. "Something is up."

"Nothing is up," Erin snapped, untwisting the top to her red nail polish.

"Erin, I've known you for ten years," Pete said softly. "We've been going steady for five years. I know you pretty well."

Erin didn't look up from her nail polish.

"Do you . . . like this guy or something?"

"He's just a friend," Erin said, polishing the nail on her pinky.

Pete stared at her some more. "You sure?"

Erin finally looked at him — at his honest, kind, loving brown eyes, at the lips she had laughed with, the first and only guy she had ever kissed. *I do love him,* she thought. *So what if Luke is gorgeous and hot and fun to flirt with? It's just a passing thing. I love Pete.*

"I'm sure," Erin said. Then she leaned over and kissed Pete. He kissed her back, and Erin felt warm and loved and protected.

"I'll miss you tomorrow night," Pete said huskily, his face buried in Erin's hair.

"I'll miss you, too," Erin said.

"We'll go to the movies this weekend, okay?" Pete said. "Maybe do something with Tara and whoever her latest guy is. What do you think?"

"Sounds like fun," Erin agreed.

Pete tipped Erin's head back and kissed her again, and Erin gave herself up to the kiss.

But even as she was pressing her lips to his and feeling his arms wrapped around her, when she closed her eyes the face she was seeing wasn't Pete's.

It was Luke Blakely's.

Noelle sat back on her bed, and watched, for the thousandth time, the videotape replay of her free-skate performance at the Midwest Regional Championships earlier this year — the performance in which she had failed to make the Nationals by one-tenth of a point.

Actually, Noelle forced herself to watch it. Because she had watched it so many times now that the videotape was starting to get fuzzy, the sound quality distorted, the picture occasionally a little jumpy.

And it wasn't as if she didn't know the entire thing by heart, anyway.

There's got to be something, Noelle

thought, watching the very end of her performance, *something I'm still missing. If I can just figure out what it is . . .*

She was supposed to be finishing her Spanish homework, but she knew neither Jack nor Sandi would ever check to see if she had done it. And anyway, she didn't have to see her tutors again until after Winterfest.

"If Love schools let out for Winterfest," Jack had told her, "we can let your tutor out for the same period of time."

Noelle hadn't argued with Jack. She wasn't really big on her schoolwork, anyway, and she could tell that Jack and Sandi had brought in the tutors for her because they had to, not because they wanted to. So Noelle did just the amount of work necessary to keep from failing, and Jack and Sandi rarely asked to check her homework or to see how she had done on one of the rare tests her various tutors administered to her.

You can only concentrate on one thing, she often said to herself, repeating yet another of Jack and Sandi's endless axioms. *And I concentrate on skating. Let other kids concentrate on high school.*

As Noelle rewound the tape, for once she

allowed herself to think about something other than skating without feeling guilty; she thought about the Winterfest athletes' dinner dance she'd be going to the next evening.

And I have the greatest dress, she thought dreamily.

Her aunt Gussie had made it — actually, her aunt Gussie made a lot of her skating costumes, too — and this time Aunt Gussie had gotten things totally right. The dress was bottle green velvet and very simple, sleeveless, with a square-cut neck, and it fell two inches above her knees. She had a matching green velvet ribbon for her hair, which for once she would be able to wear down. And tiny little emerald studs for her ears, a birthday present from Claire and Buddy. They weren't real emeralds, of course, but Noelle wouldn't have loved them any more if they had been.

There'll be real food and real guys, Noelle thought dreamily. *What will they serve? Probably roast beef. And mashed potatoes swimming in gravy. And bread. With butter. If I eat only half of everything they serve, I won't actually gain any weight. I don't think.*

And guys. Gorgeous, athletic, muscular guys from all over the country, Noelle continued, her eyes closed blissfully, a smile on her lips. *Some . . . some college skier with blond hair and blue eyes will fall madly in love with me. And I'll fly to visit him at his college, and —*

She heard the snap as the tape finished rewinding.

Keep your mind on the ball, Noelle, she told herself, sitting up and pushing the play button to watch the tape again.

There she was, flying across the ice. And then she saw it. Then she saw everything. How could she have possibly missed it before?

Ms. Connolly was right.

It was her teeth.

They were hideous.

She pushed the slo-mo button, and leaned closer to the video monitor, staring pitilessly at her mouth. Every time she smiled, now in slow-motion on the tape, Noelle saw a gaping, ugly hole in the middle of her front teeth.

"Oh, God," Noelle moaned, burying her head in her hands. "I look so ugly! How could I not have seen it! How come nobody told me until Ms. Connolly?"

Noelle hadn't said anything about it to

Jack and Sandi. She knew her parents could not afford to get her teeth capped — they barely had enough money to pay Jack and Sandi. But how could Jack not have said anything to her? Was it because he knew her parents couldn't afford it?

"I hate myself," Noelle murmured under her breath. She felt like yanking her horrid teeth out of her mouth. She felt as if she were personally responsible for her ugly, horrible, can't-win-a-medal smile.

The more she watched the tape, the more horrid she thought she looked.

Now, Noelle watched the screen intently, though the images on it were painful. She was at the end of her routine, fifteen seconds from its conclusion, and in her program was a double axel jump she had hit countless times before.

The double axel, Noelle thought. *Skate backwards, weight on my right skate, spin to the outside edge of my left skate, picking up speed. Jump into the air, spin two-and-a-half times, and land on the outside edge of my right skate.*

A piece of cake.

So why am I muffing it on the video?

On the video screen, Noelle watched herself spin the two-and-a-half revolutions in the air, and then come down to the ice again.

But she let her left skate touch the ice.

Boom. Points off. Third-place finish. Top two go to the Nationals. So Tara Lipinski and Krissi Atkinson qualified.

And I stayed home. But now I know it was more than that touchdown.

It was my teeth. My stupid, ugly teeth.

On the screen in front of her, Krissi Atkinson was taking the ice. Normally, at this point, Noelle would shut the video off, not wanting to get herself more upset by watching Krissi, who was her archrival. But now she sat watching Krissi in sick fascination, checking out Krissi's pearly white teeth.

They were perfect.

On the videotape, Krissi smiled in the direction of the judges, and Noelle felt like smashing her fist into the screen.

Krissi Atkinson had been Noelle's nemesis ever since she had begun skating competitively. Although she was the same age as Noelle, Krissi still had the looks and body of a girl four years younger.

Where Noelle was five foot three inches tall, Krissi was four foot ten inches. Where

Noelle weighed one hundred and three and one half pounds (she had just weighed herself that morning), Krissi weighed eighty-seven pounds. And where Noelle had jet black hair and usually skated in emerald green or royal blue costumes lovingly created by her aunt Gussie, Krissi was an angelic vision in her trademark all-white outfits, which were designed and handsewn by a big-name designer at ten thousand dollars a pop.

Krissi had long, lustrous, super-blond, almost white hair that came all the way down to the bottom of her back. It was always held back by white ribbons tied around it, exactly two inches apart. She had a pert little nose and blue eyes that were the color of the sky in midsummer.

Oh yes, Noelle recalled, with venom in her heart. *Krissi always signs her first name with a little heart where the dot on the letter i would be. And, to carry that theme through, there is always a little pink heart embroidered someplace on her skating outfit.*

It had become a game for the media and for her legions of young fans to find the heart.

And there were fans galore. Krissi was the darling of television and the press, and it was rumored that she had already signed a contract with the William Morris Agency for TV specials and commercial endorsements. At every event, hordes of young girls ages eight to twelve would show up, all of them with a small pink heart drawn on their right cheek as a show of support for their favorite skater.

Some TV reporter had dubbed these girls Krissi's Kids, and the name had stuck. Now, Krissi's Kids always arrived with banners and placards announcing their noisy presence. As for Noelle, her usual rooting section consisted of her parents, her brother and sister, and her aunt Gussie — that is, when they could afford to travel. But a lot of times they couldn't afford it, and the only ones there were Erin and Tara and Traci.

That's my cheering section.

Noelle took in Krissi's final pose on the videotape, and she stuck out her tongue at the screen.

"I loathe everything about you," she told Krissi's image. "Including your perfect teeth."

And it isn't because Krissi is rich and perfect-looking, Noelle told herself. *Well, not only that, anyway. She's a total witch. Once I heard she stuck coins in another skater's boots, to try and throw her off her best performance. She'll say or do any mean thing she can to undermine another skater. That's the side of her the adoring public never sees.*

But she beat me, Noelle reminded herself. *She didn't have to pull any underhanded tricks. No, Jack would say I beat myself.*

And with my ugly, stupid, hideous teeth, she's probably going to beat me again.

Noelle snapped the video off and pushed rewind, intending to put in a videotape Jack had made of her short program during practice a few days earlier. And just as she did, there was a knock at her door.

"Come in," she said, getting up to go to the stack of videos that was next to the monitor.

"Hi," Jack said, "What's up?"

"Watching videos," Noelle reported, going through the stack, looking for the practice tape.

"Helpful?" Jack asked.

"Some," Noelle answered truthfully. She smiled at Jack, but immediately felt a wave of self-consciousness at her teeth. She covered her mouth with her hand.

"Sit down, Noelle," Jack said. "I want to talk to you."

Dutifully, Noelle stopped her task, and went and sat down in the chair by her desk, while Jack plopped himself down on her bed. Behind him, over his shoulder, Noelle could see the victory poster from the 1994 Olympic women's singles skating finals, showing Oksana Baiul, Nancy Kerrigan, and Chen Lu standing on the podium, their medals around their necks, holding bouquets of flowers up over their heads, waving to the crowd.

All of them have perfect teeth, she noticed suddenly.

"I just got a phone call," Jack said to her. "It was Constance Connolly. You know her?"

"Uh . . . I think," Noelle said evasively. She hadn't said anything to Jack or Sandi about her meeting with Ms. Connolly the day before at the Mighty Cup. What was the point? She couldn't afford to have her stupid, ugly teeth capped.

Jack shook his head. "I hope you can remember your routine better than you remember meeting her," he said. "You just met her yesterday."

"Oh, yeah," Noelle muttered. "I guess I

should have told you, but . . ." The rest of her sentence died in her mouth.

"What could you have been thinking?" Jack exclaimed, not bothering to hide his annoyance. "If a judge *ever* talks to you again, you are to report to me *immediately* what that judge said. Am I completely understood?"

"Yes," Noelle said meekly. "I should have told you. I'm sorry."

"Fortunately," Jack said, "there was no damage done this time. But what if she'd asked me what you'd told me about your talk with her, what then? It could've ruined everything!"

"Yes," Noelle agreed. "I just didn't think . . ."

"She told me she told you that you should get your teeth capped," Jack went on briskly.

"My parents can't afford that," Noelle said in a low, embarrassed voice.

"She said it would help your artistic impression," Jack reported, ignoring what Noelle had just said.

"Well, *ducky*," Noelle snapped, which was something she never, but never, did in front of her coach. But she couldn't seem to stop herself. "I can't afford it!"

"Don't you want to win, Noelle?"

"Yes!" she yelled. "I want it more than anything in the world, okay?"

Jack's face brightened. "Say that again."

"I said I want it more than anything in the world," Noelle repeated, but all the fight had gone out of her.

What is the point of this, she thought. *There is no point.*

"Then we will do what's necessary," Jack said, matter-of-factly. "You're getting your teeth fixed. They don't have to be capped. They do something called bonding these days. They just fill in the spaces with a special material."

Noelle opened her mouth, but no sound came out. She shut it and then cleared her throat. "Who's going to pay for it?" she asked quietly.

"I am," Jack said. "It's not like capping."

"But — "

"No buts, Noelle," Jack cut her off. "My decision is final."

"But — "

"I thought I told you no buts," Jack repeated. "What we'll do is put it on your bill. After you win the gold at the Olympics, your parents will have all the money in the world. Fair enough?"

Sweat broke out on Noelle's upper lip. "But what . . . what if I don't win?"

Jack stood up. "Then you will have a gorgeous loser's smile, compliments of Jack and Sandi Preston." He peered into Noelle's eyes. "That's not going to happen, is it?"

"No," Noelle said. "It's not."

"Good girl," Jack said, ruffling her hair in the way that she hated. "We'll go to the dentist tomorrow afternoon. He can fix your teeth in one visit."

"What?" Noelle asked, taken aback. "But the big dinner dance is tomorrow! My aunt made me a dress!"

Jack looked at her closely. "Noelle, do you want to win Winterfest, or do you want to go to a stupid banquet with a bunch of loser so-called athletes?"

"Win Winterfest," Noelle said sadly, her dream of a great evening — and maybe even meeting a guy — dissolving into a vision of herself in some dentist's chair, her mouth shot full of Novocain.

"That's right," Jack said. "Winning is everything. We're going to win this one, Noelle, if it's the last thing that I do. Now, you with me?"

"I . . . yes," Noelle said.

What other answer could she possibly

give? She was going to get perfect teeth, just like Krissi Atkinson. It was what she really, really wanted. And what was one silly, little dinner dance? Nothing, really.

So she couldn't figure out why it was that she felt so very, very sad.

Chapter 7

"What fun, a double date!" Tara said as she waved the mascara wand over her eyelashes for the third time.

"It isn't a date," Erin insisted, pulling on her pantyhose. She had come over to Tara's house so that they could get ready for the dinner dance together. Then Tara would drive them to pick up Luke and David at the athletes' dorm.

Noelle had called Erin the night before to tell her that she wasn't going to be at the dinner dance because she was getting her teeth fixed, compliments of her coach.

"How come you don't sound happy about it?" Erin had asked her.

"I am happy," Noelle insisted. "But I really, really, really wanted to go to the dinner."

"Couldn't you get your teeth fixed on

Saturday or something?" Erin had asked.

"I have to practice all day," Noelle said. "It's better this way."

"We'll miss you," Erin had told her before hanging up.

Sometimes I really envy Noelle, she thought, *and then other times I wouldn't want her life for anything in the world.*

"Let's see, two girls and two guys," Tara mused. "Getting all dressed up, putting perfume on places we'd like to be kissed . . . I'd call it a double date!"

"Tara, stop," Erin said. "I feel horrible enough about this already."

"Because of Mr. Pete?" Tara asked, reaching into her closet for her dress.

"Stop calling him that!" Erin exclaimed. "I love him!"

Tara yawned deliberately.

"You're terrible," Erin said. "You know that, don't you?"

"I do," Tara agreed, dropping her black silk column dress over her head. "I should be boiled in oil." She turned to Erin. "What do you think?"

Erin took in the vision that was Tara — blond waves cascading over her shoulders, perfectly made-up face, and the black dress, with its sheer chiffon sleeves and neckline, that fell in a graceful column to her ankles.

"You're perfect," Erin said honestly.

"Not perfect," Tara said. "I still have ankles like two big ole cans of baked beans, but the rest of me is pretty good."

Erin laughed. "I can't believe you're so insecure about your ankles."

"Said like a woman with delicate ankles," Tara decreed, spinning in front of her mirror. "All I have to say is, David Benjamin had better be so dazzled by me above the knees that he never looks down."

"You really like him, huh?" Erin said, reaching for her dress, which was lying, covered in plastic, across the chair by Tara's desk.

"I'm not sure if I'm crazy about him or if I can't stand him," Tara said, dropping a few things into her small evening purse. "I mean, he's just so annoying. But then again, he is so gorgeous."

"Well, that's pretty shallow," Erin said, pulling her dress over her head.

"Of course," Tara agreed. "That's what's so much fun about it. Are you going to tell me you love Luke Blakely for his fine mind or his fine body?"

"I don't love Luke Blakely!" Erin insisted,

her hair caught in the neckline of her dress. Finally she popped her head out and pulled the dress down. It was ice blue satin, with a fitted waist and a low-cut back. The off-the-shoulder neckline was dotted with slender silver threads that also glinted periodically through the rest of the fabric.

"Well, he is for sure going to love you!" Tara exclaimed, staring at Erin in her new dress. "You are walking beauty, girl!"

"Really?" Erin asked, moving over so she could see her reflection in Tara's mirror. "It's not too . . . too . . ."

"Sexy?" Tara asked.

Erin turned around and peered at her back, which was almost totally bared to her waist. "Yeah, that," she said.

"It's one hot little number," Tara said. "And you look great in it. And it's not too sexy. And you are fantastic."

Erin grinned at her friend. "Such love, such support!"

"And Luke is going to drool like a fool," Tara added wickedly.

Erin reached out and slapped at Tara's arm. "Stop. I am not doing anything with Luke. Except talking, eating, and maybe dancing."

"Does this mean having him grab you on

the dance floor and kissing you passionately is totally out of the question?" Tara asked, stepping into her sexy black high heels.

"Who's kissing passionately?" Tara's mother asked, sticking her head into the doorway. She was wearing her usual jeans and flannel shirt, and her hair was messily wound around a pencil that stuck out of the top of her head.

"Erin has a hot date," Tara explained. "She's crazed for her athlete."

"What about Mr. Pete?" Mrs. Moore asked idly.

"Everything with Mr. Pete — I mean Pete — is just fine," Erin insisted, shooting Tara a killer look.

"Good," Tara's mom said. "Well, have fun. You both look very nice," she added, then walked away.

Tara shrugged. "You'd think she could be a little more enthusiastic for me."

"I guess her idea of fun and your idea of fun are two different things," Erin said lamely.

Tara pushed some hair behind her ear. "She could at least be proud of me . . ."

"I'm sure she's proud of you!" Erin insisted.

"Yeah . . ." Tara said, her voice trailing off. "Well, too bad for her. This is official fun night. In fact, fun doesn't even begin to cover it."

She grinned at Erin. "What do you say, let's go be evil."

"It's beautiful in here!" Erin exclaimed as she and Luke, and Tara and David, walked into the Kennedy Room in the student union.

With hundreds of tiny, twinkling white lights, the barren room had been transformed into a winter wonderland. The lights glimmered off of silver foil icicles and large blue-and-silver banners that read LOVE'S WINTERFEST and WELCOME ATHLETES. Round tables for six, covered with snowy white tablecloths, surrounded a small dance floor, and behind that was a stage where a band was playing a ballad by Billy Joel.

"Hey, Luke, how's it going?" a cute girl with a blond bob asked, coming over to them. "Isn't this great?"

"Yeah, it is," Luke agreed. "Oh, Gail, this is my host, Erin Kellerman. And this is her friend, Tara Moore, and David Benjamin

— he's a downhill racer from Colby. This is Gail Lowry. She's a skier from UC."

"But I'm not as good as Luke," Gail said, taking Luke's arm and pulling him close. "No one is that good!"

"Some of the girls from other schools here would disagree with you," Luke said.

"Hey, I know what I know," Gail insisted. "Want to come sit with me? I'm over at table six." She leaned close, but Erin and Tara could still hear her. "My host is some dweeby little guy who hangs on my every word. And he kind of drools. You'd be saving my life."

"Sorry, Gail, can't," Luke said lightly, extricating himself from Gail's grip. "We're assigned to table twenty. I'll catch you later."

The foursome spotted their table and made their way through the crowd.

"You could have sat with her if you wanted to," Erin said offhandedly. "I'm sure someone would have switched."

Luke looked at her sideways. "But then I wouldn't be sitting with you, would I?"

A little chill of happiness crawled up her spine. *Just let me act cool about this,* she told herself. *Just please don't let me give away how I feel.*

"So, David, how do you like the decorations?" Tara asked as David politely pulled out her chair at table twenty.

"Very nice," he said, sitting down next to her.

"I have a feeling if I asked you how you like running naked through Winterfest you'd say the same thing," Tara said.

David grinned. "Possibly," he said.

"Hey, David, they must be real psyched about you back in Israel, huh?" Luke asked, taking a sip of his water.

"My family, yes," David said. "But Israel has more important things to think about than me."

"Hi, table twenty, we're table twenty, too!" a perky girl Erin and Tara both recognized from the committee sang out. She had a mass of frizzy black hair pulled up on her head in a chignon, and she wore a red velvet dress cut so low that her ample bosom was clearly visible.

"I'm Nellie Bixom," she told Luke and David, shaking their hands heartily, "and this is my athlete, James Engles."

James was a tall African-American guy, with dancing eyes and high cheekbones, who towered over the petite Nellie.

"Hi," James said in a very deep voice, taking a seat.

"James is on the luge team from University of Michigan," Nellie gushed. "I am just so impressed with luge. Aren't you guys?"

Everyone nodded dutifully.

"So, Erin, Tara, you guys must be so psyched about the court, huh?"

"What's that?" Luke asked.

"You don't know?" Nellie asked, wide-eyed. "Tonight they'll announce the six princesses for Winterfest, and the entire Winterfest committee will pick the Queen at the final banquet. Tara will get it, for sure."

"And I'm excited for Tara," Erin added loyally.

"Wow," David said, but his voice was totally deadpan.

This subtlety was lost on Nellie. "Wow is right!" she exclaimed. "I'm hope-hope-hoping to hear my name, aren't you two?"

"Well, I'll be shocked if Tara's not on the court," Erin said. "But I'm not exactly the beauty pageant type."

"Me neither," Nellie agreed, "but this isn't just some silly pageant. This is everything! This is Winterfest!" She turned to

James and grabbed his arm. "You think I have a chance?"

"Oh, sure," James said. He seemed totally amused by her.

"I hope I hope I hope," Nellie chanted, the fingers on both her hands crossed, her eyes closed.

"Tara, would you like to dance?" David asked.

"Love to," Tara said.

"What a good idea," Luke added, getting up and holding his hand out to Erin.

"Excuse us, please," David said to Nellie, who was still chanting her "I hopes" as James cracked up next to her.

"What was that 'I hope I hope' business?" David asked, as he took Tara into his arms.

"I have no earthly idea," Tara said, leaning into David's embrace. "Mmmm, you smell good. What cologne is that?"

"I don't wear cologne," David said.

"You are ornery on purpose, aren't you?" Tara stated, pulling back to give David an arch look.

"Let me ask you something," David said, deftly turning her to the music. "Clearly you are a bright woman. Why then do you act stupid?"

Tara's jaw dropped. "I do not act stupid!"

146

"Frankly, I was surprised to see that you are so intelligent," David went on. "You do your best to hide it. It is not very attractive."

"Well, who died and made you judge and jury?" Tara fumed.

"What I mean is," David continued, "you seem to care about this beauty pageant thing. I think you must be very insecure about your looks to do this."

Tara stepped out of his arms and put her hands on her hips. "I assume if I look up pig-headed-obnoxious-know-it-all-sanctimonious-jerk in the dictionary, I will find your scowling, supercilious photo, correct?"

"I didn't mean to offend you," David said.

"Oh, yes you did," Tara shot back. "That's just what you meant to do. You have elevated bad manners to an art form!"

"You don't need to be so defensive," David said mildly. "I think I must have hit a nerve."

"Oh!" Tara yelped, her eyes blazing with fury. And since she couldn't think of anything awful enough to say to him, she simply lifted her black high heel into the air and brought it down on his toe as hard as she could.

Then she turned and marched off.

"What happened?" Erin asked as she and Luke danced up next to David, who stood there stunned.

"I don't know," he said. "We were just talking . . ."

"Did she hurt your foot, man?" Luke asked with concern.

"No," David said. "These shoes are made of thick leather."

"You're lucky," Luke said, shaking his head. "That's one hot-headed girl."

"Maybe I should go see if she's okay," Erin said, breaking away from Luke.

He pulled her back to him. "And maybe you ought to stay right here," he suggested.

She smelled the delicious smell of him, and felt his arms tighten around her, and she decided to take him up on his suggestion.

"Come on, Tara, there's no point in staying ticked off at him," Erin said, as she rubbed some lipstick off her teeth in the ladies' room.

It was two hours later. Dinner had been delicious and Erin had had a wonderful time. All the athletes had been introduced, and one by one they had stood up while the crowd applauded them. The mayor of Love made a speech. The Love College chancellor made a speech. And through it all, Tara and David had barely spoken two words to each other.

"I loathe him, I hate him, I cannot stand him," Tara seethed.

"Okay, so he'll be gone in two and a half weeks," Erin reminded Tara. "In fact, you can probably get someone else on the committee to sponsor him. I'm sure Nellie would drool over it."

"He's mine," Tara said stubbornly, brushing her hair with angry strokes.

"But you just said you hate him!" Erin exclaimed.

"Because *he* hates *me!*" Tara cried, throwing her brush into her purse. She turned to Erin. "He really, truly hates me, Erin. How can that be?"

"He doesn't — "

"He does," Tara insisted. "He thinks I'm flighty and inconsequential."

"Maybe you should drop the fact that you're valedictorian of the senior class, or that you already have a scholarship to Harvard," Erin said wryly.

"That would make it even worse," Tara

said. "He thinks I'm wasting my brains." She fiddled with the clasp on her purse. "I'm not wasting my brains."

Erin laughed. "Like I said, you're going to Harvard. I'm the one who's going to beautiful, boring Love College."

"If I could just get him to . . . see me," Tara murmured. "Maybe I'm just not his type. Maybe it's my ankles . . ."

"Oh, enough with the ankles thing already!" Erin groaned.

"Okay, okay, so I'm a wee bit neurotic," Tara said. "It's just that . . . I want him, Erin. A lot."

"I thought you hated him," Erin reminded her.

"Don't throw my words back into my face, if you please," Tara said crossly. She took a deep breath. "The truth is . . . the truth is I want to kiss him so bad that it hurts."

"You do?" Erin asked incredulously.

"Desperately," Tara admitted. "What should I do? Just grab him?"

"Well, you could — "

"Girls, girls!" Nellie yelled, running into the bathroom. "I had to come and get you. They're announcing the court!"

Tara and Erin hurried back to the table,

just as the Director of Winterfest, Dr. Leonard Smithson, was finishing his speech.

"And this year," Dr. Smithson concluded from the podium on the bandstand, "I'm sure that our six lovely girls will represent the very best of the town of Love, Love College, and, most of all, the nationally known festival of winter fun and the highest level of high school and collegiate athletic competition that is Winterfest."

"I hope I hope I hope I hope," Nellie began chanting again, her fingers crossed and her eyes closed.

"Would each Winterfest Princess come to the bandstand as her name is called," Dr. Smithson said, as he opened a sealed white envelope. "Carmella Juarez."

A pretty Hispanic girl in a silver dress stood up, grinning hugely, and worked her way up to the bandstand.

"Noelle Le Blanc," Dr. Smithson said. Someone hurried over and whispered in Dr. Smithson's ear — presumably telling him that Noelle wasn't at the dinner dance.

"Noelle!" Tara cried happily. "Oh, I'm so sorry she isn't here for this. She would have loved it."

"Yeah," Erin agreed, smiling at Tara.

"I'm so happy for her," Tara said, her eyes shining.

David turned and gave Tara a contemplative look.

"Sandra Campbell," the director said.

"Hey, that's Traci's older sister, right?" Erin said happily as a lovely, tall, slender African-American girl got up from a front table and went up to the bandstand.

"Tara Elizabeth Moore," Dr. Smithson called.

Erin squealed with delight as Tara regally got up from her chair and walked up to the bandstand.

"She knew all the time that she would be picked, didn't she?" David said.

"No, she didn't," Erin told him, over the now more desperate sound of Nellie Bixom's "I hope" chanting.

"A girl who looks like her takes that kind of thing for granted," David said.

"You are totally wrong," Erin told him fiercely. "And you ought to get to really know her before you decide you have her all figured out, don't you think?"

"Two points for you," Luke said, grinning at Erin.

"Nellie Bixom," Dr. Smithson called.

"Oh my God, did he really say it?" Nellie gasped, opening her eyes.

"He did!" Erin told her. "Honest!"

"Go get 'em, girl," James told her, and he gallantly got up and pulled out Nellie's chair. She ran up to the bandstand and hugged Tara so hard that she practically knocked her over.

"And the last girl on the Winterfest court," Dr. Smithson said, "is . . . Erin Faye Kellerman."

Erin's jaw dropped open. *He didn't really say what I think he just said,* she thought. *He couldn't have said me. Not in a million years could he have said —*

"That's you, babe," Luke said easily. He, too, stood up and helped a stunned Erin from her chair. As if in a dream, she made her way up to the other four girls on the bandstand while the whole room applauded warmly.

"Let's have one final round of applause for our Winterfest Princesses!" Dr. Smithson said.

As the whole room applauded again, Tara and Erin hugged each other.

"I just can't believe it!" Erin said in a daze. "Me on the court!"

"You deserve it," Tara said. "You are beautiful and wonderful." She looked out at their table, where Luke was still standing, staring up at Erin. "And it appears that someone else thinks so, too."

Erin turned and saw Luke, who clearly was waiting for her, then she turned back to Tara. "But what about you and — "

"Forget about that right now," Tara said. "Go be with him. It's what you want."

Erin hugged Tara again, then she walked over to Luke.

"Congratulations," he said, staring down into her eyes.

"Thanks," she said softly. "I was shocked."

"I wasn't." He took her by the hand and led her out onto the balcony. The air was cold, so cold it practically took her breath away, and all the stars were twinkling above them.

"Pray for snow, princess," Luke said, pulling Erin close to him.

"I will," she promised.

As they both stared up at the sky, a shooting star shot across the horizon, disappearing in a blaze.

"Did you see it?" Erin cried. "We both have to make a wish!"

Luke closed his eyes. "Made it," he said.

Erin closed her eyes. "I'm making it right now," she said.

But before she could open her eyes, Luke had pulled her to him, and she could feel his lips on hers.

It was the quickest any wish on a shooting star had ever come true.

Chapter 8

"Snow, snow, snow!" Erin yelled happily, pressing her face to the bay window in the living room at Jack and Sandi Preston's house. "It's really coming down out there!"

"She's a mite happy," Tara told Noelle, as she, too, stared out the window at the heavily falling snow.

"Well, it wouldn't be Winterfest without snow!" Erin said gaily. "Gosh, there must be over a foot already!"

It was the next afternoon. Noelle had spent the morning at the rink. Before she left, she had called Tara and Erin and invited them over that afternoon to look at her new skating costumes. They were due to arrive any minute from Love Cleaners, where all the skaters sent their costumes for a final cleaning and pressing before the competition.

"She's exaggerating," Tara explained to Noelle. "But we have to be understanding, because she has lost her mind."

"I guess that means you had fun last night," Noelle said wistfully, leaning against the couch.

"It was . . . so incredible," Erin said, her eyes shining.

"I'm just sorry you weren't there to hear your name read as one of the princesses on the court," Tara told Noelle. "Can you believe all three of us are princesses?"

"I never ever in a million years thought I'd be on the court," Erin said, shaking her head.

"Me, neither," Noelle agreed. "I mean, I never even considered it, since I'm one of the competing athletes."

"I don't think it's ever happened before," Erin said. "I guess this means you're beautiful *and* a champion!"

"I am not a champion," Noelle reminded them, still staring out at the falling snow.

"Hey, now that you have teeth that glow in the dark, you are a shoo-in!" Tara told her playfully. "Smile for us again."

Self-consciously, Noelle smiled her new smile.

"Beauty-pageant perfection. No spaces,"

Tara declared. "Just remember, when the judges ask you, 'What woman alive today has done more for mankind than any other?' there is only one acceptable answer, and that is Mother Teresa."

Noelle laughed. "Skating judges don't ask questions."

"True," Tara said, looking around the room for the bowl of grapes Noelle had set out for them. "They're too busy judging far more important athletic qualities, like the size and color of one's bicuspids. Where are those grapes?"

"We finished them," Noelle said with a sigh.

Actually, I ate most of them, she realized. *I know I shouldn't have, but I couldn't stop myself. All Sandi gave me for lunch was an apple and some cheese.*

"What did you have for dinner at the dinner dance?" Noelle asked.

"Forget about the food," Tara instructed her. "What you really need to hear about is what happened to Erin. In addition to being chosen for the court, Erin and Luke — "

"Hi, girls," Sandi said, coming into the living room. Her eyes immediately fell on the empty bowl on the coffee table. "What was in there?" she asked.

"Grapes," Noelle admitted, hanging her head.

"Noelle had two," Tara said quickly. "Erin and I were total pigs and ate the rest."

Sandi eyed Tara coolly, picked up the fruit bowl, and walked out.

"God, it's like prison!" Tara exclaimed. "I say we plan a breakout!"

"She's just trying to help me," Noelle said, plopping herself down on the couch. "I should have more self-discipline. Sometimes I just disgust myself!"

"Because you ate a few grapes?" Erin asked, coming over to sit next to Noelle.

"It isn't just that," Noelle said, twisting the edge of her sweater between her fingers. "I . . . I don't seem to have my mind completely on skating. I keep thinking about food. And guys."

"Two topics near and dear to my own heart," Tara agreed.

"I'm just so afraid I'll let everyone down!" Noelle exclaimed nervously.

Erin hugged Noelle quickly. "All you can do is your best, Noelle," she said.

"But what if my best isn't good enough?" Noelle whispered. "Wait till you see Krissi's routine. And she's so perfect-looking, and such a first-class witch. She beat me at regionals — "

"We've already heard that lament, Noelle," Tara said. "Time to change the funeral dirge, honey."

"You're right," Noelle said. "I know you're right. So, tell me more about last night."

"Well, David Benjamin is the most infuriating and hottest guy in the universe," Tara explained. "I probably hate him, but I'm too busy wanting to kiss him to think about it too much. And as for our little Miss Kellerman here, she is going to need to have a good long chitchat with Mr. Pete, because — "

At that moment the doorbell rang.

"I'll get it," Noelle said. "It must be the cleaners with my costumes."

Noelle hurried to the door, thinking about the three costumes her aunt Gussie had made for her for Winterfest.

Krissi Atkinson has her costumes made by the same designer who did Nancy Kerrigan's outfits for the Olympics, Noelle thought darkly, as she opened the door. *She can afford costumes that cost thousands of dollars apiece. Her parents are filthy rich.*

"Your costumes, Noelle Le Blanc," a young man with a mustache said, handing a beige plastic bag to Noelle. "Good luck, we're all rooting for you!"

"Thanks," Noelle said, taking the bag. "Drive carefully, okay?"

"No problem," the deliveryman said as the snowflakes bounced off his blue hat. "I love the snow! It's Winterfest, you know?"

Noelle walked back to the living room. "He said everyone is rooting for me!" she reported happily.

"Well, everyone is," Erin agreed. "You're the hometown girl at Winterfest."

"So, let's see the costumes," Tara said, leaning against the back of the couch.

"They're not like Krissi Atkinson's," Noelle warned her friends, leading them into the family room, "but I think Aunt Gussie did pretty good."

Noelle pulled the beige plastic covering off the three skating costumes, which were on tiny, white plastic hangers.

Noelle was right.

The costumes were not *like* Krissi Atkinson's.

They *were* Krissi Atkinson's.

The girls could easily tell that from the

perfect pink heart that had gently and lovingly been embroidered on the right shoulder of the top white outfit.

"You're going as a Krissi look-alike?" Tara asked, reaching for one of the outfits, which was still covered in see-through plastic.

"They sent Krissi's outfits by mistake," Noelle said.

"Well, let's just take the plastic off and check these puppies out," Tara suggested, lifting the plastic up.

"Hey!" Noelle protested.

"Take a chill pill," Tara advised, holding the skating outfit up to herself and admiring it. "Just tell Krissi that you had to take it out of the plastic to see if it was yours."

"Oh, sure," Noelle said. "She'll really buy that. Her outfits are all white, and mine are silver, blue, and red."

"It's really beautiful," Erin said reverently, touching the tiny white skirt. Then she thought of Noelle's feelings. "I mean, if you like things extravagant like that. It looks like it cost five thousand dollars."

"Ten thousand. I can't believe they sent me Krissi's costumes," Noelle lamented. "Do you think that means — "

The doorbell sounded again.

"It's the cleaners," Erin said. "He probably figured out his mistake."

"You want me to yank the hearts off Krissi's perfect little outfits with my teeth?" Tara asked innocently. "I could do it before I put the plastic back on."

"Krissi does underhanded things like that," Noelle said as she hurried to the door. "I don't."

"But as we all know, I am a low-down dog," Tara called to Noelle.

"The answer is no," Noelle called back. She pulled open the front door.

It was Krissi Atkinson herself.

At the curbside, a huge white van, with a pink heart painted on its side and a large KRISSI written in script, with a pink heart over the *i*, waited for her.

Noelle took in Krissi's typical Krissi Atkinson clothes — white fur après-ski boots, into which were tucked white stretch pants, and a white warm-up jacket over the whole thing with the word "Krissi" embroidered on the left breast pocket, with the signature pink heart over the *i*. Perfect prisms of snow glinted in her white-blond hair.

Krissi held a Love Cleaners beige plastic bag out to Noelle. "Hi, Noelle," Krissi said. "I understand they sent my costumes here by mistake. Here's yours."

"Thanks," Noelle said, taking the bag from Krissi.

How'd she find my house? Noelle thought.

"I called Love Cleaners just as soon as they delivered your costumes to me at our hotel," Krissi said gaily. "They gave me your address. So this is where Jack Preston and his wife ended up. It's . . . . quaint!"

"I'll get your costumes, Krissi," Noelle said grimly.

"Aren't you sweet," Krissi said. She coolly looked Noelle over, who suddenly felt utterly ugly in her old, stretched-out sweater and a pair of sweatpants.

"Aren't you going to invite me in?" Krissi asked. "It would be the polite thing to do."

I hate her, I hate her, I hate her, Noelle thought.

"Sure, Krissi," she said dutifully. "Come on in." She smiled at Krissi — or tried to — and ushered her into the house.

"Wait!" Krissi commanded. "Look at me again."

Noelle turned around.

"Now, smile."

Noelle smiled.

"You got your teeth fixed!" Krissi cried, her voice accusing.

"Yeah," Noelle said. "Yesterday."

"Well, how nice!" Krissi said, regaining her poise. "You really look so much better!"

"Thanks," Noelle replied.

"It's just a shame that you couldn't afford to have your nose done at the same time, huh?" Krissi added, her voice oozing malicious sincerity.

Noelle just stood there, stunned and stung. Involuntarily her hand reached up to her nose. At that moment, Erin and Tara walked into the foyer, carrying Krissi's costumes.

Tara handed Krissi her costumes. Noelle still had her hand over her nose. "Are you okay?" Tara asked her.

"Fine," Noelle mumbled, forcing herself to drop her hand. "Uh, Krissi, this is Tara Moore and Erin Kellerman. This is Krissi Atkinson."

"*You're* Krissi Atkinson?" Tara asked wide-eyed, her voice filled with awe.

"Why, yes," Krissi said proudly. Clearly, she was used to hearing that tone of voice when people met her.

"The same one who's on TV sometimes?" Tara asked innocently.

"That's me," Krissi said demurely. "Would you like my autograph?"

Tara burst out in laughter, as if someone had just told her the best joke she had ever heard. She laughed so hard that she bent over and couldn't catch her breath.

"You're Krissi Atkinson," Tara finally managed to gasp again, pointing at Krissi. Then she fell over again in a fit of laughter.

"I don't see what's so funny," Krissi said haughtily.

"Oh, nothing," Tara said, tears of laughter in her eyes. "I'm sorry. Truly I am. But it's just that there was this big buildup about you, and now that I actually see you in the flesh, well . . ." Tara tried to hold her laughter back, but it snorted out of her nose instead.

This sounded so funny that it started Noelle and Erin laughing, too.

"Oh, well, aren't we just hilarious," Krissi spat out, red-faced. "What have you ever done with your life?"

"Golly, not much," Tara said, managing to catch her breath. "Let's see . . . I had dinner at the White House recently, along with everyone else who got perfect scores on their SATs and achievement tests. And, hmmmm, what else? I'm going to Harvard next year on a full scholarship to study neuropsychology. But other than that, I've mostly been sitting around doing my nails. Do you like my manicure?"

Tara thrust a perfectly manicured hand up toward Krissi's astonished face and waggled her fingers. "I get so hung up between short and red or long and French. What do you think?"

"I have to go," was all Krissi could think of to say. "I'll, uh, see you on the ice, Noelle." She turned and hurried through the falling snow to her waiting van.

"Bye-bye, now!" Tara called after her. "Oh, take care of that pimple on your chin, Krissi. Is it nerves, honey? It's just so . . . unsightly!"

Noelle closed the door and turned to Tara. "I can't believe what you just did."

"I was kind of fantastic, wasn't I?" Tara said demurely.

"You totally psyched her out!" Erin said, grinning hugely.

"Who does she think she is, Saint Joan of Arc?" Tara asked. " 'Do you want my autograph?' Puh-leez!"

With that, Tara started laughing yet

again. And Erin joined in. And then, finally, Noelle.

Because Noelle realized that if she was looking for a psychological edge on Krissi Atkinson, her best friend Tara Moore may have just given her one.

"Are you excited about tomorrow?" Erin asked as she dunked the tiny marshmallows into her hot chocolate.

It was Saturday evening, and Luke had just finished his very last practice jumps before the Winterfest would officially begin the next day. Erin had watched his practice, feeling breathless and dazzled.

She could close her eyes and still feel the melting feeling of his lips on hers, his arms around her, holding her close to his pounding heart. Now they were at the Mighty Cup, which was full of the athletes and hosts who had had a similar notion of where to go after practice.

"Oh, yeah," Luke said, taking a bite of his buttered bagel. "I'm pumped."

"I heard people in the crowd saying that your only real competition is that guy from Utah, Brad Johnson," Erin said.

"Not true," Luke replied. "Brad's great, but so is the dude from Vermont, and that

Swiss exchange student, Bjorn Kurtsted, from the University of Massachusetts. And Nat Beal."

"Your last practice jump was the best," Erin reminded him, sipping her hot chocolate.

"Only once," Luke said. "It could go either way." He looked outside at the snow, which had started falling again. "I guess we got the snow we wanted, huh?"

"It's perfect," Erin said happily.

Luke smiled. "You are probably the nicest girl I ever met. Have I told you that?"

Erin blushed happily. "Oh, well . . ." she stammered.

"Seriously," Luke said, sipping his coffee. "I mean, you are totally genuine. It's so refreshing. Special."

"I never think of myself as being special, I guess," Erin admitted. She stared thoughtfully into her hot chocolate. "My two best friends — now, they're special," she said, a smile playing on her lips.

"Tara is unique, I'll give her that," Luke said wryly.

"She is!" Erin agreed. "She is the most intelligent person I ever met, and she has a photographic memory. It's amazing! And guys always underestimate her, because she's so pretty and she has that southern accent."

"Watching her and David together is a hoot," Luke said. "I think their problem is that they're too much alike."

Erin was thoughtful for a moment. "I never thought about that."

"Oh, for sure," Luke said. "They're both really smart, and they're both trying to psych each other out. The really funny thing is that Tara doesn't realize that David is pulling her leg."

"He is?" Erin asked with surprise.

Luke laughed. "You mean you don't know, either?"

"No," Erin said honestly.

"Well, then, I guess he's doing a good job," Luke said, draining his coffee. "So who is this other best friend that's so amazing?"

"Noelle Le Blanc," Erin said proudly. "She's a — "

"Figure skater," Luke put in. "I think I've heard of her."

"She's incredible," Erin said enthusiastically. "She's going to win Winterfest, and then she's going to the Olympics. I really want you to meet her."

"Hey, more power to her," Luke said. He poured some more coffee into his cup from the tiny carafe on the table. "I dream about the Olympics myself."

"Oh, Luke, that would be so awesome," Erin breathed. "I can't even imagine having that kind of talent."

"Oh, come on," Luke said. "I told you, everyone is great at something. You're smart, pretty, a sweetheart of a girl. Your boyfriend is really lucky."

Erin's heart turned over. *How can Luke be talking about Pete after he kissed me?*

"Pete isn't . . . I mean he is but . . ." Erin stammered, feeling like an idiot.

I don't want to lie and I don't want Luke to think we don't have any chance together, either, she thought desperately. *I have no idea what to say!*

"Hey, don't worry about it," Luke said easily. "We don't have to get all bent out of shape, you know?"

"Right," Erin agreed, although she wasn't really sure she knew what Luke meant at all. But just as she was trying to figure out how to get him to explain, the most terrible thing happened.

Pete Cole walked into the Mighty Cup.

Erin felt like sinking down into her seat, like disappearing through the wooden floor.

Wait, she counseled herself. *This is perfectly innocent. I am sitting here with the athlete I was assigned for Winterfest. This is what I'm supposed to be doing.*

But she felt so guilty — as if Pete could read how she really felt written all over her face.

"Hi!" Pete said, bounding over to them. "I just stopped in to pick up some espresso beans for my mom. What luck finding you here, huh?"

"It's great," Erin managed. "Uh, Luke Blakely, this is Pete Cole. Pete, this is Luke. He's a ski jumper."

"Great to meet you, man," Pete said, shaking Luke's hand. "Welcome to Love."

"Thanks," Luke said. "Pull up a seat."

No, no, no, no, Erin screamed in her head. But her face — hopefully — betrayed nothing.

"Oh, great," Pete said. He grabbed an empty chair from a nearby table and pulled it up next to Erin. "So, Luke, how do you like Love?" Pete asked.

"Seems like a cool town," Luke replied.

"Yeah, we like it," Pete said. He put his

arm around Erin's shoulders. "Erin's lived here her whole life. I moved here when I was a little kid. I fell in love with her the very first day of school."

"Yeah?" Luke said, taking another sip of his coffee.

"Yeah," Pete replied. "You know, one of those love-at-first-sight things. Right, Erin?"

Erin managed a sickly smile. "Oh, well, you know . . ."

Pete pulled Erin closer and kissed her cheek. "That's my girl," he said heartily.

"You're a lucky guy," Luke said.

"Hey, don't I know it," Pete agreed. He looked at his watch. "Wow, guess I better get going. My mom has all these friends over, and she's out of coffee." He stood up. "Nice to meet you, Luke," he said, shaking Luke's hand again.

"Yeah, the same," Luke said easily.

"Glad to see my girl's taking good care of you," Pete said. He bent down and kissed Erin again. "I'll call you later, honey," he added and walked away.

She wanted to kill Pete. Truly kill him. He had never called her "honey" before in his life. Never.

But of course he has to pull that in front

of Luke, Erin fumed. *I happen to know his mother doesn't drink coffee and never has it in the house. Somehow he knew I was here with Luke and he wanted to come ruin everything, so he made up that lame excuse. Of all the dirty, underhanded —*

"Nice guy," Luke said.

"He can be a little overbearing," Erin said. "We aren't joined at the hip."

"The guy's in love with you," Luke said with a shrug. "Don't knock it."

Pete paid for his coffee, then waved to Erin and Luke before he walked out of the Mighty Cup.

"Maybe he isn't in love with me," Erin said carefully. "Or . . ." and here she held her breath. "Maybe I'm not in love with him."

Luke just raised his eyebrows.

"I mean," Erin continued in a rush, "this might sound totally crazy to you, but . . . I've been going out with Pete since the eighth grade. Maybe . . . maybe he's just . . . a habit."

Erin ran her finger over the rim of her cup. "Tara says Pete is safe and secure, that that's why I like him."

Luke wiped his hands off with his napkin. "So, what do *you* think?"

"I think," Erin said carefully, "that being safe is highly overrated." She boldly lifted her face and looked into Luke's eyes. "Let's get out of here," she said.

And they did.

Chapter 9

"Ladies and gentlemen," a metallic voice boomed over the football stadium loud-speaker, "please give a grand Love-sized ovation for the athletes of Love Winter-fest Ten!"

With that thrilling and long-awaited announcement, the Love College marching band, assembled at the foot of the home football stands, started playing a sassy brass fanfare. Meanwhile, an impressive array of cannons, manned by the Love College ROTC brigade, dressed in their parade regalia, fired off a loud and stirring salute. Silver and pale blue helium balloons — the school colors of Love College — filled the air.

In the stands, ten thousand people filled the football stadium. They stood as one to applaud and cheer, waving their small silver-and-blue Winterfest flags as the first group of athletes competing in Winterfest X were led into the stadium. It was the bobsledders, and they were led by a lucky Love High School student, who proudly held aloft a big sign that said BOB-SLEDDERS.

Erin and Tara grinned at each other from their spot in the stands.

"It's perfect," Erin said, her eyes shining. "I'll remember this day my whole life."

It was Sunday afternoon, at precisely one o'clock. It had snowed furiously through the entire night and most of the morning — by the time the snow had quit at ten o'clock in the morning, twenty-two inches had accumulated. The sky cleared, the sun shone brightly, and tiny Love, Michigan, had been turned into a white, glorious, winter wonderland.

"I'm so proud of this town," Erin added, waving her little Winterfest flag.

"For a Yankee burg, it's not so bad," Tara said, nudging Erin's shoulder playfully. She looked around at the crowd. "We did good, huh?"

Tara was referring to the panic of the organizing committee when they realized that not only had twenty-two inches of perfect and much needed snow fallen on the Nordic ski trails and the nearby slopes of Love Mountain (site of all the Alpine ski events, including the storied downhill). Twenty-two inches of snow had also blanketed all the seats in the football stadium, the parking lots that awaited five thousand or more cars, the track around the football field where the athletes were to parade, and the field itself.

Fortunately, the organizers had prepared. Every free piece of snow removal equipment from the surrounding area had been called in for emergency duty on area roads and in the parking lots. And the organizers put out a general alert in town — the Emergency Broadcast System had actually been activated for the first time since the August tornado warnings of three summers before — for people to come with snow shovels to the football stadium for the back-breaking job of clearing all the snow from the bleachers.

The whole town had responded, including Tara and her mom, and Erin and the entire Kellerman family.

By eleven o'clock, there were more than five hundred citizens of Love in the football stadium, each one of them with a snow shovel in hand.

An hour later, the bleachers were clear of snow.

So when the first athletes made their way into the stands, the people in the crowd were cheering not only for the athletes, but also for the Herculean task that they themselves had accomplished.

"You sorry Mr. Pete's not here?" Tara teased Erin.

Pete was supposed to have joined them, but he and his family lived on a farm outside of Love, and he'd called Erin earlier to tell her that his father had taken the four-wheel-drive vehicle and that he was stranded without it.

"I'm so mad at him," Erin said. "He finally admitted to me that Nellie Bixom told him that Luke and I were at the Mighty Cup last night. Oh, God, he called me 'honey.' " She shuddered at the memory.

"Time to have it out with Mr. Pete," Tara said. "That's what I say."

Erin sighed. After leaving the Mighty Cup with Luke the night before, she figured they would go somewhere to be alone, and then she would be in Luke's arms, and everything would be perfect.

Well, they'd gone somewhere to be alone, all right. They'd parked on Lover's Hill. Only instead of making out, Luke had talked about ski jumping, and how much it meant to him, and what he was going to have to do if he really wanted to make it to the Olympics.

No kissing had been involved.

None. *Nada*. Nothing. Zippo.

It had to have been because he met Pete, Erin thought dismally. *It can't be that Luke just didn't want to kiss me. Can it?*

Tara clapped her mittened hands together. "Didn't anyone mention that snow is freezing?" she said, her teeth chattering.

"Tara," Erin said, "you left Mississippi ten years ago."

"It's my thin southern blood," Tara said with dignity, stamping her feet in an effort to get the circulation in them flowing.

"You want some tea?" Erin asked, reaching down for the thermos she'd brought.

"Intravenously," Tara quipped as Erin unscrewed the top, poured some steaming tea into the plastic cup on top, and handed it to her friend. Tara took a grateful and long sip.

As the bobsledders paraded by, the man on the public address system explained the sport for the crowd; how the bobsled, invented in the 1880s by lashing two toboggans together, was now a very, very sophisticated sled, and how the Winterfest Ten competition was limited to two-person bobsleds, which ran down a special track that had been built near Love Mountain.

"Let's move it along, y'all!" Tara sang out as the bobsledders stopped, turned, and waved to the huge crowd. "I'm freezing! I have lost all feeling in my toes!"

"Hi, Tara, hi, Erin!" a bubbly voice called out to them from the stands above. "Isn't this just fantastic?"

They both turned around. There was Nellie Bixom. She wore a purple parka unzipped halfway to her waist, over a purple bodysuit cut very low. Pinned to her parka was a huge button that read "Winterfest Princess."

Erin and Tara waved dutifully, then turned back around.

Tara leaned close to Erin. "Just out of curiosity, where do you think a girl buys a bra that large?"

Erin cracked up.

"And she must have had that 'Winterfest

Princess' button made somewhere," Tara went on. "Let's just hope the poor thing doesn't make an error and pin it to her bosom."

Following the bobsledders came the eight invited ice hockey teams — four in the high school division, four in the college division, who would be competing in the round-robin hockey tournaments.

After the hockey players came the lugers, who rode sleds much smaller than bobsleds down a modified bobsled course. "James! James!" they heard Nellie Bixom calling.

And then came the figure skaters.

They all came out together — all the skaters who would be competing in the junior and the senior divisions, both male and female.

The crowd went crazy. Figure skating was by far the most popular spectator event at Winterfest. And the junior ladies' division — the one in which both Noelle and Krissi competed — was the most popular of all.

"Where's Noelle?" Tara asked frantically, scanning the group of skaters.

"There she is!" Erin cried, spotting their friend. She was walking on the track closest to the stands — Erin could see that she was as far away from Krissi Atkinson as she possibly could be.

"She looks so darling!" Tara cried.

Erin had to agree. Although Krissi Atkinson shone in an all-white outfit, Noelle looked regally beautiful in a red velour parka over a black turtleneck, with black velvet leggings and red leg warmers. The red brought out the color in her cheeks and made her dark eyes and hair shine richly in contrast.

"Yo, Noelle!!! Woo-woo!!" Tara yelled out in her most unladylike voice, trying to catch their friend's attention, swinging her arm in the air like she was in the audience on some late-night talk show.

For a millisecond, Erin was embarrassed. Then she, too, gave herself up to the moment. "Woo! Woo! Woo woo woo!" she hooted with Tara. "No-elle, No-elle, No-elle!" she yelled.

It worked. Noelle zeroed in on the sound of their voices, scanning the stands for Tara and Erin. She spotted them and gave a huge wave.

"Go to it, girlfriend!" Tara yelled down to her. "Yo, Krissi, what's that on your chin?"

Krissi Atkinson pointedly looked the other way.

"Yea, Noelle!" Erin cried, jumping up and down, which made Noelle wave even more enthusiastically.

The whole crowd started cheering more loudly. Everyone knew that Noelle was being coached by Jack Preston and his wife.

Jack Preston was a Love legend — the first and only famous athlete to have been born and raised in Love. So Noelle Le Blanc had quickly become a Love favorite.

"It's too bad Noelle's family isn't here yet," Erin said, waving one last time at Noelle as she rounded the track.

"Next week," Tara said. Her eyes scanned the athletes. "Where's David?"

By now, the figure skaters were giving way to the speed skaters, and then came the Nordic skiers, the cross-country and biathlon competitors, whose weird event included both a cross-country ski race and the firing of a rifle at various targets along the way — the biathloners carried a rifle along with them as they skied.

And then came the ski jumpers, Luke Blakely among them. When Erin saw Luke, who saw her in the crowd and gave her a special wave, a thrill of joy and of guilt washed over her at the same time.

"Get your lips ready," Tara joked. "He's gonna need to be warmed up."

If he wants to kiss me so much why didn't he kiss me last night? Erin wanted to scream. But she felt too embarrassed about it to tell Tara.

"If David doesn't come out soon," Tara declared, her teeth chattering, "I am going to turn into a statue right here and now, and you will have to put me in the microwave to bring me back to life."

"David could bring you back to life," Erin said.

"True," Tara agreed. "I'd like to jump into his parka and snuggle up."

"Here they come!" Erin said, spotting the student who carried the sign ALPINE SKIING. Behind her came a group of forty girls and forty guys — a huge contingent — representing the skiers who'd be competing in the Alpine events.

"David told me — one of the times that he would deign to speak to me, that is — " Tara explained, "that they eliminate half the skiers in prelims the first day out . . . where is he?"

"There he is!" Erin's sharp eyes had spotted David, walking in a close-knit group of guys. David — he'd been easy to spot, because he wasn't wearing a hat, despite the cold — seemed to be scanning the crowd, looking for something or someone.

"You think he's looking for you?" Erin asked.

"Doubtful," Tara said dryly. "Maybe he's looking for Nellie 'Buxom' Bixom. I bet she's more his type."

Finally, all the athletes were assembled in ranks on the football field, which, though mostly shoveled off, still bore a thin layer of snow on it.

In deference to the cold weather, the organizers had decided to streamline the opening ceremonies, reasoning that it would not be terribly good for the games if half the athletes suffered from hypothermia before the competitions began.

There was a brief speech by the mayor, some welcoming remarks by Dr. Smithson, and then, the moment everyone had been waiting for: the lighting of a huge bonfire that had been built in the middle of the football field.

This was one of Winterfest's great traditions. Instead of an Olympic flame, the bonfire was kept burning all through the games, as an invitation for anyone — competitor or spectator — to come, warm their hands, get something hot to drink, and just be a part of it all.

The bonfire became, for the days of Winterfest, Love's town square.

And then it was time for another of Winterfest's great traditions.

Everyone in the stands reached down and made a snowball out of the snow that remained.

The athletes, who had been briefed beforehand, made snowballs of their own.

The mayor said, into the microphone, "Let Winterfest begin!"

And with that, everyone launched their snowballs — the athletes at the crowd, the crowd at the athletes. For fifteen seconds, Love, Michigan, was the home of the world's biggest snowball fight.

The games had begun.

"I want you to see her practice session," Erin explained as she, Luke, Tara, and David hurried toward the rink where Noelle was practicing. "You guys have to meet her. And we have to wish her luck!"

It was a few hours later, and the foursome had just finished having dinner together at Pizza Bob's. They had polished off a Big Bob special, as well as two orders of cheese sticks and chocolate milk shakes. David and Tara had been almost civil to each other during dinner — at least no pizza had actually been hurled across the table.

"So, David," Tara said casually, as their boots crunched through the snow toward the skating rink, "we saw you looking out at the crowd during the opening ceremonies. Who were you looking for?"

David thought a moment. "I believe her name is Nellie Bixom," he said seriously.

Tara made a noise of disgust. "Well, all I have to say is, your taste couldn't get much lower! I mean, is that girl obvious or what? Why does she even bother to get dressed in the morning? I mean — "

"Tara," David said, staring at her. "I am teasing you."

"You are?" Tara asked guardedly.

David gave her a cool look. "Maybe."

Tara threw up her hands in disgust. "Somebody just shoot him for me, would you?"

"What's that?" David asked, pointing to the Love College mascot — a lifesize papier-mâché moose — now standing on the other side of the rink.

"Come on," Tara said, taking David's arm. "I'll introduce you to Bullwinkle, the Lovelorn Moose. Maybe he'll turn out to be your type, too." She turned to Erin. "We'll be right back."

Erin's eyes scanned the ten skaters now gliding across the ice until she picked out Noelle.

"That's Noelle!" Erin cried, pointing to her friend. She leaned on the rail surrounding the rink, her eyes glued to her friend.

"Which one?" Luke asked, leaning against the rail with Erin.

"In the green," Erin said, proudly pointing to Noelle.

Noelle took a few powerful glides across the ice, then she jumped into the air, spun around twice, and came down in a perfect landing. Then she immediately jumped again, whirling around so fast she was a blur of green, and she came down in a graceful arabesque.

"Isn't she — " Erin began, turning to Luke.

"Incredible," Luke said, his eyes fastened on Noelle. "She's incredible."

"I told you she was," Erin said.

Together they watched as Noelle went

through jumps, long spins, and short spins.

"Her triple is amazing!" Luke exclaimed.

"I know," Erin agreed enthusiastically. "I just can't believe how talented she is. And she's so nice, too. I just can't wait until you actually meet her!"

"You know who she looks like?" Luke said. "Did you ever see any of those movies of Audrey Hepburn when she was young?"

"Yeah, I think," Erin said. "On cable. What was it called . . . *Roman Holiday*!"

"Right," Luke agreed, his eyes following Noelle around the rink. "I mean, Noelle's hair is darker and longer, but something about the way she moves . . . so graceful . . ."

"I know what you mean," Erin agreed.

Noelle did another jump and skated over near Erin and Luke.

"Hi," she said breathlessly, stopping by the side of the rink.

"You look incredible out there," Erin said. "Oh, this is Luke Blakely, and this is Noelle Le Blanc."

"Nice to meet you," Noelle said shyly. "I've heard a lot about you."

"I've heard a lot about you, too," Luke

said, taking Noelle's hand. "But it didn't do you justice."

"Thanks," Noelle said. "I need all the confidence boosters I can get right about now."

"Hey, you're the best one out there," Luke insisted.

"I don't think Krissi Atkinson would agree with you," Noelle said, looking over at Krissi, who was spinning so quickly she looked like a white blur on the ice.

"Take my word for it," Luke said. "You skate better, you're more graceful, and you're more beautiful."

Even though Noelle's cheeks were already red from skating, she blushed at Luke's compliments. "That's really nice of you," she said.

"Hey, Noelle!" Tara said, walking over with David. She quickly introduced them. "David just met Bullwinkle."

"He's a lovely moose," David said with a grin. He looked over at Tara and cocked his head. "Actually, there is quite a resemblance, now that I look more closely."

Tara hit David's arm. "You can see now why I hate him, Noelle."

"So, how soon do you finish practice?" Luke asked Noelle.

Noelle looked at the large clock on the wall. "Fifteen minutes and we have to be off the ice," she said.

"So, can you come out with us?" Luke asked eagerly.

"No chance," Noelle said. "Jack would kill me. I'm supposed to go right home to sleep, then get up at five for drills with Sandi." She glanced over her shoulder. "In fact, if he comes out of the john and catches me talking with you guys, I'm dead meat."

"We'll be rooting for you big-time, Noelle," Erin said fervently.

"Thanks," Noelle said. "Hey, it was nice to meet you two," she told Luke and David. "Good luck in your prelims."

Luke reached out and took Noelle's hand. "It was great to meet you, too," he told her, looking into her eyes. "Really great."

"Oh, thanks," Noelle said, a bit flustered. Then she waved to her friends and skated off.

"She is unbelievable," Luke said, his eyes following Noelle as she skated away.

He watched her unleash another perfect double axel, and shook his head, grinning.

Chapter 10

Ten years here in Love, Tara thought, gripping the steering wheel tightly in an effort to keep her car steady on the snow-slicked road, *and this is the first time I've been to Love Mountain in the wintertime.*

Well, there's a first time for everything.

She followed the line of cars snaking ahead of her up the winding access road to Love Mountain ski area, where all the Alpine skiing events were being held, including the senior men's downhill in which David Benjamin was competing.

It was the next afternoon and, with school out for Winterfest vacation, Tara had debated with herself all morning about whether to go watch David compete in the preliminary round of the men's downhill, or stay home and reread Victor Hugo's *Les*

Misérables — in the original French, of course.

She remembered her conversation with David the night before, when she'd dropped him off at his dorm.

"I suppose you'd be devastated if I didn't watch you slide down that mountain tomorrow," she told him.

"Not really," he replied. "It's only the qualifying round, you see."

"But if you don't qualify, you don't get to really compete," Tara said. "And you know I'll bring you luck."

"How will you do that?" David asked curiously.

"Like this," Tara had replied. And then she had leaned over and gently, ever-so-gently, kissed him on the cheek.

That was the moment he was supposed to grab me and pull me to him in a passionate embrace, Tara recalled with chagrin, *only he didn't. He just politely said goodnight and got out of the car.*

It has to be the ankles.

So she'd vowed to read Hugo, and forget about the infuriating David Benjamin, gorgeous, talented, brilliant Israeli skier, honor student at tough Colby College, speaker of five different languages, with eyes so blue and hair so black and a mouth that you just felt like you had to kiss and —

No. She would not-not-not think about him. She read ten more pages. She kept seeing David's face superimposed over Hugo's words. Finally she gave up, and ran to her room to dress in her warmest — and, she hoped, cutest — outfit, to go watch David ski.

According to the *Winterfest Love Letter* — a paper printed daily during Winterfest — David was scheduled to do his qualifying run at two-thirty.

Tara showered, put on some makeup, and dressed in long silk underwear under faded jeans, a pale pink turtleneck, and a hot pink mohair sweater. Then she'd grabbed her navy pea coat, pink mittens, and earmuffs and ran out the door.

Tara braked as the line of cars heading to the mountain ground to a halt. She thought about Love Mountain.

Not nearly as big as the mountains in Colorado, she recalled from her fifth grade geography class, or even some of the ones in Vermont. *But it has a vertical drop of nearly nine hundred and fifty feet, and it's very, very steep.*

It's supposed to be the hardest skiing be-

tween New York State and Colorado, she remembered, as the line of spectators' cars continued to ease its way forward, like a Slinky toy, into Love Mountain's jammed parking lots.

Tara followed the waving arms of the parking attendants and pulled her car into the slot they designated. She jumped out quickly and followed the other spectators who were walking up toward, and then past, the main ski lodge and then gathering together in a big crowd around the finish line for the men's downhill. There were even several sets of bleachers erected there for the spectators' comfort, but they were all filled by the time Tara arrived.

Where's . . . there he is! Tara thought, spotting David, off to one side, carefully and lovingly applying wax to the bottoms of his skis.

She negotiated her way through the crowd and made her way over to him.

"Hey, there. You need some help with those?"

David looked up, and a bemused smile crossed his face. "I see you decided to show up."

"I knew you'd cry if I didn't," Tara said.

196

"And I just hate to see a grown man cry. So, what do I do to help?"

"How do I know you won't sabotage me?" he asked.

"You're not Krissi Atkinson," Tara replied with dignity.

"Excuse me?" David asked, not comprehending.

"Krissi Atkinson?" Tara answered. "The figure skater?"

"I don't know her," David answered, turning his attention back to his skis. "But just as long as I'm safe, I won't worry."

"You're safe," Tara assured him. "Just don't let any girl get near your toes."

"In these boots," David joked, "I think I'm protected. Unless you're wearing high heels again."

Tara looked down at David's feet. He was already in his ski boots — bright orange plastic boots that came halfway up his shins and were fastened at the back by two huge plastic clips.

Amazing, Tara thought. *And the rest of that uni is pretty space-age, too.*

David was dressed in a one-piece, formfitting silver racing suit, with COLBY, the college in Maine that David attended, written in big block letters across the front of it. On top of that — Tara could just make out the word COLBY beneath it — was a white Winterfest bib with the number 101 stamped on it. Off to his left, two ski poles, with a weird, S-shaped curve in them, were jammed into the snowpack, and next to them, on the snow, was a motorcycle-style crash helmet the same color as the racing suit David wore.

"Next up on the course!" the loudspeaker blared, echoing off the buildings and the foothills surrounding beautiful Love Mountain. "Skier number eighty-five, Willie Singleton, from the University of Nevada at Reno."

"Watch him," David commanded.

"Where?" Tara asked.

David pointed to a huge video monitor that was set up by the finish line, on which the spectators could watch all of each skier's run, thanks to a multitude of cameras set up along the race course.

Dutifully, Tara watched as Singleton burst out of the starting gate, took a few skating steps down the course, and then went into his egg-shaped racer's tuck, his S-shaped ski poles fitting neatly around his body.

Faster and faster, Singleton flashed down

the course, flying over the snow, prejumping over bumps so that his skis remained in contact with the snow for the maximum amount of time possible, while the camera angle switched from camera to camera as Singleton successfully negotiated the course.

"Here he comes!" the loudspeaker called. A roar went up from the crowd.

Tara looked up the mountain to the trail cut out of it that was lined by spectators on all sides. Willie Singleton came into view, still in his tuck, and he stayed in it all the way down until he passed the finish line. Then he braked by turning sideways with all his might, sending a wave of snow flying up and into the spectators who pressed against the restraining ropes by the finish line.

Quickly, Singleton whipped his head around to check out his time, which was posted on the electronic board off to the side of the finish line. When he saw the time, he punched his fist in the air happily as the crowd cheered for him.

"One-thirty-seven thirty-seven," David said. "That should qualify him."

"It puts him in first place!" Tara realized with alarm. "Can you beat him?"

David smiled at her. "I didn't know you cared."

"I don't," Tara said, tossing her head. "It was a purely scientific query on my part."

"Not to worry," David replied. "Ten skiers qualify in this event. I will do my best to make sure there is a place for me."

"Well, break a leg!" Tara said cheerfully.

"You wish for me to break a leg?" David asked, his brow furrowed. "I didn't know you disliked me that much, Tara."

"It's a show business expression," Tara explained quickly. "Don't take it literally. It means — "

"Good luck," David finished for her. "I know, Tara. I was teasing you. Again."

Tara's eyes darted fire. "Oh, you think that is so hilarious, don't you?"

"Yes, I do," David said, giving a few finishing brushes to the bottom of his skis with a fist-sized piece of cork that he was using to smooth out the wax he had just applied. "See you at the finish line."

"But — "

With that, David slung his skis over his shoulder, picked up his ski poles and his helmet, and trudged over to the chairlift that would take him to the top of Love Mountain for his qualifying run.

Great. Just great, Tara thought to herself. *You are making a total idiot out of yourself. Why don't you just throw yourself down in the snow and scream "kiss me, you skiing god, you"?*

Tara clomped through the snow over to the lodge and bought herself a hot cocoa. Then she took off her parka, mittens, and earmuffs and sipped her cocoa while she listened to what was happening on the mountain via the well-informed public address system.

When skier number one hundred had been called to the start line, she put her warm clothes on and went back outside, edging her way through the throng to the restraining rope by the finish line. By this time, all but one of the racers had come down — David would have to beat at least the number eight person ranked on the board in order to be assured of a spot in the last round.

"Now in the gate," the loudspeaker announced, "skier number one-oh-one, from Israel, racing for Colby College in Maine, David Benjamin!"

Tara sucked her breath in, her eyes riveted to the video screen as David edged back and forth in the starting gate, and then slammed his way through the gate, tripping the timer, onto the course. He took five strong skating steps down the beginning of the downhill course, and then settled into his tuck.

And he was really moving.

"First third time for Benjamin," the loudspeaker announced, "thirty-one point five seconds. That's our fastest split time of the day."

The crowd cheered loudly at the announcement.

"Come on," Tara muttered under her breath, "go, go, go, go!"

On the screen, David held his tuck, edging easily through the swooping left-hand turn halfway down the course and then tucking again for the final third of the run.

Then disaster struck.

Tara watched, dumbfounded, as David took off from a bump and flew in the air. In midair, his skis separated, and David desperately waved his ski poles around, fighting valiantly to keep his balance.

It was touch-and-go. He could crash as easily as he could keep going once he made his landing.

He landed.

And he pulled it back together and kept going.

Oh please, Tara thought, her fingers clenched into tight, nervous fists inside her mittens. *Please . . .*

She watched David resume his tuck and, with seeming determination, attack the rest of the course.

Don't let that screw you up. Go, you big jerk. Go. Go!

"Go, go, go!" Tara yelled, encouraging David, even though he couldn't hear her, of course.

"Now coming into view," the loudspeaker announced, "David Benjamin, number one-oh-one."

At the top of the last stretch, David flashed into view, still in his perfect tuck. Tara kept one eye on him and one eye on the timer.

He has to beat one minute forty-one and five-tenths of a second, she thought, as the seconds ticked away and David skied in what seemed like slow-motion, despite the fact that he was being clocked at eighty-five miles an hour, toward the finish line.

And then he was across it.

He and Tara looked at the timer at the same time.

A minute thirty-eight and eighty-seven one-hundredths of a second.

Good enough for fifth place. Good enough to qualify for the finals.

"Yes!" Tara screamed, jumping up into the air. "He did it!"

David took his crash helmet off and shook his head, thankful that he hadn't bitten it completely on the middle part of the course and eliminated himself from the competition before it had really gotten started.

He had made the final round. And that's what really counted.

Tara looked over at David.

Was it possible?

David gave her a brief and poignant thumbs-up. Tara smiled the brightest smile of her life, and gave him the thumbs-up sign right back.

Then David packed up his skis and walked back to where the other skiers had assembled.

Those who had qualified, and those who had not.

* * *

WINTERFEST LOVE LETTER
TEN QUALIFY FOR
SKI JUMPING FINALS

Luke Blakely, jumping for the University of Colorado, led a field of ten jumpers from across the United States and Canada who have qualified for the final round on the seventy-meter hill. The qualifying round was held yesterday.

Blakely amassed 229.1 total points, awarded for both distance and style, easily outpointing Nathanael Beal, from the University of New Hampshire, who garnered 221.45 points. Jumpers from six other schools round out the final field of ten.

The ski jumping finals will be held on the second-to-last day of Winterfest.

Erin threw the paper down on the couch and closed her eyes. She could see it all over again — Luke up on the hill, Luke making his spectacular jumps. It had all been so wonderful. He had hugged her hard afterward.

But then he hugged everyone in sight, Erin thought with a sigh. And every female in sight hugged him back. Hard.

After that, Luke had had some interviews to do, and though Erin had volunteered to wait for him, he told her she didn't need to.

So she had driven home, only to find a message on the answering machine saying that Pete was coming over.

She had been avoiding him as much as possible, because she had no clear idea of what she wanted to say or how she wanted to say it.

She sighed and put her bunny slippers up on the coffee table, her favorite thinking position. *I just don't know what to do. How can I hurt Pete when he's —*

"And this is my sister, Erin 'Death' Kellerman," her little brother Sam intoned, leading a small group of kids into the living room. His face was painted a deathly white, with black circles drawn around his eyes. The littlest girl in the group, who looked to be about four, grabbed an older boy's hand and held it tight, staring in horror at Erin.

206

"Sam, get out of here," Erin said.

Sam turned to his group. "If I don't do what she says, she'll strangle me in my sleep," he intoned seriously. "And now on to the casket room . . ."

Erin shook her head as the kids straggled out of the room.

Thank God Sam and all my other little siblings are going to Grandma Beck's in Detroit tomorrow, she sighed.

She glanced over at the *Winterfest Love Letter* again, staring at Luke's name. Did she love him? Did she? And how did he feel about her? And why couldn't they talk about it?

"I don't even know what love is," she said out loud crossly.

"Come again?" Aunt Daisy stood in the doorway of the living room.

Fortunately she was not wearing her latex gloves.

"Oh hi, Aunt Daisy," Erin said.

"Haven't seen much of you lately, sweetie," she said, coming into the living room to sit with Erin. "What's doing?"

"Winterfest," Erin replied glumly.

"Well, jeepers, you don't sound very happy about it!" Daisy exclaimed, tucking a few stray hairs back into her bun. "I should think that what with being on the court and shepherding your young athlete around and rooting for Noelle, you'd be just beside yourself with excitement!"

"I have guy problems," Erin confessed. "I've been with Pete forever. But I really, really, really like Luke. But I don't want to hurt Pete. And . . . I don't know what I'm doing."

"Ah, well, I know quite a bit about guys," Daisy said, nodding her head. "If you want to talk . . ."

Erin stared at Aunt Daisy, who was in her early forties, had never married, lived with her brother and his family, and put makeup on dead people for a living. And she found it hard to believe that Daisy knew anything about guys.

Unless they were dead guys, of course.

"I know what you're thinking," Daisy sang out, her eyes twinkling. "You're thinking 'how could Crazy Daisy know anything about guys.' "

"No — " Erin protested.

"Oh, yes, sweetie," Daisy said. "Well, let me tell you a little story — "

Oh, no, anything but that, Erin thought.

"Gosh, Aunt Daisy, I don't exactly have

time for a story now. Pete's on his way over — "

"It's short," Daisy said, settling back into the couch. "When I was fifteen I was quite a beauty — everyone in Love said so. I had long, long red hair, and a pretty face, and a cute little figure on me!"

"Uh-huh," Erin said, her eyes glazing over.

"And these triplets came to town — exchange students from Norway — so handsome they took your breath away, they were."

"Uh-huh," Erin said, sneaking a glance at her watch.

"All three of those boys were in love with me," Daisy said. "My mother told me I had to pick one of them, that it wasn't kind to string them all along like that. And you know what I did?"

"No, sure don't," Erin said.

"I sneaked out one night and ran away from home," Daisy said. "I hitchhiked to Detroit to be with the guy I really loved. He was a student at Wayne State University and way smarter than those cute-but-dumb triplets from Norway," Daisy said with satisfaction.

Erin's eyes grew huge. "You hitchhiked to Detroit at night — by *yourself* — to see a college guy? And you were only *fifteen*??" Erin was shocked beyond belief.

"Sure did," Daisy said smugly. "It was much safer in those days. Still, how do you think I got the name Crazy Daisy?"

Erin's face flushed. "I, I always thought, I mean . . ."

Daisy laughed and kissed her niece on the cheek. "You thought it was because I beautify the dead, I know. I suppose that's what everyone thinks. But the truth is I earned my nickname because of my wild and woolly youth."

"I can't believe you never told me about this before!" Erin exclaimed.

"Well, I didn't want to shock you too much," Daisy said, patting Erin's knee. "You're young and lovely, Erin. And you're a very, very good person. And you don't have to be tied down to one boy so soon. That's the fun of being young!"

"But I love Pete!" Erin protested.

"I know you do," Daisy said. "And Luke may turn out to be a boy who's just passing through, like the triplets. Or he may turn out to be the love of your life. But you can't be afraid to follow your heart."

"I'm just not sure what my heart is telling me," Erin admitted.

Daisy patted her knee again. "That's okay, honey. You'll find out. Just don't settle at seventeen for safe because you're scared of exciting, okay?"

"I guess," Erin said, dazed.

Daisy stood up and smiled at her niece. "Well it was lovely having this chat with you, sweetie. I have to go put false eyelashes on Mrs. Kawalski. She made her husband promise she'd be buried in her lashes. I just hope I don't stick her eyes together with that glue — it can be so messy."

She leaned over and kissed Erin on the cheek, then she scampered out of the room.

"My family is certifiable," Erin mumbled to herself, as the doorbell rang.

"Hi," Erin said, opening the door for Pete.

"Hi," he said, and wrapped his arms around her. "Man, I missed you."

"I guess you finally got shoveled out up there, huh?" Erin said, padding over to the couch in the bunny slippers she always wore at home.

"What a snowstorm, huh?" Pete said. He

sat down next to her on the couch and looked at her earnestly. "Listen, I've been thinking a lot about that thing at the Mighty Cup — "

"You mean when you lied to me and embarrassed me in front of Luke?" Erin asked sharply.

"Yeah, I acted like a jerk," Pete admitted. "I apologize."

"I can't believe you — "

"But you're not exactly guilt-free in this, Erin," he added.

"Me??"

"Yeah, you," Pete said. He folded his arms. "I think you're falling for this Luke guy."

"That's ridiculous," Erin said hotly.

"Come on, Erin, this is me you're talking to," Pete said quietly. "If you weren't into the guy, you would have been glad to see me. If you weren't into the guy, you wouldn't have been so happy that I didn't have a ticket to the dinner dance, or that I couldn't make it in for the opening ceremonies."

"I wasn't happy about any of that," Erin muttered.

Pete gently reached for Erin's chin and

turned her head to face him. "You don't have to lie to me, Erin."

Tears came to her eyes. "But I love you — "

"Yeah, I know," Pete said. "But . . . what I said about Luke . . . it's true, isn't it?"

"I don't know," Erin said. She reached for the small, velvet pillow on the couch and held it tight against her chest. "I . . . I don't know what I feel! I think I'm losing my mind!"

Pete's face hardened. "Have you kissed him?"

"Pete — "

"I have a right to know," Pete said. "Have you kissed him?"

"Just once," Erin whispered. "It didn't mean anything — "

"You're not the type of girl who kisses a guy if it doesn't mean anything," Pete said. He stood up and paced around the room. "So, what do we do now?"

"I don't know," Erin said miserably.

"The thought of you with another guy . . ." Pete began, his voice choking a little.

Erin's heart was breaking. She got up and went to him. She put her arms around him. "I can't stand that I'm hurting you."

"Yeah," he mumbled.

"It's not like I'm in love with him," Erin said.

Pete looked at her. "You're not?"

"I barely know him," she admitted.

"So, what do we do now?" Pete asked again, his arms dangling at his sides.

"I think we just have to . . . see what happens," Erin said cautiously.

"Oh, great," Pete exploded. "I'm supposed to just stand around and take it while you go out with Luke? What am I, your lapdog?"

"No, Pete — "

"Don't you think I get attracted to other girls sometimes?" Pete yelled at Erin.

"I guess I never thought about it — "

"Well, think about it now," Pete said. "But when you love someone, really love someone, then you have a commitment. And you don't go around kissing other people!"

Erin hung her head. "You're right."

"So, you'll stop seeing him? I mean, except as his host?" Pete asked.

Erin gulped hard. "I . . . can't promise," she admitted.

Pete's face paled. "Then you don't even know what love is, Erin," he said.

"I know that I love you," she said, as

tears filled her eyes again. "And I know that I'm all mixed up."

Pete made a strangled sound in his throat, and he wrapped his arms around Erin, holding her tight. "I can't stand the thought of losing you," he said, his voice choked with tears.

"I can't stand the thought of losing you, either," Erin said, gulping hard. "And we won't. I mean, we don't have to . . ."

Pete stood up straight, and brushed the tears from his eyes with the back of his hand. "I don't know, Erin. You're going to have to make a choice."

"But — "

"That's just the way it is," Pete said sadly. "It's either me, or it's Luke. You can't have it both ways."

Then he kissed her once more, and he strode out the door.

Chapter 11

"Please, someone help me, I can't breathe!" Noelle gasped, as she grabbed her chest and fell to the ice. "Please, I'm — "

She gasped for air, her eyes snapping open, and sat up quickly in bed.

Her heart was pounding, her chest was heaving.

It was just a dream, she told herself, panting for air. *It wasn't real. It was just a terrible nightmare* . . .

Only the nightmare was continuing. And now she was awake, sitting up in bed, in the middle of the night.

Harder and harder and harder, her heart pounded, like she'd just skated the longest, toughest endurance workout that Jack could have designed for her, and then done another mile or so of laps at top speed.

And then something even worse happened. It felt as if her heart was vibrating in her chest instead of beating.

Noelle panicked, clutching her bedspread with trembling fingers.

"Please," she begged her heart, as she put her hand over her chest and heaved in gulp after gulp of air. "Please, heart, stop doing that!"

It was a few days later, and Winterfest was in full swing. Jack had continued to work Noelle very hard, running her through her programs over and over again. And he and Sandi had been feeding Noelle practically nothing. A fat-free yogurt, an apple, and a half can of tuna was a big eating day. Sometimes they forced her to eat even less.

The food regime had its desired effect. Noelle was now down to one hundred and one and three-quarter pounds. She knew that, because she had done her nightly ritual of weighing herself — in front of Jack and Sandi — before she went to sleep.

The vibrations stopped, but still her heart was beating too fast. She loosened her death grip on her bedspread just long enough to turn on the bedside lamp and look at the clock. It was two forty-five in the morning.

And her heart kept pounding.

"Something is wrong with me," she gasped, more afraid than she'd ever been in her life. "Something is very, very wrong."

She hunched over, breaking out into a cold sweat. Beads of perspiration formed on her forehead, illuminated by the harsh light of a halogen bulb in her bedside lamp.

I should tell Jack, Noelle thought. *But what if I can't compete? But didn't I just go to the doctor? What is Jack going to do? And didn't I just have a bad dream? What if I'm upset about that?*

Noelle's heart raced on. And then, finally, thank God, it started to slow down.

Noelle breathed a deep sigh of relief, as she felt her heartbeat slowly, surely, return to normal. She lay down in her bed, utterly exhausted.

I'm just freaked out about the competition, she told herself. *And I've been on this stupid starvation diet. That has to be it.*

That has to be.

"Come on, Noelle," Jack implored her from where he stood at rinkside. "Jump! Let's see some air here, okay, hon?"

Noelle waved to him, as she skated backwards, ready to unleash yet another double axel, under his practiced and watchful eye.

It was eight hours later — nearly eleven o'clock the next day, and Noelle was running through her private morning workout with her coach. Because there were only two rinks in Love, each skater had been assigned a half hour each day to practice in private with his or her coach. Noelle's half hour went from ten thirty in the morning until eleven. After eleven, the rink was open to any serious figure skater for a group skate.

I didn't tell Jack about last night, Noelle thought, as she powered her skates over the ice. *But I woke up feeling totally normal. And the first twenty minutes of my workout went so well, only now . . .*

Now I can't catch my breath again.

No, please, God, don't let this be happening to me . . .

Noelle pumped her legs harder, determined to overcome whatever it was she was feeling.

It's nothing, she told herself, even as she struggled to get a deep breath of air. *Only losers give in to every little physical thing, that's one of Jack's most famous axioms. And I'm not a loser.*

"Air, Noelle," Jack called to her, his hands cupped around his mouth. "Let's see some air."

Noelle waved back to him again.

Air, she thought to herself. *Maximum air.*

She circled the ice, ready to do another double axel. But when she turned forward again, after shifting her weight back onto the outside edge of her left skate, and launched herself, she got very little air at all.

Certainly not enough to double the axel.

She singled it, which would have meant points off in competition.

Damn, she thought. *Damn damn damn damn damn.*

Noelle stopped, and bent over, breathing hard.

"What's wrong with you?" Jack yelled with annoyance.

Noelle couldn't move from her bent-over position to reply. She was too busy just trying to suck in enough air to breathe.

"You okay, Noelle?" Jack called to her. "You need a breather?"

Noelle forced herself to straighten up.

She waved her hand and shook her head no, still trying to catch her breath.

"I said, take a breather!" Jack ordered. "I'm going to make a phone call. Take five and then we'll finish up."

Slowly, tentatively, Noelle skated to the entrance to the ice, and stepped off. Heavily, she sat down on the bench and bent over again, taking deep breaths that didn't seem to be helping her feel any stronger.

"You okay?" a worried voice said from behind her.

Noelle looked up. It was her friend Traci, a half-eaten candy bar in her hand.

"Yeah, sure," Noelle half-said, half-gasped. "I'm fine."

"I came for the free skate at eleven," Traci said, staring at Noelle with concern. She sat down next to her friend. "You don't look so fine to me."

"I said I'm fine," Noelle protested.

"And I say you're a big liar," Traci commented.

"I'm just tired," Noelle responded, trying to take another deep breath. She felt so weak, so puny, as if she had the worst flu in the world.

"Right," Traci scoffed, looking closely at

her friend. "I've seen you practice for eight hours straight, and you don't even breathe hard, so what's wrong?"

"Nothing's wrong!" Noelle cried. "Just leave me alone!"

Traci just stared at her.

"Okay," Noelle finally said. "I'll tell you. But you have to promise me that you won't tell anyone."

"That is stupid, Noelle — "

"Promise!" Noelle gasped out. "Or I won't tell you anything!"

"You are some piece of work," Traci chided her.

"I mean it," Noelle said. She was beginning to breathe a little easier, and it made her feel even more stubborn, not so weak and vulnerable and scared.

Traci considered for a moment. "Only if I can tell you what I think you should do. And only then if you'll at least consider listening to me."

"Deal," Noelle said. She looked around to make sure Jack wasn't anywhere near them. "Last night, I woke up in the middle of the night, and my heart was, like, totally out of control, hammering, like, and then it, like, vibrated instead of just beating."

"What??" Traci cried.

"Keep your voice down!" Noelle hissed. "I got so scared, Traci, that something was really, really wrong with me."

"That's the first intelligent thing I've heard you say!" Traci exclaimed.

"But it went away," Noelle said. "And now I'm fine."

"You're not fine," Traci insisted. "I saw you just now. You couldn't breathe!"

"That's just because I slept so badly," Noelle said. "And Jack has me on this prison diet — "

Traci's brown hand reached for Noelle's pale fingers. "Noelle, please listen to me," Traci began. "I checked with my mom about your heart thing — "

"You didn't have any right to do that!" Noelle cried, pulling her hand away from Traci.

"Oh, chill out," Traci snapped. "I didn't tell her it was you. She checked with a friend of hers who's a heart specialist. And he said that what you've got isn't always nothing — sometimes it's something. Something serious."

"Come on, I got checked by Jack's doctor!" Noelle protested.

"Yeah, Jack's doctor," Traci said. "Whose side do you think he's on? Jack's doctor would probably certify my grandmother to skate, and she's got emphysema so bad she can't walk across a room without wheezing."

"You are totally blowing this out of proportion," Noelle said. Her breathing was fine now. She felt normal.

She swung her head back toward the doors and to the pay phone outside, to make sure that Jack was still on the phone.

He was, but he was just hanging up.

"I gotta go," Noelle said. "Jack's coming."

"Noelle, you can't just ignore this — "

"Stop worrying," Noelle told her. "All I need is some food." With a quick glance over her shoulder at Jack, who was now deep in conversation with Sandi, Noelle reached for Traci's candy bar and took a quick bite, chewing it as fast as she possibly could.

"You know you're crazy, don't you?" Traci asked her.

"One mouthful of chocolate and I'm a new woman," Noelle said. "Oh, wow, that is the best thing I ever tasted."

"Noelle," Traci said, as she gathered up her stuff, "you've got to go to a doctor. Another doctor. Get yourself checked out. Please?"

"All I need is another bite of chocolate," Noelle said. She glanced furtively at Jack, and quickly took another bite, then handed the candy bar back to Traci.

"Noelle — "

"Quit worrying, Mom," Noelle teased, skating backwards away from her friend. She felt perfectly fine now, and all her former worries seemed ridiculous.

"A doctor," Traci mouthed.

Noelle waved her off and skated toward Jack, who was waiting for her now on the other side of the rink.

"So, champ," Jack called to Noelle, as he came through the archway into the rink area. "You feeling better now?"

"Yes," Noelle said, as brightly as she could muster. She was careful to make sure she stood far enough from him so that he couldn't smell her breath, just in case he could sniff out the two bites of chocolate. "I feel great!"

"Then let's get out there!" Jack declared. "You've still got three minutes."

Noelle went back out onto the center of the ice.

But Traci's words rang in her head.

You've got to go to a doctor. Another doctor. Sometimes it's something. Something serious.

Noelle flew across the ice, preparing for a triple axel, a jump she attempted only rarely. She flew through the air, around and around and around . . .

It was perfect. *She* was perfect.

Yes! There is absolutely nothing wrong with you that two bites of chocolate wasn't able to cure, she told herself.

Traci is totally, completely wrong.

"Y'all," Tara said, as she piled yet another huge snow shovel full of snow onto the enormous pile that she and her friends had already put together, "this is either incredibly fun or incredibly stupid. I'm not sure which."

"Shut up and shovel," David said to her, as he and Luke together pushed one of the wooden restraining walls they'd improvised around the pile of snow.

"You are not in the Israeli army now, sir," Tara replied. "You don't get to order me around." She shoveled another load of snow. "I guess you'll have to go, though, after you finish college."

It was around three o'clock that same afternoon, and Tara, Erin, David, Luke, Noelle's friend Traci, and a whole group of Love residents and visiting athletes were involved in one of the most fun traditions of Winterfest, the annual snow sculpture contest.

"How do you know so much about Israel?" David asked, digging his shovel into the snow again.

"Well, other than the United States, I think it's the coolest country on the planet," Tara remarked. "I've read a lot about it."

"And you remember everything you read," David said, dropping another load of snow on the pile. "I've noticed that about you."

"Imagine, gorgeous and brainy," Tara said blithely. "How can you possibly resist me?"

"Sometimes I think you think you're a character out of *Gone With the Wind*," David said, digging his shovel into the snow again.

"I'll take that as a compliment," Tara said prettily.

"It wasn't meant as one," David said.

Tara leaned on her shovel and contemplated him. "I'm just curious. Is your obnoxiousness a family trait, or are you the black sheep of the family?"

A smile twitched around David's lips. "I have a brother, Ari, who is one year younger than me. Ari really *is* in the Israeli army. And according to our mother, we are equally impossible."

Tara made a face at David. "I like your mother already."

"Hey, Traci, didn't you win this event last year?" Erin asked, as she dropped a load of snow on their ever-growing pile.

"My team did," Traci said. "The theme was animals, and we made a fifteen-foot-long, eight-foot-high wolverine, and since the wolverine — "

"The wolverine is the state animal of Michigan," Tara explained to David. "That's why they picked the wolverine. Wait, don't tell me, you already knew that."

"Frankly, I had no idea," David admitted.

"This is killer on your back," Erin said, rubbing the small of her back gingerly.

"You need to bend your knees more as you shovel," Luke explained. He rubbed his fingers into her back. "Better?"

"Much," she told him.

And don't take your hand away, she

wanted to add. *Put your arms around me instead!*

"I know I always say I hate the cold," Tara said, staring out at the Love College football field where four teams of snow sculptors were getting ready, "but this is kind of fun. In a frigid sort of way."

"I wonder what the other teams are doing?" Traci mused, shoveling hard. "I should scout out the competition."

At three other locations around Love, other teams were also building their sculptures. The competition would be fierce. It was every year.

The theme for this year's contest was *America*, and this year, the judges had added a special twist: not only were the contestants supposed to build a snow sculpture, but they were also supposed to sing a song in front of it for all the judges.

What would the winners get? A ton of baby food and a check for two hundred dollars, both donated by the Gerber baby food company, which had a big plant in Michigan, to the charity of their choice.

"My arms are killing me," Erin said, shoveling up another huge mound of snow.

"Yabba-dabba-do, one more for the rockpile," Steve Ward grunted as he dumped a huge shovelful of snow. He was a burly guy with a short goatee who played goaltender for the State University of New York at Binghamton's ice hockey team.

Luke laughed. "You know, you look kind of like ol' Fred Flintstone, Steve," he said, going for some more snow.

"I dig Fred big-time," Steve replied. "Now, that was a great cartoon show, huh?"

Luke dropped his arm around Erin's shoulders. "How about you, Erin? You a Fred and Wilma fan?"

"Oh, sure, who isn't?" Erin replied. "I watch it on cable. Dino is my fave."

"My kind of woman," Steve approved.

Luke laughed and went back to shoveling.

What is going on? Erin thought miserably. *He's nice to me, but he acts as if we never kissed, as if we're just buds!*

And Pete's making me choose between the two of them. But now I don't even know if Luke really likes me at all! All I do is think about Luke. But I still love Pete.

And I have to choose. I wish Luke would just talk to me. Tell me the truth. No, I don't. Yes, I do.

"You know, it's too bad Noelle isn't here," Luke said. "She'd really enjoy this."

Why are you thinking about Noelle? Erin wanted to scream, then she immediately felt guilty. *Noelle is your best friend,* she reminded herself. *Luke is just being nice.*

"Too bad Noelle can't do anything," Erin agreed, "but her coach keeps her locked up like a prisoner."

"Sometimes that's what it takes to become a champion," Luke said. "I admire her guts, you know?"

"I do, too," Erin admitted. "And her talent. I can't wait until the figure skating competition."

"Me neither," Luke agreed. "So long as it's after the ski jumping finals!"

Both of them smiled, because they knew that Luke meant that if the ski jumping had been scheduled after the ice skating, he'd never be able to enjoy watching it. As it was, the only reason he could be building the snow sculpture was that his coach had given him a day off from training.

Someone in the stands blew a whistle.

"Okay, guys," Traci called to the group, "gather 'round and listen up. That means it's time to start building."

Before they'd gotten going at around noon, Erin and her team had engaged in a furious, friendly debate about exactly what American thing they should sculpt.

"A New York Jets football helmet," Steve the hockey goaltender had suggested. "They stink, but I love 'em."

"How about an American eagle?" Luke offered.

"Too hard," someone else had said. "What about a relief map of the United States?"

"What about the Statue of Liberty?" David mused.

"Wrong, wrong, all wrong," Tara sang out, after the suggestions died out. "There's only one thing we can do that will assure us of winning."

"What's that?" Traci had asked.

Tara started whistling the theme from *The Flintstones* cartoon show.

"*The Flintstones?*" Steve Ward had asked incredulously. "I'm a total Flintstones nut! I think I'm in love!"

"I don't know if *The Flintstones* is such a good idea," David had said.

"David," Tara said slowly, "we will do Fred and Wilma in their *car*. The automobile is an American invention, the half hour television cartoon is an American invention, New York City is definitely an American invention, and it has the largest natural history collection of fossilized dinosaurs in the world, and said dinosaurs once roamed the earth right here in the good ol' US of A. Besides, Hanna-Barbera is an American company, hence an American invention."

Fred and Wilma Flintstone it would be.

Traci had quickly sketched the two of them in their Stone Age car, complete with Dino the pet dinosaur sitting on the front hood.

And now they were ready to get to work. According to the rules, they had only four hours to do the sculpture itself.

So they gathered around their big pile of snow and waited for the starting whistle.

The whistle in the stands blew again, signaling that the sculptors should start sculpting.

"Flintstone!!!" Steve yelled, so loud that everyone on the football field stopped what they were doing around their own teams' sculptures and looked at him. "You're fireeeeeeeed!!!!!"

Everyone on the team threw a snowball at Steve, and then they got to work.

Four hours later, Fred and Wilma had been magnificently constructed out of snow, and Erin and her friends waited in a tight little knot in the now floodlit football stadium for the team of three judges from the college to come over, evaluate their snow sculpture, and make their award of points.

"America, America," the group at the other end of the football field sang out loudly, saluting the American flag that flew at the top of the stadium as they sang, "God shed his grace on thee, and crown thy good with brotherhood, from sea to shining sea!"

"I told you we should have made the Statue of Liberty," David grumbled good-naturedly as the other group, which included Nellie Bixom, finished their song. "That's what they did."

"Then there'd be two Miss Liberties, so kindly shut up and go over the words," Tara instructed him as Bixom's group finished "America, America," to the wild applause and cheers of the group of about five hundred spectators who'd gathered to watch the judging.

"Well, that's our cue," Tara told the group as the judges and spectators came walking over to them. "You ready, Steve?"

"Hey, show biz is my life," the burly

hockey player said. "Flintstone!!!!" he shouted again at the top of his lungs, doing his best imitation of Mr. Slate, Fred Flintstone's ornery boss at the quarry. "You're fiiiiiirrrreeeed!!!"

And then the team all burst into a parody of the famous theme song.

Flinstones are in Love town,
It's the place that they just love to be.
Who needs boring Bedrock,
'Cause right here we're makin' history.

Erin looked over at Luke as she sang, a huge smile on her face. Luke winked at her, and joy filled her up.

I will remember this moment forever, she thought, as she continued to sing lustily. *I will remember every wonderful thing about it.*

But then, to Erin's shock, an even more wonderful thing happened.

The entire crowd, and at least two of the three judges, was grinning happily and singing along as well.

When you're here in Love town,
You'll have a good time, a yab-ba-do time,
You'll have a LOVE-LY time!

And then, for the big finish, Steve dropped to one knee and shouted, "Willllllll-maaa!" at the top of his lungs.

The crowd roared its approval and applauded like mad, and everyone on their team hugged one another.

"That's it for the judging!" a voice boomed out over the stadium loudspeaker. "Check the *Winterfest Love Letter* for the posting of the results."

"Uh-oh," David said, tugging Erin's sleeve.

"What?" Erin asked.

He motioned to the third judge. Erin recognized him — Roger Debard, the chairman of the classics department at Love College, and well known as being the hardest grader in the entire college. Erin knew better than to sign up for a course with him when she enrolled.

Debard was shaking his head, scowling, and jotting furious notes in his little notebook.

"Second place," David predicted. "High marks for technical merit, but low scores on artistic impression."

"He probably loves Buxom Bixom and her Statue of Liberty as much as you do," Tara told David.

David just shrugged his shoulders.

Tara fumed silently. *Why does he do that? Why doesn't he just say, "Tara, I like you so much more than that obvious cow Bixom. Now, kiss me!"*

Tara sighed with frustration and leaned close to Erin. "Did I get old and ugly in the last few days?"

"Don't give up," Erin whispered back, but her mind was on Luke, who had strolled over to the bonfire. "Excuse me."

"Hi," she said, walking over to Luke.

"Hi there," he said, holding his hands out to the warm fire.

"That was fun, huh?"

"Yeah," Luke agreed.

"So, can I give you a ride back to the dorm?" she offered nervously.

"I'll just catch the athletes' bus back with David," he said. "It'll be here in a few minutes."

"I'd be happy to take you," Erin offered again.

"No need," he replied. "Isn't this fire great?"

"Yeah," Erin said. "It's great."

Suddenly, Erin felt like crying. How had it gone so wrong? Why didn't he like her anymore?

I can't stand it, Erin thought. I have to ask him what happened.

"Luke, I . . ."

"Yeah?"

She couldn't do it. "Nothing."

"See you soon, I hope," Luke said as he smiled that winning smile at her.

"Me too," Erin couldn't help saying, as Luke reached over and gave her a friendly kiss on the cheek, which she returned. Then she turned and started walking to her car.

I didn't even say good-bye to Tara, she realized. *But if I did I'd probably start crying.*

She pulled her car out of the parking lot.

I can't go home now, she thought. *Someone in my family will want to know how everything went. And then I'll just start bawling like an idiot.*

So for the next hour and a half, Erin drove herself around Love, thinking, thinking, and thinking some more.

She drove out to the ski jump hill, and looked at it all lit up in the floodlights, as a few jumpers made some practice jumps.

She drove and looked at the other snow sculptures, none of which, she decided, were even in the same league as the one her group had created.

She drove past the Mighty Cup and thought about going in and drinking a cup of cocoa by herself, but the place looked jam-packed.

And all the time she was driving, she was thinking.

About Luke.

About Pete.

About herself.

I need an objective opinion, she finally decided as she fiddled with the knob on the radio absentmindedly, trying to tune in one of the Detroit alternative-music stations. *Someone totally objective, not even like Aunt Daisy.*

I know, she thought suddenly. *I'll talk to Noelle. She doesn't have a boyfriend, and there isn't any guy she's interested in. She'll be completely objective. That is, if Jack will let her talk to me.*

Erin turned the car around and headed down Main Street toward the area of town where the Prestons lived. Slowly negotiating the streets clogged by Winterfest traffic, she finally came to the Prestons' sprawling ranch house.

Erin pulled her car into the big driveway, next to their Ford Bronco with the personalized plates that read ONLY GOLD, and hopped out of the car.

To get to the front door from the driveway, she had to walk past the picture window that framed the family room, where she, Noelle, and Tara would hang out on the rare occasions that Jack let Noelle have friends over.

As she walked by the huge window, Erin could see into the warm, inviting living room. There was a fire in the fireplace. And two people sat on the couch.

Jack and Sandi?

"No!" Erin cried, unable to stop the sound of pain that exploded from her heart.

Because it wasn't Jack and Sandi Preston at all.

It was Noelle.

And Luke Blakely.

Chapter 12

Erin tightened her scarf around her neck and looked up the hill, hoping to catch a glimpse of Luke amid the other jumpers milling around near the top. The final competition was coming to an end. All about her, on bleachers that had been erected hastily around the landing and stopping zones of the jumping hill, spectators were packed in as close as they could possibly be, both to allow the maximum number of spectators to sit and to maximize the amount of body heat generated.

The electronic scoreboard displayed the time and temperature. It was just about noon, and the temperature read 20° Fahrenheit.

Erin scanned the jumpers again. She couldn't pick him out. As Tara, David, and the entire crowd packed in around her chatted and cheered on their favorite jumpers, Erin's mind drifted far away.

I can't believe that so many days of Winterfest have passed, she thought. *It was just beginning, and now it's almost over. I thought everything was going to be so perfect, but it isn't.*

She could still see that horrible scene of Noelle and Luke together on the couch at the Prestons' house, still feel the clutch of pain and betrayal in her heart.

And I didn't confront them, Erin thought. *Not that night and not in all the days since. What could I say? Luke isn't mine. So he kissed me once — I guess it didn't really mean anything to him after all. I guess I'm just so young and stupid and inexperienced that I thought he was falling in love with me the same way I was falling in love with him.*

And Noelle. My best friend. But she didn't know how I felt about Luke. I never got a chance to tell her. And now . . . well, now it's too late.

Tara doesn't even know that I saw Luke and Noelle together. I can't bring myself to tell her. And Pete is barely speaking to me. I haven't even seen him since he told me I had to choose between him and Luke.

I am totally, completely mixed up about everything.

Except this. Every time I see Luke, my heart feels like it's breaking.

"You know, this Winterfest is really a very fun thing," David said, smiling at Erin. "You are fortunate to live in Love, you know?"

Erin nodded and tried to smile, even though at the moment she didn't feel very fortunate at all.

Just snap out of it, she told herself. *Think about all the "fun things" you've done over the past few days!*

They had come in second in the snow sculpture contest, as David had predicted, being beaten by Nellie "Buxom" Bixom's patriotic Statue of Liberty. At the awards ceremony in Love's town square, the crowd had good-naturedly booed the winners, and then had sung *The Flintstones'* theme song in honor of the very popular second-place team.

Then there was the hilarity of seeing Nellie "Buxom" Bixom in one low-cut outfit after another, campaigning all over Love for votes for Winterfest Queen. Every place Erin went — in every store, on every street corner, in the bowling alley, at the ski lodge, around the athletes' dorms, and especially nonstop by the bonfire in the football stadium, Nellie was there, sucking up to anyone and everyone. Since every Love citizen over the age of twelve was allowed to vote, she had her work cut out for her.

I wouldn't be surprised if she'd come to our cemetery and etched the names off the tombstones onto Queen of the Court ballots, Erin thought with a smile. *But I still don't think she'll beat Tara.*

Erin thought back to the parties, the gettogethers and sleigh rides, the ice-fishing contests out on Love Lake, and the cafeteria tray-riding race down the hill in front of the college president's mansion. Like a film going through her mind she saw the huge barbecue-in-January that featured hamburgers, hotdogs, baked beans that had been baking for forty-eight hours, and (for the adults) beer that was served in beer steins left over from when their grandparents had moved to Love.

There were the hockey games — Steve "Flintstone!!! You're fired!!!!" Ward and his team from SUNY–Binghamton was actually in second place in its division, and Erin had gone with Tara to two of Steve's games.

And it was all so wonderful, Erin thought, a catch in her throat, *but still there's this terrible ache in my heart. All those days Luke was right there next to me, but he wasn't mine. He was just my friend. He is just my friend. And me, being the gutless wonder that I am, I don't know why.*

"Noelle's family arrives tomorrow morning, don't they?" Tara asked, stomping her feet to try and warm them up.

"What are they like?" David asked, curious.

"Bizarre," Tara said. "Her parents fight a lot. Her aunt Gussie has hair the color of a fire engine and she chain-smokes tiny little cigars. They always make Noelle extra nervous when they show up."

"That is difficult when you are trying to concentrate," David said.

"I imagine so," Tara agreed. "I'm blessed to have only one die-hard feminist mother to deal with, myself."

"Where is your father?" David asked.

"He moved on to greener pastures," Tara said lightly. "I think the politically correct poetry circle in our living room got to be a little bit too much for him. He never was very socially aware."

"You don't see him?" David asked.

"It's utterly unimportant to me," Tara said blithely. "Believe me, it's poor Noelle and her cloying family I feel sorry for."

Well, I don't, Erin thought coldly. *Noelle is a superstar. Noelle is gorgeous, talented, famous, and she looks like young Audrey Hepburn.*

And Luke wants her and not me.

Erin sighed and wrapped her mittened hands around her body for warmth. *So what if she called me the day after I saw her and Luke together in Jack Preston's family room? And so what if she's called me twice since then and I haven't called her back?*

Because I don't know what to say.

"Erin!" Tara said. "Hey, wake up!"

Erin turned to her friend, a sheepish look on her face.

Tara peered at her closely. "Have you got the vapors, sweetie? I only said your name five times."

"I was thinking," Erin said quickly.

Tara gave her a funny look. "Have you been acting real strange lately, or is it my imagination?"

Erin just shrugged.

"Are you okay?" Tara asked.

"Yeah, sure," Erin said.

"Things okay with you and Luke?" Tara pressed.

"Winterfest is almost over," Erin said, instead of answering Tara's question. "Luke's going back to Colorado."

"Well, last I heard they still had phone lines and airplanes that connected us to that part of the world," Tara said.

Erin pressed her lips together. "You haven't . . . talked to Noelle lately, have you?"

Tara shook her head. "What does that have to do with you and Luke?"

"Nothing," Erin said quickly. "I just wondered."

"Jack isn't letting her make calls, take calls, or see anyone until after tomorrow," Tara reported. "You know that."

"Yeah, right," Erin agreed.

"Luke's third in line to jump," David said, cocking his head toward the hill. "He is going to win. I am sure of it."

"Well, he said it was a perfect day to jump," Tara reminded David.

Erin looked up. There wasn't a cloud in the sky. It was cold enough so that the inclined jumping track wouldn't get mushy or slushy, and there was no wind to hold a jumper up, knock him off balance, or cut down on his distance.

That's what Luke had told her, anyway.

"All I've got to do is win," he'd said intently, before he embraced Erin, Tara, and David in turn. "Thanks for coming to watch me. It means a lot."

"Too bad Noelle couldn't come," Erin had said. She couldn't help herself. It was like having a toothache and not being able to stop yourself from wriggling your tongue where it hurt.

"Erin, I — " Luke began.

"What?"

Luke glanced at David and Tara, then back at Erin. "This isn't the time, I guess."

"No," she'd agreed quietly. "All you should be thinking about now is winning."

He smiled at her — and something in his eyes told her he wanted to say more — but he didn't. He just turned and headed for the van that would take him up the mountain.

Now, true to everyone's predictions, Luke was leading the competition going into the second, and final, competitive jump of the day. In the landing area, off to one side, judges had inserted colored poles to indicate the distance of each competitor's first jump.

Luke's red pole was the farthest away from the jumping ramp by a good five feet or so.

"Next to jump," the voice on the loud-speaker announced, "Gilbert Gaston, from McGill University, Montreal, Canada."

A hush fell over the crowd as Gaston stepped into the gate. Then he leaned forward and started down the hill, gathering speed each foot of the way.

When he hit the takeoff he exploded into the air, trying to squeeze every bit of distance he could out of the jump.

He landed to loud cheers from the spectators, but he was a good three feet short of Luke's first jump.

"Come on, Luke," Erin said under her breath.

There was only one jumper ahead of Luke — Nathanael Beal from the University of New Hampshire. Beal had qualified second to Luke in the prelims, and Luke had said that he considered Beal his most dangerous competitor.

"Now jumping, Nathanael Beal, from the University of New Hampshire," the announcer said.

Beal stepped into the slot at the top of the gate.

He jumped.

And when he landed, he was a foot past Luke's first-round jump.

The small contingent of fans from New Hampshire went absolutely crazy with glee as the other fans cheered Beal on.

"Everyone loves an upset," David observed.

"Well, Luke's just going to have to beat it," Tara said firmly. "Come on, Luke!"

Erin held her breath.

I might not know what's going on between us, Erin thought, *but I know one thing: I want him to win.*

She reached over and took Tara's hand in her own, squeezing it tightly.

Tara squeezed back.

"Now jumping, Luke Blakely, from the University of Colorado," the announcer said.

"Come on," Tara whispered.

"You can do it, Luke," David said.

Luke got into the starting gate and gave a little push to get going down the ramp, as a fresh breeze blew over the bleachers and up the mountain, filling the wind sock — which told the skiers how windy the conditions were — that was attached to the bottom of the jump.

"Oh, no," David muttered. "The wind just came up."

Luke sped down the ramp, looking like the experienced champion jumper he was. He hit the takeoff area and flew into the air, spreading his skis into the now familiar V-shape that allowed for maximum loft.

The gust of breeze hit Luke head-on.

His skis wobbled a bit, and he had to wave his hands to catch his balance.

It cost him.

He landed four feet short of his earlier effort. His jump was only the third-longest of the day, behind both Nathanael Beal and Gilbert Gaston.

"Oh, no," Erin cried when she'd seen what had happened.

"He didn't see the wind sock," David groaned.

Luke knew he had blown it. He skidded to a stop, snapped out of his bindings, and stomped disgustedly away, not even waving to his friends in the stands.

"I can't believe it," Tara said.

"I can," David said, shaking his head. "This is sports. Anything can happen."

"What should we do?" Erin asked, feeling sick inside.

"Ladies and gentlemen, we have the final results of the ski jump," a voice boomed over the loudspeaker. "First place, Nathanael Beal, University of New Hampshire, second place, Gilbert Gaston, McGill University," the announcer boomed over the PA system. "Third place, Luke Blakely, University of Colorado. Let's have a hand for all our contestants!"

Everyone in the crowd stood and cheered, including Erin and her friends.

But they all knew that Luke was not going to feel as if they had anything to cheer about.

"Man, I can't believe I did that," Luke muttered for about the hundredth time. "I had it, I really had it, and then . . ." He shook his head with disgust yet again at his third-place finish. "I stink."

Luke, Erin, Tara, and David were in the restaurant in the lodge at the bottom of Love Mountain, where the downhill finals were soon to take place. It was a cozy room with a huge, crackling fireplace and wooden tables into which, over the years, many athletes had carved their names and

the year they had participated in Winterfest. The salt and pepper shakers were
wooden, too, carved into the shape of two
tiny skiers, one male, one female. Up above
the bar was suspended a large TV, clearly
visible to all the tables. Currently it was
tuned to MTV, but the sound was turned
down.

After Luke's third-place win, they
watched the medal ceremony, when the
bronze medal for ski jumping had been
placed around Luke's neck. At Winterfest,
unlike the Olympics, all three medalists
stood on the same level to receive their
medals, instead of having the gold medalist
stand highest, then the silver, and then the
bronze. The idea was to honor all the athletes in some sense equally, and it worked.

For a while Luke barely spoke, just
silently agreeing to go to lunch with them
at the lodge. But once they'd arrived, he
kept going over and over what had happened to him, reliving every awful moment
of what he saw as his "defeat."

The foursome had ordered the pasta special; David's coach insisted his athletes
carbo-load before an event. To drink, they
chose carrot juice, also ordered by David's
coach.

"Third place isn't so bad," Erin said, sipping the carrot juice.

"I could have won it," Luke said, his hand clenched around his glass of juice.

"It wasn't your fault," David said. "You were already in your crouch when the wind came up. You couldn't see the wind sock. There was nothing you could do."

"I should have been able to feel it," Luke said. "I was just so sure that there was no wind."

"Well, we're proud of you," Tara said. "Now, stop brooding and eat your pasta."

"We really *are* proud of you," Erin added, touching Luke's hand.

Luke tried to smile, but he was only half successful.

I don't know what to say to make him feel better, Erin thought miserably. *I bet Noelle would know.* She stared at a dancer in an MTV video up on the TV, who looked depressingly like the lithe Noelle.

After all, they have so much in common. I don't know anything about being a serious athlete. The only thing I know about is the perfect rouge for the newly deceased. I can't really blame Luke for choosing Noelle over me. After all —

"Hey, Erin, did you hear anything I just

said?" Tara asked, daintily swirling some pasta on her fork.

"No," Erin admitted, tearing her eyes away from the MTV dancing Noelle look-alike. "Sorry. What?" She forced her mind away from the same painful thoughts that had been plaguing her for days and days.

"I said we should go to that palm reader — you know, the woman out on Rutgers Road — and find out how David and Noelle are going to finish."

"The future isn't written before we live it," David said, slurping up a mouthful of spaghetti. "I wouldn't believe her."

"Well, that just shows what you know," Tara scoffed at him. She picked up his left hand and studied it. "It just so happens that Madame Dupré taught me everything she knows about palmistry. I can read your future right now."

"I think you are only saying that so you can hold my hand," David said, reaching for his carrot juice with his free hand.

Tara pushed his hand away from her. "Honestly, you are the most egotistical boy I have ever met. You think every member of the opposite sex is after you, don't you?"

Luke smiled, clearly making an effort to throw off his disappointment. "Tara, you sound like you're talking about yourself."

Tara's mouth opened in outrage. *"Moi?"*

"Oh, perish the thought," David teased.

"You know, I don't even know why I hang out with y'all," Tara said. She took a sip of the carrot juice and made a face. "And here I am drinking this swill just to keep you company before you race, David."

"We have to be nice to him before he skis," Erin said.

"I *never* have to be nice to him," Tara informed her.

"We're supposed to be building up his confidence," Erin reminded Tara.

"Erin, David has cornered the market on confidence," she said dryly. "His confidence overfloweth." She turned to David. "I really want to know, is your brother, Ari, as disgustingly cocky as you are?"

"He is a much nicer person than me," David said.

"I'll bet he's better-looking, too," Tara added. "I may just have to fly over to Israel and look him up. And when he falls madly in love with me, David, you'll remember that you once had your chance, and you blew it."

"He has a girlfriend," David informed Tara.

"Beautiful, I suppose?" Tara asked, taking another sip of her juice.

"Yes," David agreed. "Her name is Yael. They are in the army together."

"So, I suppose you and Ari both only like Israeli girls who look perfect without mascara, who look great in those little shorts y'all wear over there, and who've been certified by the Israel Defense Forces in Uzis and carbines," Tara sniffed.

"Correct," David said gravely. "And if they ever enter a beauty pageant, we drop them immediately."

Tara gave David a withering look. "I know that was your pathetic attempt at humor. I think."

"David, man," Luke interrupted. "I wish you would just kiss Tara to shut her up. She's getting kind of relentless."

"Hey!" Tara objected. "I — "

"Anyone want coffee? Dessert?" a waitress asked, coming over to the table, her pen poised over her order pad. "We've got some killer homemade apple pie."

"No caffeine and no sugar," David said. He looked at his watch. "I ski very soon."

The other three passed on coffee and dessert, and the waitress left the check after wishing David luck.

"So, you cool, David?" Luke asked. "You ready?"

"I am," David said. "I feel strong."

"Confident, you mean," Tara translated.

"Too bad we can't give some of it to Noelle, huh?" Luke asked, reaching for the check. "She's really flipped out about her short program tomorrow."

"How do you know?" Erin asked, keeping her voice light.

"I called her this morning," Luke reported. "She had to sneak to even speak with me. Jack is getting really crazy."

"He just wants her to be a champion," Erin said, an edge to her voice. "I guess you know all about that."

Luke gave her a funny look. "Yeah, I do."

"How much do we owe you, Luke?" Tara asked, reaching for her purse.

"This one is on me," Luke said, waving off their money. "To wish you luck, David — we're pulling for you."

"Thanks," David said. He gave a small shrug. "Believe it or not, I'm not always as totally confident as Scarlett O'Hara here would have you believe."

"Aha!" Tara cried. "So you admit to a human weakness after all! Well — "

"Shhhh!" David said sharply, turning his

head to the TV on the wall. Someone had changed the channel to CNN and turned up the sound. CNN put up its "Breaking News" logo, and then the news anchor Reid Collins was on the air.

"We now go to Richard Blystone in Tel Aviv with this live report," Collins said.

The screen switched to a scene of utter devastation. A car bomb had obviously recently exploded in the area, and people were lying in the street, dead or wounded and bloodied, and many emergency vehicles, their sirens wailing, were going back and forth.

"This is Richard Blystone in Tel Aviv." Blystone's voice narrated the action. "Just minutes ago, a terrorist car bomb exploded here in Dizengoff Square in Tel Aviv. What you are looking at is the destruction that this bomb has wrought."

The camera panned around the square. There were buildings with windows blown out, cars still on fire, and, as before, the dead and wounded in the street.

"It was around nine P.M. local time when the bomb exploded," Blystone narrated. "Local cafés were packed with people."

The camera zoomed in for close-ups on some of the bodies in the street.

"Adonai," David said. "My God!"

"What is it?" Tara asked him. David's face had gone completely white.

"My God," David repeated, his hand over his mouth and tears in his eyes. He pointed to a bloodied body on the screen. "That is my brother, Ari."

Chapter 13

They all just sat together, silently staring at the television set in the cafeteria of the Love Mountain ski lodge. They had already watched the same footage over and over and over.

At tables all around them, Winterfest athletes and hundreds of spectators were chatting, laughing, eating, joking, roughhousing, flirting, and, above all, eating and drinking.

As if the world were still normal, Tara thought, looking over at David. *But it's not. Oh, David . . .*

Silently she reached for his hand. He let her take it, still staring blankly at the horrible images on the TV screen.

It was forty-five minutes later, and CNN was still focusing its coverage on the car bomb attack. They were replaying the footage they'd filmed over and over, as if putting it up on the screen again and again would somehow make what happened seem more real.

Immediately after learning of the attack, David had gone to try to call Israel. There was no answer at his home, and the switchboards at both the Tel Aviv police department and the government offices he had tried in Jerusalem were jammed.

David had told Tara that Israel was such a small country that it felt like everyone knew everyone else, and when a terrorist bomb went off or some other tragedy happened, it seemed like it was happening to a member of your own family.

Hence the phone calls and the jammed phone lines. And it wasn't likely to get better anytime soon.

"Hey, man, do we have to watch that?" a high-spirited guy from two tables over yelled. "Someone change the channel. We're celebrating here!"

"Yes, we have to watch it," Tara said fiercely, turning around to stare the loud guy down.

"Well, what's your problem, honey?" he asked nastily.

"Anyone who gets up to change the channel will die," Tara said, then she turned back to her friends.

Someone across the room ran over to the loud guy and quickly whispered something in his ear while looking over at David. Then the guy got up and walked over to their table.

"Hey, man, I'm sorry, I didn't know you're Israeli," he said, putting out his hand to David.

David managed to shake it.

"My apologies, man," the guy said earnestly. Then he returned to his own table.

Tara looked over at David, who was staring straight ahead at nothing.

If that guy only knew, Tara thought. *Not only is it David's country, it's David's brother.*

"I think I will try to call again," David said abruptly, pushing his chair back.

"Would all athletes participating in the final round of the men's senior downhill event please proceed to the registration table for final check-in," a man with Winterfest organizer credentials announced through a bullhorn as he stood at the doorway to the cafeteria.

"I have to ski," David said, his voice tight and controlled.

"But — " Tara started to say.

"Last call," the man with the bullhorn said. "All skiers in the final round of the downhill must proceed now to registration."

"I have to ski now," he repeated, getting up from the table as if he were on auto-pilot. "I'll see you all after the first run."

"Is there anything we can do, man?" Luke asked him, getting up from his chair.

David shook his head.

"Are you sure?" Erin asked. They were all standing now.

"You can pray," David said.

And it was very clear that he wasn't re-ferring to prayer about his skiing.

Tara, Erin, and Luke watched David leave, then they sat down again. Then Tara, who was not used to praying at all, closed her eyes and sent up a silent missive. When she opened her eyes, she noticed that Erin and Luke had their eyes closed, too. They opened them, and the three friends stared at one another.

"Tell me how they score the skiing again," Tara asked Luke, since none of them wanted to talk about Ari when there was absolutely nothing they could do and no way to get any information at the moment.

"David will get time to change," Luke said, "then he'll have some time on the mountain to warm up. After that he'll do the first of two runs."

Tara nodded. "Go on," she said.

"He'll do his final run tonight," Luke explained. "Then the times from his two runs will be combined to come up with a total score."

Tara nodded again. She bit her lower lip. "I can't stand this. I want to do something! If I had David's home phone, I'd try to call his parents."

"They're probably at the hospital in Tel Aviv now," Luke said, fiddling with the skier-shaped pepper shaker on the table. "They live there."

"I just can't understand how David can ski now," Erin blurted out.

"I can," Luke said in a low voice. "If it were me, I'd do the same thing."

"But it's just a stupid sport!" Erin cried, her voice cracking with emotion. "His brother could be dead, and he's — "

"Skiing in a race," Luke finished. "Unless you're as committed as David is, I guess it's hard to understand. But if Ari is anything like his brother, he'd want David to run this race."

"Well, I'm sorry," Erin said. "I couldn't do it!"

No one said anything for a long moment. All around them the noise, excitement, and high spirits of Winterfest continued, and in the center was a trio of silent, ashen-faced mourners.

"Life can change just like that," Tara said, as if she were speaking to herself. "And you never know . . ."

"You never know," Erin echoed sadly.

Tara took a deep breath and stood back up. "Y'all, we better go find a seat in the bleachers outside," she said softly. "I want to sit in the very front."

"He won't be able to see you no matter where you sit," Luke said, pushing his chair in. "He'll never know."

"I'll know," Tara said.

"Now in the gates," the announcer said, "skier number one-oh-one, David Benjamin, of Tel Aviv, Israel, skiing for Colby College, Waterville, Maine."

Tara reached for Erin's hand. Without thinking, Erin reached for Luke's hand. The three of them sat in the front row of the bleachers, connected, not speaking.

The scoreboard told the story. David was to be the fifth skier coming down, since he had qualified in fifth place. Normally, Luke had explained to them, this would be a perfect position. He'd have an opportunity to see how the other skiers performed, what lines they took in some of the turns, and what waxes they were using on their skis.

Normally.

But nothing about David's first downhill run was going to be normal.

On the scoreboard, the times of the runs had been getting faster and faster, Tara could see. The first skier had come down the course in a minute and thirty-four and fifteen one hundredths of a second. The fourth skier had crossed the line in 1:32.

"This is it," Luke muttered, his gloved fingers squeezing Erin's.

All three of them had their eyes glued to the giant video monitor that Tara had watched so closely during David's qualifying run.

And now David was off. He took his by now familiar five skating steps down the mountain and dropped into his tuck.

He easily cruised through the upper section of the course.

"I can't believe it," Tara said. "He's holding it together."

"Awesome," Luke agreed.

The announcer put David's split time over the loudspeaker — he had the fastest time so far.

Go, David, Tara rooted silently, as if she could will him quickly and safely down the mountain. *Go.*

David held his tuck in good position until he got halfway down the run, down to the same point where he'd had his slight bobble in the preliminaries.

And disaster struck again.

David missed his prejump over the rolling bump, so the bump threw him into the air, controlling him instead of his controlling the jump.

"No!" Tara cried, biting her lower lip hard.

"Damn," Luke muttered.

"Come on, David!" Tara yelled, even though she knew that he couldn't hear her.

He lost his balance badly on his landing. His ski tips crossed, and it looked like he was going to crash at sixty miles an hour. Amazingly, he didn't crash, but instead veered far to the right on the left-hand turn, picking an inopportune line, narrowly missing the orange restraining fence that stopped skiers from skidding into the woods.

Then, amazingly, he recovered and got back into his tuck. But by then it was too late. Far too late. When he reappeared at the top of the final incline heading down the finish line, the speed gun clocked him at eighty miles an hour instead of the eighty-five he had done in his qualifying run.

He crossed the finish line in 1:37 exactly.

He was seven seconds slower than the fastest skier of the day so far. Unless the rest of the skiers didn't ski at all, it was now practically a foregone conclusion that he'd finish tenth out of ten, by a wide margin.

Last place.

David's Winterfest was over.

For a long time Tara, Erin, and Luke just sat there silently. They couldn't move, couldn't speak.

"Well," Tara finally said, her lower lip trembling, "this just truly bites it."

She stood up quickly. "I'll see y'all later."

"Where are you going?" Erin asked.

"To David," she said. "Maybe he needs me."

"Thank you, operator," David said into the phone. "I will try again later."

It was an hour later. David and Tara were in David's dorm room. David had finally gotten through to the largest hospital in Tel Aviv, feeling certain that that was where his brother would have been taken. And, miracle of miracles, the switchboard operator had confirmed that Ari Benjamin had been brought in to Emergency. But when she had tried to connect David to the emergency room, he had been disconnected.

He dialed back quickly, but when the operator connected him, he got a busy signal. After three more attempts, he was still getting a busy signal.

David sat on the edge of his bed, his hands dangling uselessly at his sides.

"At least now you know where he is," Tara said. She sat down next to him. "And they wouldn't have brought him to the hospital if he was . . ."

I can't say "dead," Tara thought. *I just can't.*

"Yes, they would," David said, his voice

flat. "That is exactly what they would do. They would officially try to resuscitate him, then he would need to be pronounced dead by a doctor."

"He's not dead," Tara said harshly.

David was silent.

"He's not," she said more quietly. "I would know if he was dead."

David turned to look at her. "*That* is a stupid thing to say."

"I never say anything stupid," Tara replied. "And I don't care how much you insult me. I just have this feeling that I would know."

"You don't even know him," David said.

"I know him," Tara said. "A little, anyway. If he's like you."

David's face hardened, and he lashed out at Tara. "You don't know me at all. Don't pretend that you do."

"You're wrong — "

"I'm not wrong," David insisted, his eyes cold. "You play more games than any girl I ever met. You hide behind your perfect hair and your perfect manicure, like it will protect you from something real. And it does. No one ever touches you, and you never touch anyone."

"If it makes you feel better to take your pain out on me, go ahead," Tara said, her voice steely.

"I am just telling you the truth," David insisted. "I don't even know why you're here. Because I am a challenge to you, I suppose. Because I am the only guy who does not fall at your feet because you're beautiful and brilliant. But you waste it all with your shallowness, your pageants, your silliness — "

David stopped. He was breathing hard, his hands clenched into tight fists, tears in his eyes.

"You have everything," David continued, his voice low now. "But you feel nothing. Not really."

The silence in the room felt thick, like humid summer air. Tara stared down at her perfect manicure — pale pink, which matched the pale pink ribbon in her hair.

Tara took a deep breath, still staring at her fingers. "I feel . . ." she began haltingly, "I feel . . . everything. That's the problem, you see. Like when my father left . . . I knew it had to be because I wasn't a perfect enough girl for him to stay. Once he called me and said he would send a dozen roses for my birthday, a perfect gift for a perfect girl. The roses never came. Nothing came."

She stood up and stared out the window. Snow was beginning to fall again, lightly dancing to the ground. "He never called me again. Once, he wrote to say he had a new family — a new daughter. More perfect than me, is what I imagined. And my mother, well, I just guess I'm a big disappointment to her, too. We're nothing alike. We're not friends. The only thing we seem to have in common is a gene pool."

She turned to look at David. "I know you think I'm silly and flighty and ridiculous. But I know what it feels like to hurt, to hurt so badly that you don't feel as if the hole in your heart can ever mend. I know that every wound doesn't heal, and you have to find a way to go on anyway.

"So maybe you don't like me very much, David Benjamin, and I guess that's okay. I can't make you like me. And I can't make your brother be okay. I wish I could . . ." Tara's voice caught, and she forced herself to continue. ". . . do both those things. But the only thing I can do is to tell you how much I care about you, and that as long as I live I will see your face in my dreams."

With a strangled cry of pain, David

launched himself toward Tara, his arms open wide, and in a moment she was in them, but she was holding him more than he was holding her, and she let him cry in her arms.

"I'm sorry," David sobbed. "I'm so sorry . . ."

"It's okay," Tara crooned, rocking him in her arms. "It's okay."

They stood like that a long time, finally moving to his bed. Tara wiped the tears from David's cheeks. He lay down on his back, and she lay with her head on his chest, listening to the pounding of his heart, his arms wrapped around her.

"Luke was right about us, you know," Tara said softly. "We are too much alike."

"I know," David said, stroking her hair. "I think I will try the hospital again."

They both sat up, and David dialed the number one more time.

Please, God, Tara prayed, sending up a silent prayer. *Please.*

David spoke in rapid Hebrew into the phone. Tara sat on the bed, her arms wrapped around herself, watching his face. The conversation seemed to go on and on. Then — it was so wonderful — she saw a change in his face, a light come into his eyes. And then finally he hung up and turned to her.

"I spoke with my mother," David said, his eyes shining. "My brother is alive!"

"Oh, David!" Tara cried, running into his arms.

He held her tight. "He is not safe yet. He is in surgery now. The blast pierced his left lung, ruptured his spleen. It's not good, but he has a chance. A chance."

"Yes, a chance," Tara whispered. She lifted her face up to gaze into David's blue, blue eyes. "A chance."

David looked at her, and now, for the first time, his eyes were naked and vulnerable. "Do you realize I've never kissed you?" he asked in a low voice.

"It's occurred to me," Tara admitted.

Then David Benjamin of Tel Aviv, Israel, pulled Tara Moore, originally of Starkville, Mississippi, to him, and he kissed her until they both weren't even on the planet Earth at all.

Chapter 14

"Here they come," Erin said quietly. She put down the handful of popcorn she'd taken from the box on the cafeteria table that she had been sharing with Luke, Traci, who had shown up a half hour earlier to watch the racing finals, and — to Erin's surprise — Aunt Daisy.

"Poor guy," Traci said under her breath. "How do you think he's doing it?" Traci wondered as they watched David and Tara walk across the cafeteria. "I'd be a wreck."

"He *is* a wreck," Luke said firmly. "But he's also a pro."

Erin sighed. *I'll never understand that attitude,* she thought.

And then another thought flew, unbidden, into her mind.

Noelle would understand.

"People are stronger than you think, Traci," Aunt Daisy observed. "I've seen it time and again. I remember when Mr. Percival fell off his roof and broke his neck. Mrs. Percival had agoraphobia — she hadn't been out of the house in years — and don't you know she planned a lovely funeral and made sure Mr. Percival was buried in his favorite blue shirt and his favorite hairpiece. The one that made him look like Frank Sinatra, she said."

Everyone just kind of stared at Erin's aunt, who smiled cheerfully at all the young people.

It was seven o'clock that evening. Huge throngs of people had gathered at Love Mountain for the second, decisive run of the men's senior downhill, to be held under the lights.

Decisive for everyone but David, of course, who had so totally screwed up his first run that he was out of medal contention. Nonetheless, he insisted that he was going to compete.

Erin had stopped home during the afternoon, and Tara had called her there and reported everything she knew. David's brother was alive, but it could go either way. And David was going to ski.

Erin watched David and Tara make their way over toward them.

David's saying "excuse me" for people to give him some room, and when they see who it is, they instantly shut up and move away to let him through!

"Everyone knows, I guess," Traci said.

"I wish people had kept their mouths shut about it," Luke muttered.

"Well, you know people," Aunt Daisy observed. "Private tragedy becomes a public event sometimes. People don't mean anything bad by it."

Erin nodded.

Aunt Daisy might be crazy, but she's right this time, Erin thought. *Somehow everyone knows about David's brother. People have come over to this table to ask us about it ever since we sat down.*

"It reminds me of Dan Jansen," Luke murmured as David stopped to talk with someone on his ski team.

"The skater," Traci said, nodding.

"Who's Dan Jansen?" Erin asked.

"Speed skater," Traci explained. "1984 Olympics. He was favored to win a bunch of gold medals. His sister died right before the games. He blew every event."

"But he didn't quit," Luke said firmly. "That's the important thing."

I guess that's a mentality I'll never understand, Erin thought. *It's as if we speak completely different languages.*

Finally, David and Tara reached the table.

The first thing Erin noticed was that they were holding hands.

"Hi," Traci said, giving David a warm smile.

"Have you heard anything else?" Erin asked as David and Tara pulled chairs up to the table.

"Nothing," David said. "My mother said she would call me as soon as there was news. I thought I would hear by now."

Erin reached out for David's hand. "You know, you don't have to race tonight. You can withdraw."

"I am not withdrawing," David said steadfastly. "There is no way."

"Look, I don't want to interfere, here," Traci began hesitantly. "I mean, you don't even know me. But . . . I ski a lot. My sister competes. And I know you'll be going eighty-five, ninety miles an hour down that hill. If you're not totally concentrating when you're racing, you can hurt yourself. Really hurt yourself."

"I am not crashing," David declared, "and I am not withdrawing."

At that moment, another of the competition organizers came into the cafeteria to make the same announcement that had been made earlier in the afternoon to get the racers headed to the registration area to pick up their bibs and prepare for the final downhill run.

But he added a twist this time.

"Would all racers *choosing* to compete in this evening's final downhill run of the men's senior downhill please proceed to race registration immediately," he said into his bullhorn.

Choosing to compete? Erin thought. *He must have added that for David. Even the organizers meant to make sure David knows he can gracefully withdraw from the race.*

Rather than the excited buzz that had met the announcement earlier in the afternoon, a complete hush fell over the cafeteria.

Hundreds of pairs of sympathetic and even pained eyes swung toward David, waiting to see what he would do.

He stood up.

He picked up his silver COLBY racing helmet, which was on the table in front of him, and he slowly, with great dignity, began to walk directly toward the man with the bullhorn.

"That's my guy," Tara said with pride.

Erin raised her eyebrows. "You must have had some afternoon!"

Tara smiled. "You could say that." She turned back to David, who walked so tall and proud toward the door with his fellow skiers.

Tara slowly began to clap her hands.

The sound reverberated through the ski lodge cafeteria like a gunshot.

She clapped again.

And again. And again.

And then Erin was clapping with her. And then Luke, and Traci, and Crazy Daisy, and Nellie "Buxom" Bixom with her athlete, James, joined in from the next table, and more and more people, Steve Ward and his entire hockey team, Dinky Deederman and his friend Caleb, everyone, athletes and fans alike, applauded as one for the courage of David Benjamin.

Tara's eyes welled up with tears. "Y'all, I can't do this," she managed to choke out. "I didn't even wear waterproof mascara."

David showed no signs of being moved by the display of emotion. He walked over to the man with the bullhorn and said something to him.

The man nodded and handed the bullhorn to David. A hush came over the crowded room.

David put the bullhorn to his lips. "My name is David Benjamin," he said, in a clear, strong voice. "I dedicate my race tonight to my brother, Ari Benjamin."

Then he handed the bullhorn back to the Winterfest organizer, turned, his head held high, and headed for the door.

"Now in the starting gate," the loudspeaker voice boomed, echoing as it had before off the hills and the ski lodge, "racer number one-oh-one, David Benjamin, racing for Colby College in Waterville, Maine."

Erin, Tara, Traci, Luke, and Aunt Daisy were jammed together in the finish line bleachers. It had been agony for all of them, waiting for David to race. Because he had finished last in the afternoon run, he was going to race last in the evening. Which meant, potentially at least, that the course was going to be more rutted, more skied-out, and that much harder than it had been in the afternoon.

Tara took a quick look at the scoreboard. In this heat, the fastest time had been a minute twenty-nine and thirty-six one hundredths of a second, turned in by Willie Singleton.

Come on, David, she prayed as she watched him on the video monitor — watched him put a gloved hand over his eyes for a moment, as if he were saying a little prayer. *Come on!*

"He's off!" the loudspeaker voice said, as Tara saw David burst through the starting gate, take five skating steps down the mountain, and drop into his characteristic racing tuck.

He flashed through the uppermost part of the course magnificently, hardly slowing in the few turns, maintaining his perfect tuck, his speed increasing.

"Go, man," Luke said, his voice low and intense.

"He's jamming!" Traci cried.

This time it was Tara who reached for Erin's hand. She squeezed so tightly that Erin's fingers felt as if they could burst, but she didn't care.

The loudspeaker announced David's first split time.

He was fastest through the upper part of the course by a second and a half.

And then he was into the dangerous middle part of the run where he'd encountered so much trouble on his two earlier runs.

His prejump was picture-perfect, over the long, rolling bump that had tossed him about like a bucking bronco rider that afternoon. He landed on the downside of the bump, picking up additional speed, staying in his tuck.

"Unbelievable," Luke whispered, watching the monitor.

"Come on, David!" Tara yelled, as David kept his aerodynamic tuck intact through the final swooping S-turn that led to the bottom part of the course.

"Go!" Aunt Daisy yelled, her fist in the air.

"Go!" Erin yelled, and she put her fist in the air, too.

Now, David was coming into view — a silver bullet, no, a silver blur, at the top of the final, steep pitch that led to the finish line.

The crowd was going crazy, cheering, clanging cowbells they had brought, imploring David to go faster, faster, faster. A string of firecrackers went off, adding to the cacophony.

David flashed across the finish line and snapped to a stop, sending a small moving wall of snow three feet up in the air with his ski edges.

There's a problem with the clock, Tara thought, as she looked at his time.

1:26 and two one-hundredths of a second.

That's amazing. That's three seconds faster than anyone else!

But there was nothing wrong with the clock. The crowd, stunned silent for a moment by David's enormous, blockbuster, inspiring run, burst into wild applause and cheers at his incredible performance.

And down in the stopping area past the finish line, David just stared at the finish line timer, absolutely shocked by what he had just done.

"It's better than winning," Luke said, in absolute awe. "I didn't think it was possible . . ."

Tara had tears streaming down her face. So did Erin and Traci. Even Luke's eyes welled up with tears.

"You did it, you big jerk," Tara whispered. "You did it."

And then, David turned his head away from the finish line. He scanned the crowd. Finally, his eyes found Tara's eyes. And he gave a thumbs-up with his right hand, and his face shone with happiness and love.

Then he was besieged by the other nine skiers competing, including the apparent medal winners, who ran over to him, clapping him on the back and swinging their fists in the air in shared triumph.

He'd placed fifth overall, the scoreboard said.

No medal for David Benjamin.

But the crowd knew that he was the true winner. And that was all that mattered.

Chapter 15

Boom-boom-boom-boom-boom.

Noelle could feel her heart pounding in her chest.

Too fast. Too hard. Too scary.

She took a huge gulp of air and willed it to slow down.

Please, don't, she thought. *Please.*

Her heart didn't listen.

She knew, in the tiny little corner of her mind that she allowed to know, that her heart had been pounding more and more lately. She had nearly fainted again during her practice the day before.

She had woken up the last three nights in a row with that terrible racing feeling, bathed in a cold, clammy sweat of fear.

Please, Noelle thought again. *She reached for the edge of the table to steady herself. Her hand was shaking.*

Think about good things. Think about Luke.

"Lemme look at my girl, the champion!" Noelle's dad boomed, coming over to her and spinning her around.

She forced a smile onto her face. He held her at arm's length. "You're something else, dollface, you know that?"

"Thanks, Dad," Noelle said, her smile tight. "But I'm not a champion yet."

It was almost nine o'clock the next morning. Noelle's family had arrived in their rented camper an hour earlier — the camper was now parked in the Prestons' driveway.

Noelle had called Tara at seven o'clock — waking her up, actually — to tell her that Jack said she could have her closest friends over, along with her family, for breakfast.

And I felt fine at seven, Noelle recalled. *My heart was normal, my breathing was fine, and again it all just seemed like a bad dream.*

As her father prattled on about the interview he'd done for the *Detroit Free Press,* Noelle replayed her conversation with Tara in her mind.

"Jack's letting you have *company*??" Tara

had asked in shock. "That doesn't sound like Jack at all. Maybe Jack's nice twin has taken over his body."

"I think it's because he knows how nervous my family makes me," Noelle explained. "He can't stop them from being here. So he probably figures they'll make me less crazy if I have some friends around."

"You've got the guy figured out, all right," Tara had agreed.

"So, you'll come?" Noelle asked. "I know it's not much notice — "

"Sweetie, I'm already there," Tara had assured her. "Can I bring David?"

"Sure," Noelle said. "Luke told me about David's brother — I'm so sorry."

"Actually, he got a call late last night that his brother made it through the surgery with flying colors," Tara reported.

"That's great," Noelle said warmly. "I know Luke was bummed-out about finishing third, but I heard David was a superstar on his last run."

"Listen," Tara said, sitting up in bed, "just out of curiosity, when did you and Luke get so chummy?"

"We've . . . kind of been hanging out," Noelle admitted.

"Hanging out like how?" Tara had asked carefully. "I have a feeling we have some catching up to do, sweetie."

"After today, I promise," Noelle said. "But today I just can't think about anything except skating."

"I understand," Tara had agreed. "Did you call Erin yet?"

"Could you call her?" Noelle asked. "I still have to call Traci."

"Uh . . . Noelle," Tara said slowly, "have you and Erin talked much lately?"

"Not at all," Noelle said. "You know that. Until last night I hadn't talked to anyone but Jack and Sandi for three days. And Jack doesn't talk, he lectures."

"Maybe you and Erin need to have a little chitchat," Tara suggested.

"Is she mad at me or something?" Noelle asked with concern. "Because I tried to call her days ago, and — "

"Let me hit you with another question," Tara interrupted. "Are you and Luke, like, an *item*?"

Silence.

And then, "I really, really, really like him, Tara," Noelle confided, her voice low with happiness. "And I think he likes me, too! Isn't that fantastic?"

"Sure," Tara said. "It's just . . . great!"

"Why did you hesitate?" Noelle asked anxiously.

"Nothing," Tara said quickly. "It's great. Everything's great!"

"Oh, Tara," Noelle breathed, "isn't Luke fantastic?"

"Sure is," Tara agreed. "What a guy."

"He said he'd invite me to his college for a weekend," Noelle said. "I'm going to go, too, whether Jack likes it or not!"

"Go, girl," Tara had said, but to Noelle something in her voice sounded . . . odd.

"So listen, Noelle, I'll call Erin and we'll see you in a couple of hours," Tara said.

"Are you sure everything is okay?" Noelle asked.

"Absolutely," Tara lied. "You just concentrate on your skating."

Okay. I'll concentrate on my skating, Noelle thought to herself. *Right. I can't think about my friends. Or Luke. Or my health. All I can think about is skating.*

She forced her mind back to the endless story her father was telling.

". . . and this reporter asked who you took after," her father continued, "so I says 'my daughter is just like me, we act alike, we think alike, except she's better lookin'!' "

Noelle smiled dutifully at her father.

"Well, look at me going on and on like an idiot," her father said. "Hey, it's just an old man's pride, honey. I always say, we ain't got much, but we got Noelle, and Noelle is pure gold."

Noelle smiled again, then she looked over her father's shoulder toward the front door of the house, willing her friends to walk through the door.

I can't take much more of this, she thought desperately, her heart pounding in her chest. She breathed in deeply, forcing her shoulders to relax. *Your heart is only pounding because of the tension, she told herself. It's just the pressure.*

"Hey, you're going for the gold, dollface!" Noelle's father insisted, hugging his daughter again. "So, did you eat anything yet?"

Sandi had put out a breakfast spread of bagels, muffins, juice, and coffee.

She had also instructed Noelle to eat one half of a bran muffin, no butter, and a small glass of orange juice. Period.

"I'm fine, Dad," Noelle said.

"My baby," Noelle's mom cried, her mouth full of muffin. She wiped her mouth with her napkin and planted a kiss on her daughter's cheek.

"I love these muffins," Aunt Gussie said, coming up next to her sister. "I could eat a dozen!"

"You already have," Noelle's dad sniped.

"Hey, Jimmy, cut it out," Noelle's mom chided him, putting her large, dimpled arm around her sister.

"The two of you could eat anyone out of house and home," Jimmy said with disgust.

"Traci!" Noelle cried, when she spotted her friend coming in the front door. She ran over to her, anxious to get away from her feuding family.

"Hi," Traci said, hugging Noelle hard. "How you doing?"

"Hanging in," Noelle said. "Frankly, I'd like to take my whole family and stick them outside in the camper."

Traci looked around. She had met Noelle's family before, and knew just what they were like. "Where's Buddy and Claire?"

"In the basement playing video games," Noelle said. "Lucky them."

Traci looked around to make sure no one could overhear them. "So, how's your heart?"

"It's fine," Noelle said, a bright smile on her face.

Traci peered into her eyes. "You look funny."

"I don't look funny," Noelle insisted. "I'm just nervous."

"Would you lie to me about it?" Traci asked, still peering closely at Noelle.

Noelle didn't reply.

"Of course you would," Traci said. "You're lying to me right now." She grabbed Noelle's arm. "Did you see another doctor like I told you to?"

"I don't need a doctor, Traci," Noelle said, shaking her friend off.

Traci pulled Noelle back to her. "Look, I know you don't want to talk about it, okay? But I'm not going to let this slide. I care about you too much. You have to tell me the truth!"

"Noelle, honey-bun, come on over here!" her mom called. "Aunt Gussie wants to talk to you about what makeup will go with your skating costumes!"

"Just a sec, Mom," Noelle called back to her mother.

Traci's hand held Noelle's arm fast. "Tell me," Traci insisted. "Or I'm walking into the dining room right this minute and I'm making an announcement to everyone."

"All right!" Noelle cried, her voice hushed and tense. "Sometimes I feel like it's beating too fast. And sometimes it scares me. Sometimes it scares me a lot, okay? And no, I didn't go to see another doctor. All I have to do is get through today, Traci, and then I promise — "

"How do you know if you should even be skating today?" Traci asked, her voice as low and tense as Noelle's.

"Please, Traci," Noelle begged. "This is the most important day of my life. I have to show everyone that I'm Olympic material. It means . . . everything. Don't you see that?"

Traci was silent.

"I promise I'll go see a doctor next week. You can ask your mom to recommend someone for me to see, okay?"

"Noelle!" Luke said happily, coming in the front door. He shook some snow off his hair. "It started snowing again. That's lucky, you know?" He leaned down and kissed Noelle lightly. "You look gorgeous," he added.

Traci stared hard at her friend. And Noelle's eyes begged her silently: *Do it my way. Please.*

"I love you, Noelle," Traci said softly, giving her a hug. She walked away quickly so Noelle wouldn't see the tears in her eyes.

"I'm so glad you're here," Noelle told Luke, taking in his gorgeous face, his lean, muscular body clad in jeans and an off-white cable-knit ski sweater over a blue turtleneck.

"Today is your day," Luke told her warmly. He touched her cheek softly with one finger. "I know you're the hometown face, but I'll be the guy in the stands rooting for you louder and harder than anyone."

Noelle leaned into the warmth and safety of Luke's arms. "That means so much to me," she whispered.

"So, who's the young man?" Aunt Gussie bellowed, coming over to them. "My, what a looker!"

Noelle smiled ruefully at Luke. She had already told him all about her family. "Aunt Gussie," she said softly, "I want you to meet Luke Blakely."

"Well, hi!" Erin said with surprise, her brush halfway to her hair. Tara was standing in her doorway. "You weren't supposed to pick me up until nine o'clock, and it's only eight-thirty. Or did I screw up the time?"

"I came early," Tara said. She sat down on Erin's bed. "Before we go see Noelle, we need to talk."

"You sound serious," Erin said lightly, even though she had a sinking feeling that she wasn't going to want to talk about whatever it was they had to talk about "before they saw Noelle."

"So what's up?" Erin asked, sitting in the chair at her desk. "Did you and David have a fight?"

"David and I are destined to live happily ever after and have brilliant but argumentative children," Tara said. "I wanted to talk about you and Luke."

Erin looked away, and picked some imaginary lint off her bedspread. "What about us?"

"Well, I've been so wrapped up in my own crazy romance with David that I have a feeling I missed something about the two of you somewhere along the way," Tara said. "So . . . are you on, or are you off?"

"Did he say something to you?" Erin asked.

"No," Tara replied. "But Noelle did."

"What did she say?" Erin asked.

Tara hesitated. "Maybe I shouldn't be doing this. Maybe you and Noelle should be having this conversation."

"You started it now," Erin said sharply. "You need to finish it."

Tara hesitated again. "Does Noelle know about you and Luke? I mean, is it possible that she thinks y'all are just friends?"

"Probably," Erin admitted, her voice low. "I never got a chance to tell her about the night Luke kissed me at the dinner dance."

"Erin Kellerman," Tara said, "you have been holding out on me. What is going on?"

Erin sighed. "God, Tara, I don't know. One day Luke and I were this couple, and the next day we weren't. He just totally changed! Like suddenly I was just his bud, you know? And I felt like such a fool I didn't tell you."

"You're not supposed to hold out on your best friend, you know," Tara said.

"I just felt so dumb," Erin admitted. "I know Luke liked me! I'm not crazy! It's not like I threw myself at him!"

"You're right," Tara agreed. "I'm the only one in this room who did anything like that."

"And you ended up with David," Erin said bitterly. She stood up and paced to the window. "If I only knew what happened! It's been driving me nuts. I go over and over everything in my mind. Luke and I were having coffee at the Mighty Cup. And Pete came in, and — "

"And *Pete* came in??" Tara asked incredulously. "He saw you with Pete?"

Erin nodded slowly. "Pete was all over me, too." The light was dawning. "You think that's it?"

"Is the Pope Catholic?" Tara replied. "I could have saved you days of mooning around like a sick heifer. And after that is when Noelle and Luke got together, I assume."

Erin nodded miserably. "I saw them together," she confessed. "At the Prestons'." She quickly explained about the night she had shown up, unannounced, to see Noelle. "Noelle called me a couple of times after that, but I didn't return her calls," Erin concluded.

"Whoa," Tara said, throwing herself back on Erin's bed. She stared up at the ceiling. "This is soap-opera central."

"I know Noelle didn't know about me and Luke," Erin said, "but I've been so mad at her."

"How about being mad at Luke?" Tara

suggested, sitting up again. "He's the one who kissed you and then ditched you."

"Yeah," Erin agreed faintly. "I guess."

"You guess?" Tara echoed. "Erin, you and I and Noelle are the Three Musketeers. We stick together through thick and thin. You can't let a mere *guy* come between us! You just can't!"

"I know," Erin agreed reluctantly. "But, you know, it still hurts." She gulped hard. "I mean, it still really, really hurts."

Tara hugged Erin hard. "I know."

"Pete said I had to choose between him and Luke," Erin said, wiping a tear off her cheek. "I guess the choice has been made for me already."

"Mr. Pete isn't so bad," Tara said. "I just tease you about him, you know."

"I know," Erin said. "And I haven't been very nice to him lately."

Tara handed Erin a Kleenex from the box on her dresser, and Erin blew her nose. "You ready to go face the music?" Tara asked her.

Erin nodded. "It's like Aunt Daisy said, people are tougher than they look, and I guess that includes me. Let's go."

* * *

"I'm so glad you guys are here," Noelle said, hugging Erin hard as she, Tara, and David came into the front hall of the Prestons' house.

"Me, too," Erin said, hugging her back.

"Is your family driving you loony-tunes?" Tara asked.

"Yeah," Noelle admitted. She sneaked a glance over at Luke, who was standing near the buffet table talking with Noelle's dad. "But having all of you guys here really makes it easier." She reached for David's hand. "I'm so sorry about your brother, David."

"He's going to be okay," David said. He wrapped an arm around Tara's shoulder. "I am feeling good."

"That's because I gave him an hour-long back rub last night," Tara reported. "He owes me big-time."

Noelle looked at Erin, who was staring past her at Luke. "Erin," she began hesitantly, "is everything okay? I mean — "

"Everything is okay," Erin assured her. "But I need to talk with Luke. Excuse me." She strode over to him.

"Hi," Luke said. "Today's Noelle's big day, huh?"

"Right," Erin agreed. Her heart was

pounding with nervousness, but she forced herself to keep her voice steady. "Luke, could I speak with you privately for a minute?"

An uncomfortable look flickered across his eyes. "Uh . . . sure."

"We can go to Noelle's room," Erin said. "Excuse us, Traci."

"Sure," Traci agreed, sipping her cup of coffee.

The walk to Noelle's room seemed long and endless.

And very, very silent.

"So, what's up?" Luke asked when they reached Noelle's room. He turned to face Erin.

"We haven't talked very much, have we?" Erin began nervously.

"We talk," Luke maintained.

"Not about what we need to talk about," Erin said. She took a deep breath.

Why does it have to be so hard? she wondered.

"I . . . really like you, Luke," Erin said. "And I thought that you really liked me."

"I do like you," Luke said. "Remember when I told you that you're probably the nicest girl I've ever known?"

"I remember," Erin said.

"It's still true," Luke said. "You're ter-rific."

"Then why . . . then what happened?" Erin asked, her voice catching. "I know about you and Noelle. What I don't know is why."

Luke rubbed his chin self-consciously. "I'm not very good at this stuff."

"Me, either," Erin agreed. "But I still have to know."

Luke sat down on Noelle's bed. Erin sat in the plump red-and-white-gingham-covered chair under the window. She waited.

"You and I were having fun, right?" Luke said. "But the very first day that I arrived, when I asked you about being in Love, you went on and on about Pete — remember?"

Erin nodded.

"And the more I got to know you," Luke continued, "the more I thought, 'that Pete is one lucky son-of-a-gun, 'cuz this is a great girl.' "

Erin nodded again.

"And then, at the dinner dance . . . well, I guess I forgot that there *was* a Pete. I just felt so jazzed, and we were having such a great time, and you were so terrific, and . . . well, you know."

"You kissed me," Erin said softly.

"Then the next day, I got a quick dose of reality," Luke went on. "Pete. In the flesh. Nice guy. Clearly crazy about you. And I already knew you were crazy about him — "

"But you should have asked me!" Erin cried.

"I didn't have to!" Luke shot back. "You had already told me how you felt, right? And I thought about it. I didn't have any right to come in the middle of that. I mean, it wasn't fair. So I figured I'd just chill out about us."

"Why didn't you say anything?" Erin asked plaintively. "How was I supposed to know?"

Luke scratched his chin again. "I guess I didn't think it would mean that much to you," he admitted, his face troubled.

"Well, it did," Erin admitted. "And then you and Noelle — "

"That was after I saw you and Pete together," Luke said quickly. "And . . . look, I don't want to hurt you, Erin, but . . . I've never felt about a girl before the way I feel about Noelle. I can't even put it into words."

"Do you love her?" Erin asked softly.

Luke shrugged. "We've hardly gotten to

spend any time together yet," he admitted. "But . . . from the first moment I saw her, I felt something special. And the more I get to know her, the more special it is."

The lyrics to an old song Erin's mom used to sing when she was putting the dishes in the dishwasher ran through Erin's mind. *"It hurts so bad . . . you know it hurts so bad . . ."*

"I'm sorry, Erin," Luke said. "I'm really sorry I didn't say anything. I guess I kind of wussed out. But please believe me, I never meant to hurt you."

"I know," Erin said. She willed herself not to cry. "You and Noelle have a lot in common. I can see that."

"We do," Luke agreed.

"You know, Noelle has been really sheltered by Jack," Erin began.

"Strangled is more like it," Luke put in.

"What I mean is, he hasn't let her date or anything," Erin went on. "She's never had a boyfriend before."

"She didn't tell me that," Luke admitted.

"Well, it's true," Erin said. "And she is the most terrific, kindest, coolest girl in the world, and she deserves the very best." Now she forced herself to stare Luke directly in the eye. "So I just want you to know that you have to be really, really good to her. Because if you break her heart, Luke Blakely, I'll kill you."

Luke stood up and walked over to Erin, pulling her gently to her feet. He hugged her softly. "Like I said, you are the nicest girl I ever met in my life," he told her.

"Thanks," she managed, fighting back her tears.

Someday your broken heart will mend, she promised herself. *Someday.*

Erin took Luke's hand and smiled at him. "Let's go see Noelle."

Chapter 16

"Ladies and gentlemen," the announcer intoned sonorously through the speaker system, a faint but discernible British accent coloring her words, "there will now be a fifteen-minute intermission before the long program performances of our final three competitors in the junior ladies' individual competition. Please be sure to return to your seats by nine o'clock in order that there not be an unwarranted delay. Winterfest thanks you."

The lights in the Love College hockey arena, which had been dimmed for the first three groups of skaters, went back on as all around the arena a buzz of excited conversation began. The final three skaters were Krissi Atkinson, Marie-France McDonald, from the small town of Moose Jaw,

Saskatchewan, in Canada, and, of course, Noelle Le Blanc.

Noelle was skating last.

"Almost time," Tara said to Erin.

"Why do I feel like I've spent the last two weeks with my stomach in a knot," Erin asked, "watching my friends do winter sports?"

"Because you have," David said, as he stood and stretched. "But there is nothing as intense as figure skating. Nothing."

"I'm dyin' here," Luke admitted, nervously drumming his fingers on his knee. "I'm more nervous for her than I was for me."

"I'm sure Noelle's dyin' herself," Tara mused, looking around at the huge crowd. "This is worse than a beauty pageant!"

"Of course," David said. "These women have to actually have talent."

"I thought you would be nicer, now that Ari is out of danger, but I was wrong," Tara said.

"True," David agreed, trying not to smile.

Tara gave David a cool look. "I'll have you know that in the Miss America Pageant talent counts for a major portion of the winning score."

"Oh, that's right," David said gravely. "I forgot. The one who has prepared night and day to sing 'I'm a Yankee Doodle Dandy' in a costume she sewed herself."

Tara cracked up and threw her arms around his neck. "You disgust me with every fiber of my being," she told him, and then they kissed.

Erin sneaked a look over at Luke, but he was too busy drumming his fingers and worrying about Noelle to even notice Tara and David.

So I guess everyone gets to live happily ever after, she thought to herself. *Tara and David, Noelle and Luke, Erin and Pete.*

Erin and Pete.

The thought didn't fill her with happiness, though. She closed her eyes and tried to remember the last time she and Pete had kissed so passionately that she felt as if she would die from bliss, the way she had felt kissing Luke.

It had been a very, very long time.

But maybe that's mature love, Erin mused. *Maybe that kind of thing never lasts for anyone.*

"Hey, Erin!" Tara called to her gaily. "Isn't it going to be the most hilarious thing later on tonight when Mr. David Benjamin here has to dance in front of everyone with Miss Tara Moore when she's named Queen of Winterfest?"

"I have to do that?" David asked, feigning great shock.

"Oh, shoot, you'll love it," Tara teased him. "We'll make sure we send photos of you and your beauty queen back home. Everyone will be so disappointed in you!"

"You're only going to win if Buxom Bixom didn't stuff the ballot boxes," Erin told Tara. "And I wouldn't put it past her."

"I can be a gracious runner-up, if called upon to do so," Tara said regally, her arms around David's neck. She kissed him on the cheek. "Some things are much more important, you know."

Winterfest is almost over, Erin realized. *Just women's junior skating finals and then the midnight closing ceremonies and party on the Love town square.*

Erin stared out at the ice, now being groomed by a large machine. The junior figure skating competition was the hardest ticket to come by in all of Winterfest, harder even than the senior women's figure skating. That's because, as Noelle had explained to Erin and Tara many times, the trend in figure skating judging had been, for several years, to reward the smaller, thinner, younger skaters at the expense of those who had gone through full puberty and were now truly young women.

"That's why Jack wants me to be so thin," Noelle had told them, even before Winterfest had gotten under way. "In a competition between a great junior and a great senior, the great junior wins every time. And the great junior gets to go to the Olympics."

"But that's not fair," Erin had countered. "The senior skaters have so much more experience."

Noelle had laughed and hugged Erin hard. "That's what I love about you, Erin," she had said. "You still think the world is fair."

"Well, it should be," Erin had grumbled.

"The world of skating hasn't ever been fair," Noelle had said with a shrug. "And that's the only world I know."

Now each seat in the five thousand–seat hockey arena was filled. Erin had heard that people were scalping their tickets for fifty dollars each outside the arena.

And if it weren't for the fact that Tara and I are on the organizing committee, I don't even know if we'd be here, she thought.

She looked down at the white program she'd been handed when she came into the hockey arena.

It says it all, she thought, rereading the program notes on the inside front page.

JUNIOR WOMEN'S SKATING TRUE TO FORM; ATKINSON AND LE BLANC LEAD AFTER ORIGINAL PROGRAM

Seventeen-year-old skater Krissi Atkinson, from Le Soeur, Minnesota, and local favorite Noelle Le Blanc led the field of skaters coming out of this afternoon's original program. Also joining them in the final group of three skaters performing tonight is fifteen-year-old Marie-France McDonald, from Moose Jaw, Saskatchewan, competing for the first time at Winterfest.

Atkinson, who skated her original program to music from Disney's *The Lion King,* led Le Blanc by a mere tenth of a point at the end of the original program. Le Blanc's performance, to Paul Desmond's jazz standard "Take Six," brought the hometown crowd to its feet, but Atkinson seemed to make a stronger impression on one of the judges, Constance Connolly, who gave the Minnesota skater a grade of 5.9, as opposed to her 5.8 for Le Blanc.

McDonald also skated well, and seems a shoo-in for the bronze medal, unless Atkinson or Le Blanc are to falter badly in tonight's competition.

Erin looked up when Tara ran her hand back and forth on the open page in front of her, blocking her from reading any more.

"Check out Noelle's family," Tara instructed her, motioning with her chin across the arena. "Her dad looks as nervous as a rooster in the henhouse."

David laughed. "That is one of your better quaint southern expressions, Tara," he told her.

Erin looked across the ice, which had been painted a magnificent white with the words WINTERFEST X written in dramatic red script across it, to where Noelle's family was ensconced in a box fifteen rows behind the judges' scoring tables.

Noelle's mom was eating a huge pink cotton candy, and her dad was standing up, pacing, while he drank beer from an enormous, 32-ounce green paper cup. Aunt Gussie was brushing Claire's hair, and little Buddy was standing on his seat, jumping up and down.

"I know her family is kind of wacky," Luke said, "but they are totally behind her, which is cool, you know?"

"Must be nice," Tara said lightly. "My mother never comes to my pageants."

Way over to the left, at one end of the hockey arena, a bunch of preteen girls — maybe forty or fifty, all dressed in white, each with a pink heart painted on her right cheek — suddenly broke into song, to the melody of "The Song That Never Ends" from the kids' TV show, the "Shari Lewis Show":

We're Krissi's Kids through thick and thin!
Oh yes we hope that she will win!
We'll go anywhere to watch her
If it's hot or if it's cold
And if you want to know just what we want
It's her Olympic gold . . .

Over and over and over.

Through all of this, they waved banners and held up signs that said "KRISSI'S KIDS!"

314

"I say we get us a bunch of really gooey pies and pie those little darlings," Tara said sweetly. "That would shut 'em up."

We're Krissi's Kids through thick and thin! Oh yes we hope that she will win . . .

"Doesn't that song ever end?" Luke groaned.

"Hope," Erin replied. She'd heard Krissi's Kids sing that song for what seemed like hours at other skating events in which Noelle had competed.

"You know, y'all," Tara drawled, a devious glint in her eye, "we could just slip over there, erase the apostrophe in their signs, and their little signs would read 'KRISSI SKIDS!' "

"You are a sick and demented person," David said to her with a laugh. "I like that in a woman."

The arena lights dimmed suddenly, indicating that the competition was going to resume soon. Krissi's Kids treated it as a cue to turn their volume up a notch.

We're Krissi's Kids through thick and thin! Oh yes we hope that she will win . . .

"Ladies and gentlemen," the British voice intoned through the sound system, "please return to your seats, please return to your seats."

Krissi's Kids finished one last rousing round of their song, and then some adult — also dressed in white with a pink heart on her cheek — shepherded them all to their seats.

"Ladies and gentlemen," the announcer said, "welcome to the final round of skaters in the women's junior competition. Please welcome, from Moose Jaw, Saskatchewan, Marie-France McDonald!"

Marie-France McDonald skated out to warm applause from the audience. She was just a wisp of a girl, no more than four feet eight, no more than eighty pounds. She wore an emerald green skating outfit with ruffles that accented her tiny stature, and a matching green ruffled ribbon around her short, dirty-blond bob.

Marie-France skated smoothly to the Beatles' "Here, There and Everywhere," segueing into "Yellow Submarine." Her jumps were high, light, and miraculous.

"She's really, really good," Erin whispered nervously to Tara.

But she fell on a daring triple axel not

more than twenty-five seconds into her program. And then she fell again, a minute later, on a triple lutz. And though she concluded her program strongly, she was in no position to challenge either Krissi or Noelle, if they skated as expected. Her scores were mostly 5.7s and 5.8s, both for technical merit and artistic impression.

"Call me a bad sport," Luke said, wiping nervous perspiration from his brow, "but when she fell, I wanted to cheer."

The lights came up for five minutes, and then they went back down again. Then the announcement came:

"Ladies and gentlemen, please welcome, from Le Soeur, Minnesota, Krissi Atkinson!"

Krissi's Kids went wild, clapping, screaming and cheering, and the rest of the audience gave Krissi an enthusiastic round of applause. The Kids began to throw dozens of pink roses on the ice, which tuxedoed ushers skated out to gather.

"Please," Tara prayed, "don't start that song again or I will have to come over there and wring your darling little necks."

Krissi, meanwhile, delayed her entrance until the last possible second. Then she stepped out into the spotlight that had been focused on the entrance to the ice.

There was an audible intake of breath from the audience, and then they applauded again.

"She's perfect-looking," Erin breathed.

"She's okay," Luke commented.

"She's a witch," Tara snapped, as Krissi skated out on the ice for a few warm-up laps.

"That costume," Erin said, leaning forward in her seat. "It's just so unbelievably beautiful!"

"That's not the one we saw," Tara said.

"I guess this one was behind that one," Erin said.

Krissi's outfit was, of course, all white. But this costume was a series of sheer, gossamer layers of chiffon, each overlapping the last, so that when Krissi skated it appeared as if her dress was somehow skating with her. The tiniest rhinestones had been sewn into the hem of the skirt, as well as being scattered throughout the material. White, rhinestone-studded ribbons tied back Krissi's long, white-blond hair, and other rhinestones were somehow suspended in her hair. The bright lights of the arena glinted off the rhinestones. And on the very corner of the hem of the second layer of white chiffon was Krissi's trademark — the tiniest pink heart.

Krissi was a fairy princess come to life.

"I hope she belches really loud when she does her first arabesque," Tara said.

The others were too nervous to laugh. They just sat with their hands clenched and watched.

Now Krissi was ready to skate. She stood at center ice, her hands above her head like a ballerina, as her music began.

Krissi was skating to an old song from the 1940s, "Boogie Woogie Bugle Boy," that featured lots of trumpet flourishes and upbeat sections.

And, even Tara had to admit, she skated brilliantly.

Her program neatly mixed dance steps with several double jumps, including a difficult double axel/triple toe loop combination. And Krissi shone all the way through, her characteristic broad smile never leaving her face.

"Watch what she does when she skates by the judges," Tara hissed to Erin. "Her smile is extra big and fake."

"Did she just *wink* at them??" Erin asked incredulously. "You're not allowed to wink! Are you?"

Krissi's fast, sassy music segued into the final strains of the slow and dramatic Andrew Lloyd Webber hit from the Broadway musical *Cats,* "Memory."

As the final haunting notes rang out, Krissi finished with a spectacular layback spin, her blond hair whipping around and around as her head and shoulders dropped backward and her back arched.

The song ended, and Krissi lay, a perfect white flower, on the ice.

The crowd cheered. Krissi's Kids threw more pink roses onto the ice. Krissi gracefully got to her feet, bowing to everyone and blowing kisses to the crowd. Then she skated over toward her Kids and hugged one of them, who leaned especially far over the barrier that separated spectators from the ice.

"She knows how to play the crowd, that's for sure," Luke sighed. He ran his hand over his face.

"She only did two triples," David pointed out.

"Let's see her scores," Erin said tensely. "It's not over yet."

As if the judges had heard Erin's cue, the scores were posted on the scoreboard, to thunderous applause from the crowd.

5.9 5.9 5.9 5.9 5.8 5.8 5.9 5.9

Mostly 5.9s on the scale of 1 to 6, Erin thought, *but there were two 5.8s! And Connolly gave her a 5.8!*

Then, Krissi's scores for artistic impression were posted, to more applause.

ARTISTIC IMPRESSION
5.9 5.9 5.9 5.9 5.8 5.8 5.9 5.9

Krissi came out to the edge of the rink, smiling broadly, and waved happily to the crowd, blowing more kisses.

"Can Noelle beat that?" Erin asked nervously.

No one answered her. Because they all knew how tough it would be.

"She can still do it," Luke finally said. "It's not impossible."

"The long program counts twice as much as the short program," David said. "If she gets all five-nines, she wins."

"She can do it," Erin breathed. "I know she can. I just know it!"

The lights went up to indicate another five-minute intermission before Noelle would skate — the last skater of the competition.

"This waiting is the worst," Luke said.

"Hey you guys," said a voice from behind them.

They all turned around. It was Traci, dressed in a conservative skirt and a blue sport jacket, with official Winterfest credentials hanging around her neck. Traci was helping out behind the scenes at the skating competition.

"Hey," Tara said to her. "You ready to watch our girl win?"

"I have to talk to you guys," Traci said instead of answering. Her face looked pinched and anxious.

"What's wrong?" Erin asked.

"It's Noelle . . ." Traci began, then she hesitated.

Luke grabbed Traci's arm. "Something happened to Noelle?"

"Oh, God," Traci muttered. "I promised I wouldn't say anything. She'll hate me forever."

"What is it?" Erin demanded. "You have to tell us."

"I swore to Noelle I wouldn't say anything," Traci said, her voice low and tense. "But . . . some things are more important than your word."

"Look, you're scaring the hell out of us,"

Tara said. "So just spit it out!"

Traci bit her lower lip, a million conflicting emotions skidding across her face. Then, finally, she spoke.

"Noelle went to the doctor," Traci began, "before Winterfest. She went to see Jack's doctor. Because she was feeling weak, and couldn't catch her breath — "

"She never told us anything about this!" Erin exclaimed.

"I know that," Traci agreed. "I'm the only one she told." Now that she'd started, the words just poured out of Traci's mouth.

"The doctor said that she had a heart murmur, but that she could compete, and that she should maybe eat more," Traci said nervously.

"She doesn't eat anything," Luke said, his brow furrowed. "She lives on air!"

"I know that," Traci agreed. "Anyway . . . I knew she had to be really bad off to tell me about it, and I could see that she wasn't herself, you know? So I checked it out with my mom at the medical center, and . . . what Noelle has can be dangerous! I mean really dangerous!"

"Oh, God," Luke groaned.

"I saw her in practice this week, and she still couldn't catch her breath," Traci continued, her voice hurried and anxious, "and just now, I saw her downstairs, waiting to skate, and . . . she looks terrible. I tried to talk to her, but she just waved me off."

"Didn't she tell Jack?" Luke demanded.

"Of course not," Traci replied. "You know how Noelle is. She'd never tell him."

"But she can't skate if there's something wrong with her heart!" Luke protested. "We have to stop her!"

"How can we?" Traci asked. "We can't make her not skate! God, I shouldn't have let it get this far."

"I have to go talk to her — " Luke said. He began to move past Erin to get out of the bleachers.

"I'm coming, too," Erin said.

Now all of them were on their feet, ready to head down to Noelle.

But it was too late. The lights dimmed in the arena, and the woman with the British accent was back on the public address system.

"Ladies and gentlemen," the announcer said, "we shall now have our final skater of the competition. Please welcome, from Love, Michigan, Noelle Le Blanc!"

Noelle's friends just stood there, feeling helpless.

It was too late to stop Noelle.

Finally, silently, they sat back down.

Traci gave them a long, pained look, and then she hurried away.

The arena cheered and screamed out their support for Noelle, the local favorite.

Erin looked at Tara. "She's probably okay," she said. "She probably just hasn't been eating enough."

"I could kill Jack Preston," Luke growled. "I'd like to put my fist through his face."

Now some local kids from Love were throwing flowers out onto the ice for Noelle. They were mostly carnations, and there weren't nearly as many flowers as there had been for Krissi.

Noelle skated into the light and assumed her opening pose.

"She doesn't look sick," Tara whispered hopefully.

"Maybe she ate a candy bar or something," Erin said. "That would help, right?"

"God, she's beautiful," Luke breathed.

She is, Erin had to agree. *Even if I do still wish Luke felt that way about me, instead of Noelle.*

Noelle had on a red velvet costume, simple except for its dramatic coloring. It appeared to be sleeveless and strapless, but

Erin knew there was really nude mesh material that went all the way up to Noelle's neckline, material that was sheer enough so that it couldn't be seen by the audience. The skirt was assymetrical — longer on one side than on the other — with tiny, delicate white seed pearls sewn around the border. Noelle usually skated with her hair in a bun, but now she had put only the front up, away from her face, and the back fell in lovely, dark waves around her shoulders.

Please be okay, Erin prayed.

She looked over at Tara, whose eyes were closed.

Tara opened them and gave Erin the smallest smile. "I seem to pray a lot more than I used to," she whispered to her friend.

Without speaking, the foursome reached out for one another, clasping hands as Noelle's music, Ravel's *Bolero,* began.

The music was slow, haunting, sensual, and that was exactly the way Noelle skated. In contrast to Krissi's all-white image on the ice, Noelle was dramatic and vivid, a vision in scarlet.

Jack and Sandi Preston stood just off the ice. Jack's arms were folded, and Sandi's were clasped around her body. Both of them had looks of utter concentration on their faces, as if, through sheer force of will alone, they could help Noelle skate the perfect program she would need to beat Krissi Atkinson for the gold medal.

Fifteen seconds into her program, she nailed a triple axel, and the crowd cheered.

Forty-five seconds later, she unleashed a triple toe loop combination.

Perfection, and more loud cheers from the crowd. A double salchow, followed by a triple lutz. Magnificent.

"God, she's so amazing," Luke breathed.

"Her program is tougher than Krissi's," David whispered with excitement.

Halfway through her four-minute, twenty-second program, the music swelled dramatically. And though it didn't seem possible, Noelle's skating grew stronger and surer — whirling, spinning, jumping. Each move seemed to give her more confidence and fuel her energy and her courage.

She was breathtaking perfection.

Thirty seconds to go now. Erin's hand clenched Tara's so tightly that circulation was cut off, but neither girl noticed.

A sit spin, one leg extended, as the recorded sounds of the Orchestre de Paris brought the music full circle, for one more go at the main melody.

And then, the dramatic conclusion. Noelle had told her friends all about it. She, Jack, and Sandi had decided before Winterfest that they were going to go for broke — actually, Jack and Sandi had decided this. Noelle was going to unleash that most difficult of jumps, a triple axel, with fifteen seconds left in her program.

She would be exhausted. She would be gulping air. No other junior woman did a triple axel that late in her program. If she failed, she would lose.

But if she succeeded, after nailing all her other jumps, she would win the gold.

OLYMPIC GOLD MEDAL, Erin recalled the words of Jack's handmade sign in Noelle's trophy case. IF IT'S NOT HERE, ALL THE OTHERS AREN'T WORTH DOODLY-SQUAT.

Go, Noelle, she urged her silently. *Go for the gold.*

Bolero swelled. Noelle turned backwards, and turned forward again, launching into the axel.

Her friends held their collective breaths. The arena held its collective breath.

Yes. Her takeoff was letter-perfect.

Noelle spun around in midair, one, two, three and a half times.

It was a triple axel of such perfection, so late in an incredibly difficult program, that people who witnessed it would talk about it for years to come.

And now there was only the landing.

Noelle was in perfect position, ready to touch down on her right blade, to skate the final few beats and spin her final spin to the glory of the gold.

Only it didn't happen.

Noelle's right blade touched down, and then, almost in slow motion, Noelle simply crumpled and fell to the ice, a shapeless rag doll, a tiny figure in ruby red velvet, who slid across the ice on her stomach, landing in a heap, lifeless.

"Oh my God!" Luke cried, jumping to his feet.

Erin and Tara held on to each other, feeling too stunned and sick to even cry.

Jack Preston and other officials were on the ice heading for Noelle as the audience watched in horrified shock and the final notes of *Bolero* played on.

Then, one horrified voice cried out. It was Noelle's mother, Shirley White.

"Noelle!" she screamed, as she ran down the aisle stairs toward the ice. "Oh, God, my baby!!!"

But Noelle couldn't hear her mother's cries.

She couldn't hear a thing.

Chapter 17

"Dr. Williams, Dr. Williams," a soft, disembodied voice called over the public address system of the medical center. "Dr. Thomas Williams, dial four-six-four, Dr. Williams, four-six-four."

The voice calling for Dr. Williams echoed through the jammed emergency room waiting area.

It was almost midnight, and though the waiting area was full, everyone was silent. No one had come out to tell them about Noelle's condition yet.

Noelle's entire family was there, and Jack and Sandi Preston, Erin, Tara, Luke, David, Traci, and a large delegation of officials from the Winterfest organizing committee. There were even a couple of newspaper reporters who'd sensed a story.

They'd all been standing around or sitting around, waiting for news about Noelle. Any news. Only there hadn't been any news for an hour and a half now. The only thing that they'd been told — and that was right after they'd all streamed into the emergency room — was that Noelle was alive, that she'd regained consciousness during the ambulance ride from the skating rink to the medical center, and that she was now undergoing tests.

"It might well be a long wait," a senior nurse had announced to the hushed room. "So I suggest you just sit down and be patient. The doctors are working as fast as they can."

The medical center had tried to accommodate the huge crowd by adding extra folding chairs in the waiting room so that people wouldn't have to stand, and by putting out a few pots of coffee and some stale cookies left over from a recent New Year's get-together, but no one in the room was taking anything.

Erin looked at her watch for perhaps the twentieth time. It was only ten minutes later than the last time she had checked.

"This is my fault, you know," Traci said, twisting a Kleenex between her fingers. "I should have said something. I shouldn't have promised her."

"You can't blame yourself," Erin told her. "You didn't know anything was really wrong."

"I suspected," Traci said. "Why did I listen to her? Why?"

"Noelle was the one who had to decide," David told her gently. "Not you."

"He's right," Tara told Traci. "Now, let's just concentrate on Noelle's getting well, okay?"

More endless minutes ticked by. Luke paced. Noelle's mother sniffled into a Kleenex. Aunt Gussie kept shushing Buddy, who wanted to go in and see his big sister.

Erin checked her watch again, just for something to do. "It's after midnight," she told Tara softly.

Tara nodded, her face tense.

"It seems so bizarre," Erin went on. "I mean, out there Winterfest is continuing, I suppose. Everyone is at the celebration in the square, and they're announcing the Queen — "

"And it all seems utterly unimportant," Tara concluded.

Erin nodded. "That's what I was thinking, too." She gave Tara a sad smile. "I guess you're going to miss your own coronation."

"Honestly, Erin," Tara said, "right now I couldn't care less."

"She's got to be okay," Luke muttered. His face was pinched and completely white. "What is taking them so long?"

"Maybe she just fainted from lack of food," Erin reasoned. "She hardly ate anything at all over the last two weeks."

"I knew he was starving her," Traci said, rocking back and forth in her chair. "I knew about everything, and I didn't do anything to stop it."

"Traci, you have to quit blaming yourself!" Erin told her firmly. "It doesn't help, you know!"

"I was the only one who knew . . ." Traci continued, seemingly unable to stop her litany of regret. "I was the only one — "

"That's bull," Luke snapped. "Jack knew. Sandi knew. They're responsible for this. They just cared more about making her into a champion than they cared about her, and we all know it."

"Shhhh," Tara hissed, looking over at Noelle's family. "There's no point in accusations now, and you'll just upset her family even more."

"Dr. Raggio, Dr. Raggio," the voice on the P.A. system called. "Dr. Tanya Raggio, dial three-eight-one, Dr. Raggio, three-eight-one."

Erin looked over at Jack, who was standing by the nurses' station, as if that would speed the flow of information coming out of the area where the doctors were now working on Noelle. The always-in-control Jack Preston was biting his fingernails down to the quick.

"I can't stand this anymore!" Noelle's father yelled, throwing his hands up in the air. "I want to hear some news already!"

Outside a siren grew louder and louder as it approached the emergency entrance, then cut off suddenly. A bunch of people in green hospital scrubs ran toward the emergency entrance as the doors swung open, and two paramedics in white uniforms rolled a portable stretcher-on-wheels through the emergency room doors.

"Make way, people," one of the doctors shouted to the big crowd in the emergency room.

It was an unconscious man who seemed

to be in his twenties. He was bleeding profusely from a wound on his head.

Erin shuddered. So did Tara.

No one said a word.

The doctors and paramedics wheeled the new patient into the emergency room itself, one of the paramedics holding an intravenous drip into the patient up in the air. The waiting area doors closed with a whoosh of air.

It's like a movie, Erin thought. *Only now it's real.*

"Excuse me, ladies and gentlemen?"

Erin and her friends turned toward the nurses' station, where the same severe-looking senior nurse who'd spoken with them earlier now stood, holding a clipboard.

"Ladies and gentlemen," she said, looking down at a paper on her board, "the doctors are ready to see you concerning Noelle Le Blanc."

Erin and Tara looked at each other nervously. Their hearts pounded.

"Oh, God," Noelle's mother moaned, clutching at her sister. "Oh, God."

The nurse looked back down at her piece of paper. "Would Jack and Sandi Preston,

Jimmy and Shirley White, and Gussie Larson," the nurse intoned, "please follow me to the first-floor conference room, where you'll be meeting with Dr. Westfall and Dr. Raggio."

"Is my baby okay?" Noelle's mother cried, lumbering to her feet.

"The doctor will give you all the information," the head nurse said smoothly.

"I wanna see Noelle!" Buddy whined, pulling on his mother's sleeve.

"I'll watch the kids for you," a nursing assistant said, quickly coming around the nurses' desk.

"I'll be back soon, honey," Mrs. White said, patting Buddy absently. "Stay with Claire now."

Then the head nurse looked back down at her sheet of paper. "And would Erin Kellerman, Tara Moore, Traci Campbell, and David Benjamin please follow Nurse Goldner?"

The nurse pointed quickly to a much younger nurse, in her early twenties, who was standing several feet to her right.

"Noelle can see you now, in her room," the senior nurse continued.

Erin and Tara looked at each other in

shock. They hadn't expected this. *Was this because Noelle was actually well enough to have visitors already?*

Or are we saying good-bye? Erin wondered, a terrible lump in her throat.

Erin and Tara got up and hurried toward the younger nurse, David close behind.

"Hey!" Luke called.

They turned around.

"What about me?" His face was a mixture of disbelief, pain, and sorrow.

The nurse looked down at her sheet of paper. "Who are you?"

"Luke Blakely," he said, and his voice sounded small and fragile. "She . . . she didn't want to see me?" Luke's eyes filled with tears.

The nurse scanned her paper again. "Ah, my mistake," she admitted. "You're on the list. Right this way."

Mr. and Mrs. White, Aunt Gussie, and Jack and Sandi Preston filed into the first-floor conference room. The nurse closed the door behind them.

Dr. Westfall was the same cardiologist Noelle had seen before Winterfest. With him was a plump African-American doctor in her early forties, with short hair and horn-rimmed glasses. Both were sitting on one side of the long conference table.

Dr. Westfall nodded at the Whites and the Prestons as they entered. The woman doctor was poker-faced.

"Have a seat, please," Dr. Westfall said, his voice somber.

The Prestons and the Whites immediately took seats across from them, along the length of the wooden table. Directly overhead, an array of fluorescent lights bathed them all in harsh light, and along the far wall, there were images from a magnetic resonance imaging machine backlit by a white, lighted board.

"I'm Dr. Paul Westfall," he said. "I'm the chief of cardiology — "

"What's that?" Aunt Gussie asked.

"Hearts," Dr. Westfall said, unaccustomed to being interrupted. "I'm a heart doctor. And this is Dr. Raggio. She is also a heart doctor, specializing in surgery."

Noelle's mother gripped her sister's arm with one hand and held her husband's hand with the other.

"So, Paul, let's cut to the chase," Jack said briskly. "How's my skater?"

"Not as good as when we saw her before," Dr. Westfall admitted, a tense tick appearing in the corner of his mouth.

"You saw her before?" Aunt Gussie asked, her voice tremulous.

"Gussie, can it," Noelle's father barked at his sister-in-law.

"I will *not* can it!" Aunt Gussie retorted. "This doctor just said he's seen Noelle before! Did you know about that?"

"Well, no," Shirley White said, shredding another Kleenex between her fingers. "Noelle never said anything, but I'm sure if it was serious, Jack would have — "

"May I please continue?" Dr. Westfall interrupted, his voice steely.

"Yeah, continue," Aunt Gussie said, her voice hard.

"Jack," Dr. Westfall said, again addressing his words to the coach, "I'm going to give it to you straight. She's got an atrial septal defect. It doesn't look good."

"What the hell is that?" Jack answered.

Here, Dr. Raggio spoke up for the first time. "It's a hole in her heart," she said, "between the two upper chambers."

"So, wait," Aunt Gussie said, "how come you didn't already know about this thing?"

Dr. Westfall's face tensed. "It's not always detectable. I saw no signs of it before."

"But it was there before, that's what you're saying," Gussie continued doggedly.

Dr. Westfall took off his glasses and rubbed the bridge of his nose between his eyebrows. "What I'm saying is that this did not show up on the earlier echocardiogram," he explained. "I'm sorry, but that happens sometimes. But here it is, on the MRI. Clear as day."

He got up out of his seat and walked over to the computer-generated pictures on the far wall, taking a long pointer and raising it to one of the pictures.

There it was, clear as day. A hole.

"It's called an ASD, Jack," Dr. Westfall said. "Usually there're no symptoms until puberty, when the body puts some extra demands on the heart."

"It gets worse over time," Dr. Raggio added gravely. "It can be fatal if not treated."

Dr. Westfall shot the other doctor a warning look. "You get intolerant to exercise, you get irregular heart rhythms, et cetera, et cetera."

"Like Noelle," Jack muttered, hitting himself in the head. "Good God, there's my gold medal down the tubes! Unless . . . what do we do to fix her up?"

"I recommend surgery," Dr. Raggio said. "It's her best chance."

"Or we might be able to patch it up with a cardiac catheter," Dr. Westfall added. "It depends."

"That sounds better," Jack said, "less invasive, she'll be over all this sooner, right?"

The doctors were silent.

"She can skate again, can't she?" Jack demanded. "Can't she?"

"She's gotta skate," Jimmy White added.

Everyone stared at the doctors.

"Tough to say," Dr. Westfall mumbled, unwilling to meet Jack's eyes.

"From my point of view, it's lunacy," the heart surgeon said distinctly. "She shouldn't have been able to skate now. I'm amazed, frankly."

" 'Cuz my girl has heart," Jimmy White said. "She's a champion."

"She never should have been out there!" Aunt Gussie exclaimed.

"Maybe that cath thing you said could fix her up," Shirley White said hopefully. "In time to train for the Olympics. Right, Jack?" She looked over at Jack Preston, hoping for an encouraging look back from him.

"Bottom line," Noelle's father said, "how

long before my kid can skate again?"

"I don't know if you hear what we are saying — " Dr. Raggio began.

"We would have won tonight," Noelle's mother said, desperation in her voice. "We beat Krissi Atkinson. Even her snooty parents knew it. I saw the looks on their faces. We had it won, right, Jack?"

"Hey, she'll get it back," Noelle's dad insisted, his voice too loud. "We don't worry about Noelle, right, Jack? We call her E.T. down at the bar, for 'extra tough.' She'll be back. Right, Jack?"

"It's gonna take work," Jack began. "A lot of work."

"We can do it," Shirley insisted.

"Just tell us what we need to do," Jimmy added.

"Excuse me, people," Dr. Raggio said, "you must listen to what I am saying — "

"How about if you listen to what *I'm* saying?" Aunt Gussie bellowed, her face red, her eyes narrow slits of anger.

Everyone stopped talking, and stared at her. She stared right back at her sister and brother-in-law.

"Jimmy, Shirl, listen to yourselves. Your little girl is lying in this hospital, five minutes away from dying, practically, and you're talking about whether she's going to skate again!"

Jimmy and Shirley White just looked at her blankly.

"This is little Noelle," Aunt Gussie said, her voice full of pain. "This isn't some . . . some horse you bet on at the track! She ain't a robot! She ain't your toy! And she sure as hell ain't *your* damned gold medal!"

Now Gussie turned to Jack, staring him dead in the eye.

"She's spent her whole life on them skates, Jack Preston," Gussie said. "She would die rather than disappoint you — " Now she turned to Jimmy and Shirley. "Any of you. And tonight, she almost did. So I'm suggesting you stop acting like a couple of idiots and start acting like the parents you are, and I'm suggesting you start right about now."

"Well put," Dr. Raggio said in a low voice. "Now — "

"And you, Jack Preston," Gussie said, turning back to Noelle's coach. "I don't know who's worse, Jimmy and Shirley or you. Now, I made all those skating costumes for Noelle, and I've put every single cent I could afford into helping to pay for your coaching, and coming to see Noelle skate all these years. I believed in you, just as much as Jimmy and Shirley done."

Gussie took a deep breath, her massive chest heaving, and then she continued.

"I would never, *never* imagine that you'd take Noelle to the doctor without calling Jimmy and Shirley first. No, sir, Mr. Man. Just because you act like you walk on water doesn't mean that you're allowed to play God."

The room was silent for a long moment. Gussie stared hard at her sister and brother-in-law.

Finally, Jimmy stood up. "Doctors," he said, slowly and with dignity. "When can we see our daughter? You haven't told her any of this yet, have you?"

"No," Dr. Westfall said. "We haven't."

"Good," Jimmy replied, brushing his hair back off his face. He stood up straight and tall. "Because this father needs to be there when you do."

"Noelle?"

Erin leaned over the hospital bed. The others were gathered around, too, staring at the tiny, white-faced figure in the hospital bed. Noelle's eyes were closed, and an intravenous needle was stuck in the back of her right hand, leading to a plastic bag filled with clear fluid that slowly dripped into the line.

Noelle's eyes flickered open.

"Hey," Tara whispered.

Noelle blinked twice. "What were my scores?" she croaked out.

They all laughed tension-filled laughter.

"Straight sixes, as far as we're concerned," Luke said.

"I would have won," Noelle whispered hoarsely.

"Shhh, don't try to talk," Erin said, a huge lump in her throat.

Noelle's eyes closed, then flickered open again. "Wh . . . what's wrong with me?"

"No one told us anything yet," Erin said. "Your parents are with the doctors."

"Everyone must be . . . so mad at me," Noelle said faintly.

"No one is mad at you," Tara said firmly.

"I let everyone down," Noelle said. "Jack is going to hate me."

"You should have eaten more of my candy bars," Traci said, trying not to sound as desperate as she felt.

"Yeah," Noelle said, "guess I messed up." She closed her eyes again. "So tired . . ."

"We should let you rest," David said.

Noelle's eyes sprang open. "No, don't go." She managed to smile. "I'm just run down, I'll bet. Just . . . you know . . . tired . . . that's all." She looked around for Luke. "Luke?"

"I'm right here," he said, stepping forward to take her hand.

"I guess I look pretty awful now, huh?" She smiled faintly.

"You're beautiful, Noelle," Luke said huskily.

"Noelle?"

It was Dr. Westfall, standing in the doorway. With him were Noelle's parents. No one else.

Luke moved slightly away from the bed. "I'm still here," he whispered to her reassuringly.

Dr. Westfall and Noelle's parents walked into the room.

"How's my dollface?" Noelle's father said tenderly, stroking his daughter's hair off her face.

"I'm fine," Noelle said. "Just a little tired. "I'm . . . so sorry I messed up. Where's Jack?"

"He'll see you later," Noelle's mom said. "We asked him to wait."

Dr. Westfall looked around at Noelle's friends. "Perhaps you would all like to go back to the waiting area," he said.

"No," Noelle said sharply, her voice breathless. "I want them to stay."

"All right," Dr. Westfall said. He pulled a chair up to Noelle's bed. "Well, Noelle, you've had a rough time."

"I just fainted, is all," Noelle said. "It's nothing, right?"

Dr. Westfall cleared his throat. "I'm afraid, honey, that it's something. You have what is called ASD, Noelle. What it means, basically, is that there is a small hole in your heart."

"A . . . a hole?" Noelle echoed fearfully.

"Right," Dr. Westfall said. "We're going to need to correct it. We have a couple of options for that, which we'll discuss when you're feeling a little stronger."

"But . . . I can skate again, right?" Noelle asked.

The room was deadly silent.

"Dr. Westfall, can I skate?" Noelle asked, her eyes huge in her white face. "Please, please, I have to skate . . ."

"We'll just have to take this one day at a time," Dr. Westfall said, clearly uncomfortable. "First we'll get you in better shape, then we'll decide on treatment, then — "

"You're not answering my question!" Noelle cried in anger and disbelief. "Answer me!"

Everyone looked at Dr. Westfall.

"I don't know," he mumbled, looking down at his hands.

"You didn't say no," Noelle began.

"Noelle, you must be realistic about this — " the doctor began.

"I *will* skate again," Noelle said fiercely. "I'll do everything you tell me to do to get better. And then I'll train again. I can do it . . ." She looked beyond the doctor, to her mother. "I will, Mom. I won't let you all down. I promise."

Noelle was breathless from exertion. Her head fell back on the bed.

"Oh, my baby girl," Noelle's mother said, rushing to her daughter. "You could never let us down! If you never put on a pair of skates again, we would love you just the same. My baby . . ."

Jimmy White rushed to the other side of his daughter's bed. Then both of Noelle's parents carefully wrapped their arms around their daughter, and the three of them rocked together and cried for the loss of their dream.

Chapter 18

I don't think I've ever been this tired in my life, Erin thought, as she lay her head back on the ugly orange plastic chair in the waiting room.

Noelle's parents were still with her in her room, as were Gussie and Claire. Even Buddy had been allowed in for a few minutes. Noelle had sent out word that she wanted to see her friends again, one more time, and so they were waiting.

"There's Dr. Westfall," Erin said, as she watched the doctor hurry over to Jack and Sandi.

"Y'all, I'm listening in on that conversation," Tara decided. "I don't trust him."

Tara marched over to the doctor and stood there, her arms folded.

"Can I help you, young lady?" the doctor asked, his tone cold.

"I want to hear whatever you have to say to Jack and Sandi," Tara said.

Now Erin, Traci, Luke, and David hurried across the room, too.

"So do we," Luke agreed in a steely voice.

"This is a private conversation," Dr. Westfall said, his voice cold.

"Not anymore, it isn't," Erin said. "Were you lying when you told her you didn't know if she could skate again? Because I got this feeling that you were lying to her."

"Noelle is in no shape now to hear that she will never skate again," Dr. Westfall snapped.

"So it's really over?" Jack asked wearily. "After all these years, it's just . . . over?"

"I'm not telling you it's impossible," Dr. Westfall said. "Doctors talk in terms of probability, Jack. Noelle will *probably* never skate again. I'm sorry."

"She knows," Tara said, her voice low.

"She couldn't know," Dr. Westfall said. "I didn't tell her."

"She knows anyway," Tara insisted. "If we could tell that you weren't telling her everything, then she could tell, too."

Dr. Westfall rubbed the bridge of his nose again. "I'm sorry. I wish I had better news for her. If the surgery goes well, it's possible that she could have a reasonably long and nearly normal life . . ." His voice petered out.

"I'm sorry," he said again, and then he hurried away.

"What a night," Jack said, shaking his head. He turned to Sandi. "We ought to let her rest, we'll see her tomorrow."

"But she'll feel terrible if you don't see her!" Erin cried. "She'll be so sure that she disappointed you."

Jack gave Erin a long look. "What do you want me to say, kid?" he asked, his voice harsh. "I put years into that girl, all my time, all my hard work, all my dreams . . . and now . . . pfffft! Like that, all gone."

Luke walked up to Jack and stood so close to him that their chests were practically touching. "You make me sick, you know that?" Luke said, his voice dripping with disgust.

"News flash," Jack said bitterly. "I don't give a tinker's damn what you think." He grabbed Sandi's arm. "Come on, we're outta here."

Jack and Sandi hurried to the exit.

"She's going to feel so terrible," Erin cried. "I can't believe — "

"I can," Traci said. "Jack just lost his gold medal. And that's all he's ever cared about."

At that moment the doors to the emergency room swung open, and Nellie Bixom hurried in. She was wearing her formal — apple green chiffon and black velvet, cut halfway down to her navel in front. Over that she had her unzipped purple ski parka, clearly thrown on in haste. In her arms were a dozen long-stemmed red roses.

And with her — to Erin's utter shock — was Pete Cole.

All Erin could do was stare at him.

"How's Noelle?" Nellie asked breathlessly.

"She'll live," Tara said, eyeing the odd couple.

"Thank God," Nellie said. "So she's okay?"

"Not okay," Traci said. "But she'll live."

"Well, thank God for that!" Nellie said. She glanced over at Pete. "Oh, I guess you're wondering about us. I mean, there is no us."

"I decided to show up for the end of Winterfest," Pete said with a shrug. His eyes darted from Erin to Luke, then back to Erin again. "I heard about what happened to Noelle — everyone was talking about it —

so I decided to come over here to see how she was, only my stupid car wouldn't start."

"So I told him I'd drive him over, as soon as the Queen was crowned," Nellie continued. She turned to Tara. "You lost!" she cried triumphantly.

"Congratulations, Nellie," Tara said, taking in the beautiful roses in Nellie's arms. "I'm happy for you."

"Oh, I didn't win," Nellie explained. "I was so sure I would, but . . . well, what can you do?"

"So, who won?" Erin asked, completely exhausted. She was still looking at Pete out of the corner of her eye, not knowing what she felt, or how she felt, or what to do.

"You did," Pete told Erin quietly.

Erin's mouth fell open. "I . . . *what*?"

"You won!" Nellie cried. "Imagine that! I guess people don't necessarily think about you and death in the same breath anymore, Erin. You're the Queen of Winterfest!" She handed Erin the roses, and kissed her on the cheek.

"I never, ever, in a million years . . ." Erin began, too stunned to even finish the sentence.

Slowly, Pete walked over to Erin, who stood there, too shocked to move. "Would it be okay if I give you a congratulatory hug?"

"It would be stupendous," Erin said. She handed her roses to Tara. And when Pete hugged her, she hugged him back as hard as she could.

"I'm so happy for you, sweetie," Tara said, and she hugged Erin close.

Luke leaned over and kissed Erin's cheek. "You deserve it," he said.

Pete put his hand out to Luke. "Hey, no hard feelings, man. I mean, if it's you Erin wants, then — "

"Luke is Noelle's boyfriend," Erin said.

Pete looked totally confused. "Come again?"

"It's true," she said.

Luke nodded. "You and Erin belong together."

Erin took a deep breath. She was about to do the hardest thing she had ever had to do in her life.

"Pete, could I talk to you privately for a minute?" she asked him.

"Sure," Pete said.

They walked to the far corner of the room.

"You're the Queen," Pete said, touching Erin's hair. "Kinda cool, huh?"

"Yeah," Erin admitted. "It's hard to take it in right now, with what happened to Noelle, but . . . yeah."

"Hey, you were always my queen," Pete said, his hands in his pocket.

"I know I've treated you terribly," Erin said, "ever since Winterfest started. I'm really, really sorry."

"Apology accepted," Pete said.

"And I love you, Pete. You're the most terrific guy I ever met. But . . . but things can't go back to the way they were."

"What do you mean?"

"I mean," Erin began, "that we've been together since eighth grade. I don't know what it's like to date anyone else, and neither do you. We're only seventeen, you know? We don't even know what's out there."

"Other guys, you mean," Pete said.

Erin struggled for the right words. "All my life, all I wanted was to be normal and fit in. I hated that everyone called me 'Death' Kellerman. I didn't want to stick out, to be the girl who lived at the cemetery . . ." She took a deep breath, and forced herself to continue.

"I was so happy, so relieved, when you became my boyfriend," she said. "And I . . . I kind of . . . held on to that, I guess, because it felt so safe, and it seemed so normal —"

"Ah, Erin," Pete began, reaching out for her.

"No, let me finish, or I'll lose all my courage," Erin said. "I haven't been fair to you *or* to me. Because now I see that nothing is safe, not really. Hiding out, or trying to be 'normal,' just means you never know if what you have is what you really want."

Erin gazed into Pete's eyes. "And you deserve better. And so do I. So . . . so I think we should see other people, Pete. Even if . . . even if we don't know what will happen."

"I agree," Pete said.

Erin was stunned. "You do?"

Pete smiled. "I pretty much decided that even if you and Luke weren't a couple, that I was going to tell you the same thing."

"You were?"

"I thought about it a lot while we were apart," Pete said. "I don't believe that we'll stop loving each other at all. I guess I have a lot of faith . . . that once we both see what's out there, we'll realize we had it all, all the time."

Erin's eyes filled with tears. "You are amazing."

"You, too, you Queen of Winterfest, you," Pete said. He kissed her then, a kiss of such sweetness that it took Erin's breath away.

They walked back to their friends, hand in hand.

"Hey, kids," Gussie said, hurrying over to them. "Noelle wants to see Erin and Tara," she said. "She just kicked all us adult types out of the room."

"Tell her," Luke said, grabbing Erin's arm, "tell her I love her."

Erin and Tara hurried to Noelle's room. As soon as they tiptoed in, she opened her eyes.

"Hi," she said. Then Noelle noticed that Tara's arms were full of long-stemmed roses. "You look like you just won another beauty pageant," she told her friend.

"Not me," Tara said, handing the roses to Erin. "Erin is Queen of Winterfest."

"Wow, that's so terrific," Noelle managed.

"I don't know how it happened," Erin confessed.

"Because everyone in Love knows how wonderful you are," Noelle said, her voice still weak and breathy. "Everyone has always known. You were the only one who didn't."

Erin gently laid the roses on the windowsill. Then she walked back to Noelle and took Noelle's small, pale white hand in her own. "I love you, Noelle," she said, choking back her tears.

Tara went around the bed, and she carefully held Noelle's wrist, above the IV line. "Me, too," she added.

Noelle's eyes closed. "I am going to skate again," she said. Her eyes opened defiantly. "I am."

"Never say never," Tara said tremulously.

"Skating is all that I love," Noelle said, a tear sliding down her cheek.

"You love us," Tara said. "And your family. And maybe Luke . . ."

"It's not the same," Noelle said, a sob in her voice.

"No, it isn't," Erin agreed. For the second time that night, she struggled to find the right words to say to someone she loved. "You have more guts than anyone I ever knew. No matter what you do, no matter what dreams you lose or what new ones you find, you'll still be a champion, Noelle. Because that's who you really are."

"Dang, but that was eloquent," Tara said with admiration, her lower lip trembling.

Erin let go of Noelle's hand and walked over to her roses. She picked the most perfect one, and carried it over to the bed. "For you," she said, handing it to Noelle. "For a champion."

Erin took Noelle's hand again. And so the three of them were joined, hand to hand to hand.

The tears fell down all of their cheeks, but their hands held fast, as old dreams died and new dreams took their place.

The future belonged to them. Three girls in Love.

Romances

Dreamy Days... Unforgettable Nights

☐ BAK50966-7	Another Time, Another Love	$3.99
☐ BAK54335-0	Bridesmaids	$3.99
☐ BAK46314-4	First Comes Love #2: For Better, For Worse	$3.50
☐ BAK46315-2	First Comes Love #3: In Sickness and in Health	$3.50
☐ BAK46316-0	First Comes Love #4: Till Death Do Us Part	$3.50
☐ BAK46574-0	Forbidden	$3.50
☐ BAK45785-3	Last Dance	$3.25
☐ BAK45705-5	The Last Great Summer	$3.25
☐ BAK48323-4	Last Summer, First Love #1: A Time to Love	$3.95
☐ BAK48324-2	Last Summer, First Love #2: Good-bye to Love	$3.95
☐ BAK46967-3	Lifeguards: Summer's End	$3.50
☐ BAK46966-5	Lifeguards: Summer's Promise	$3.50
☐ BAK20354-1	Malibu Summer	$3.99
☐ BAK25947-4	Once Upon a Dream: At Midnight	$3.99
☐ BAK25948-2	Once Upon a Dream: The Rose	$3.99
☐ BAK45784-5	Saturday Night	$3.25
☐ BAK45786-1	Summer Nights	$3.25
☐ BAK47877-X	Unforgettable	$3.95
☐ BAK47610-6	A Winter Love Story	$3.50
☐ BAK48152-5	Winter Love, Winter Wishes	$3.95

Available wherever you buy books, or use this order form.

Scholastic Inc., P.O. Box 7502, 2931 East McCarty Street, Jefferson City, MO 65102

Please send me the books I have checked above. I am enclosing $_____ (please add $2.00 to cover shipping and handling). Send check or money order — no cash or C.O.D.s please.

Name _____ Birthdate ___/___/____

Address _____

City _____ State/Zip ___/_____

Please allow four to six weeks for delivery. Offer good in the U.S. only. Sorry, mail orders are not available to residents of Canada. Prices subject to change.

R596